Nathaniel Hawthorne

Young
Goodman Brown

Edited by
Thomas E. Connolly
State University of New York
at Buffalo

The Merrill Literary
Casebook Series
Edward P.J. Corbett, Editor

Charles E. Merrill Publishing Company
Columbus, Ohio
A Bell & Howell Company

For Margaret Gould

Library of Congress Catalog Number: 68-55804

1 2 3 4 5 6 7 8 9 10 — 72 71 70 69 68

Printed in the United States of America

Foreword

The Charles E. Merrill Literary Casebook Series deals with short literary works, arbitrarily defined here as "works which can be easily read in a single sitting." Accordingly, the series will concentrate on poems, short stories, brief dramas, and literary essays. These casebooks are designed to be used in literature courses or in practical criticism courses where the instructor wants to expose his students to an extensive and intensive study of a single, short work or in composition courses where the instructor wants to expose his students to the discipline of writing a research paper on a literary text.

All of the casebooks in the series follow this format: (1) foreword; (2) general instructions for the writing of a research paper; (3) the editor's Introduction; (4) the text of the literary work; (5) a number of critical articles on the literary work; (6) suggested topics for short papers on the literary work; (7) suggested topics for long (10-15 pages) papers on the literary work; (8) a selective bibliography of additional readings on the literary work. Some of the casebooks, especially those dealing with poetry, may carry an additional section, which contains such features as variant versions of the work, a closely related literary work, comments by the author and his contemporaries on the work.

So that students might simulate first-hand research in library copies of books and bound periodicals, each of the critical articles carries full bibliographical information at the bottom of the first page of the article, and the text of the article carries the actual page-numbers of the original source. A notation like /131/ after a word in the text indicates that *after* that word in the original source the article went over to page 131. All of the text between that number and the next number, /132/, can be taken as occurring on page 131 of the original source.

Edward P.J. Corbett
General Editor

General Instructions
For A Research Paper

If your instructor gives you any specific directions about the format of your research paper that differ from the directions given here, you are, of course, to follow his directions. Otherwise, you can observe these directions with the confidence that they represent fairly standard conventions.

A research paper represents a student's synthesis of his reading in a number of primary and secondary works, with an indication, in footnotes, of the source of quotations used in the paper or of facts cited in paraphrased material. A *primary* source is the text of a work as it issued from the pen of the author or some document contemporary with the work. The following, for instance, would be considered primary sources: a manuscript copy of the work; first editions of the work and any subsequent editions authorized by the writer; a modern scholarly edition of the text; an author's comment about his work in letters, memoirs, diaries, journals, or periodicals; published comments on the work by the author's contemporaries. A *secondary* source would be any interpretation, explication, or evaluation of the work printed, usually several years after the author's death, in critical articles and books, in literary histories, and in biographies of the author. In this casebook, the text of the work, any variant versions of it, any commentary on the work by the author himself or his contemporaries may be considered as primary sources; the editor's Introduction, the articles from journals, and the excerpts from books are to be considered secondary sources. The paper that you eventually write will become a secondary source.

Plagiarism

The cardinal sin in the academic community is plagiarism. The rankest form of plagiarism is the verbatim reproduction of someone else's words without any indication that the passage is a quotation. A lesser but still serious form of plagiarism is to report, in your own words, the fruits of someone else's research without acknowledging the source of your information or interpretation.

You can take this as an inflexible rule: every verbatim quotation in your paper must be either enclosed in quotation marks or single-spaced and inset from the left-hand margin and must be followed by a footnote number. Students who merely change a few words or phrases in a quotation and present the passage as their own work are still guilty of plagiarism. Passages of genuine paraphrase must be footnoted too if the information or idea or interpretation contained in the paraphrase cannot be presumed to be known by ordinary educated people or at least by readers who would be interested in the subject you are writing about.

The penalties for plagiarism are usually very severe. Don't run the risk of a failing grade on the paper or even of a failing grade in the course.

Lead-Ins

Provide a lead-in for all quotations. Failure to do so results in a serious breakdown in coherence. The lead-in should at least name the person who is being quoted. The ideal lead-in, however, is one that not only names the person but indicates the pertinence of the quotation.

Examples:

> (typical lead-in for a single-spaced, inset quotation)

> Irving Babbitt makes this observation about Flaubert's attitude toward women:

(typical lead-in for quotation worked into the frame of one's sentence)

> Thus the poet sets out to show how the present age, as George Anderson puts it, "negates the values of the earlier revolution."[7]

Full Names

The first time you mention anyone in a paper give the full name of the person. Subsequently you may refer to him by his last name.

Examples: First allusion—Ronald S. Crane
          Subsequent allusions—Professor Crane, as Crane says.

Ellipses

Lacunae in a direct quotation are indicated with *three spaced periods,* in addition to whatever punctuation mark was in the text at the point where you truncated the quotation. *Hit the space-bar of your typewriter between each period.* Usually there is no need to put the ellipsis-periods at the beginning or the end of a quotation.

Example: `"The poets were not striving to communi-`
`cate with their audience; . . . By and`
`large, the Romantics were seeking . . .`
`to express their unique personalities."`[8]

Brackets

Brackets are used to enclose any material interpolated into a direct quotation. The abbreviation *sic,* enclosed in brackets, indicates that the error of spelling, grammar, or fact in a direct quotation has been copied as it was in the source being quoted. If your typewriter does not have special keys for brackets, draw the brackets neatly with a pen.

Examples: `"He [Theodore Baum] maintained that Con-`
`fucianism [the primary element in Chinese`
`philosophy] aimed at teaching each indi-`
`vidual to accept his lot in life."`[12]

`"Paul Revear [`<u>`sic`</u>`] made his historic ride`
`on April 18, 1875 [`<u>`sic`</u>`]."`[15]

Summary Footnote

A footnote number at the end of a sentence which is not enclosed in quotation marks indicates that only *that* sentence is being documented in the footnote. If you want to indicate that the footnote documents more than one sentence, put a footnote number at the end of the *first* sentence of the paraphrased passage and use some formula like this in the footnote:

[16] `For the information presented in this and the`
`following paragraph, I am indebted to Marvin`
`Magalaner, `<u>`Time`</u>` `<u>`of`</u>` `<u>`Apprenticeship`</u>`: `<u>`the`</u>` `<u>`Fiction`</u>` `<u>`of`</u>
<u>`Young`</u>` `<u>`James`</u>` `<u>`Joyce`</u>` (London, 1959), pp. 81-93.`

Citing the Edition

The edition of the author's work being used in a paper should always be cited in the first footnote that documents a quotation from that work. You can obviate the need for subsequent footnotes to that edition by using some formula like this:

⁴ Nathaniel Hawthorne, "Young Goodman Brown," as printed in <u>Young Goodman Brown</u>, ed. Thomas E. Connolly, Charles E. Merrill Literary Casebooks (Columbus, Ohio, 1968), pp. 3-15. This edition will be used throughout the paper, and hereafter all quotations from this book will be documented with a page-number in parentheses at the end of the quotation.

Notetaking

Although all the material you use in your paper may be contained in this casebook, you will find it easier to organize your paper if you work from notes written on 3 x 5 or 4 x 6 cards. Besides, you should get practice in the kind of notetaking you will have to do for other term-papers, when you will have to work from books and articles in, or on loan from, the library.

An ideal note is a self-contained note—one which has all the information you would need if you used anything from that note in your paper. A note will be self-contained if it carries the following information:

(1) The information or quotation *accurately* copied.

(2) Some system for distinguishing direct quotation from para-phrase.

(3) All the bibliographical information necessary for documenting that note—full name of the author, title, volume number (if any), place of publication, publisher, publication date, page numbers.

(4) If a question covered more than one page in the source, the note-card should indicate which part of the quotation occurred on one page and which part occurred on the next page. The easiest way to do this is to put the next page number in parentheses after the last word on one page and before the first word on the next page.

In short, your note should be so complete that you would never have to go back to the original source to gather any piece of information about that note.

Footnote Forms

The footnote forms used here follow the conventions set forth in the *MLA Style Sheet*, Revised Edition, ed. William Riley Parker, which is now used by more than 100 journals and more than thirty universities presses in the United States. Copies of this pamphlet can be purchased for fifty cents from your university bookstore or from the Modern Language Association, 62 Fifth Avenue, New York, N.Y. 10011. If your teacher or your institution prescribes a modified form of this footnoting system, you should, of course, follow that system.

A primary footnote, the form used the first time a source is cited, supplies four pieces of information: (1) author's name, (2) title of the source, (3) publication information, (4) specific location in the source of the information or quotation. A secondary footnote is the shorthand form of documentation after the source has been cited in full the first time.

Your instructor may permit you to put all your footnotes on separate pages at the end of your paper. But he may want to give you practice in putting footnotes at the bottom of the page. Whether the footnotes are put at the end of the paper or at the bottom of the page, they should observe this format of spacing: (1) the first line of each footnote should be indented, usually the same number of spaces as your paragraph indentations; (2) all subsequent lines of the footnote should start at the lefthand margin; (3) there should be single-spacing within each footnote and double-spacing between each footnote.

Example:

[10] Ruth Wallerstein, *Richard Crashaw: A Study in Style and Poetic Development*, University of Wisconsin Studies in Language and Literature, No. 37 (Madison, 1935), p. 52.

Primary Footnotes

(The form to be used the *first* time a work is cited)

[1] Paull F. Baum, *Ten Studies in the Poetry of Matthew Arnold* (Durham, N.C., 1958), p. 37.

(book by a single author; p. is the abbreviation of *page*)

[2] René Wellek and Austin Warren, *Theory of Literature* (New York, 1949), pp. 106-7.

(book by two authors; pp. is the abbreviation of *pages*)

[3] William Hickling Prescott, History of the Reign of Philip the Second, King of Spain, ed. John Foster Kirk (Philadelphia, 1871), II, 47.

(an edited work of more than one volume; *ed.* is the abbreviation for "edited by"; note that whenever a volume number is cited, the abbreviation p. or pp. is *not* used in front of the page number)

[4] John Pick, ed., The Windhover (Columbus, Ohio 1968), p. 4.

(form for quotation from an editor's Introduction—as, for instance, in this casebook series; here *ed.* is the abbreviation for "editor")

[5] A.S.P. Woodhouse, "Nature and Grace in The Faerie Queen," in Elizabethan Poetry: Modern Essays in Criticism, ed. Paul J. Alpers (New York, 1967), pp. 346-7.

(chapter or article from an edited collection)

[6] Morton D. Paley, "Tyger of Wrath," PMLA, LXXXI (December, 1966), 544.

(an article from a periodical; note that because the volume number is cited no p. or pp. precedes the page number; the titles of periodicals are often abbreviated in footnotes but are spelled out in the Bibliography; here, for instance, *PMLA* is the abbreviation for *Publications of the Modern Language Association*)

Secondary Footnotes

(Abbreviated footnote forms to be used after a work has been cited once in full)

[7] Baum, p. 45.

(abbreviated form for work cited in footnote #1; note that the secondary footnote is indented the same number of spaces as the first line of primary footnotes)

[8] Wellek and Warren, pp. 239-40.

(abbreviated form for work cited in footnote #2)

[9] Prescott, II, 239.

(abbreviated form for work cited in footnote #3; because this is a multi-volume work, the volume number must be given in addition to the page number)

[10] Ibid., p. 245.

(refers to the immediately preceding footnote—that is, to page 245 in the second volume of Prescott's history; *ibid.* is the abbreviation of the Latin adverb *ibidem* meaning "in the same place"; note that this abbreviation is italicized or underlined and that it is followed by a period, because it is an abbreviation)

[11] Ibid., III, 103.
(refers to the immediately preceding footnote—that is, to Prescott's work again; there must be added to *ibid.* only what changes from the preceding footnote; here the volume and page changed; note that there is no p. before 103, because a volume number was cited)

[12] Baum, pp. 47-50.
(refers to the same work cited in footnote #7 and ultimately to the work cited in full in footnote #1)

[13] Paley, p. 547.
(refers to the article cited in footnote #6)

[14] Rebecca P. Parkin, "Mythopoeic Activity in the Rape of the Lock," ELH, XXI (March, 1954), 32.
(since this article from the *Journal of English Literary History* has not been previously cited in full, it must be given in full here)

[15] Ibid., pp. 33-4.
(refers to Parkin's article in the immediately preceding footnote)

Bibliography Forms

Note carefully the differences in bibliography forms from footnote forms: (1) the last name of the author is given first, since bibliography items are arranged alphabetically according to the surname of the author (in the case of two or more authors of a work, only the name of the first author is reversed) ; (2) the first line of each bibliography item starts at the lefthand margin; subsequent lines are indented; (3) periods are used instead of commas, and parentheses do not enclose publication information; (4) the publisher is given in addition to the place of publication; (5) the first and last pages of articles and chapters are given; (6) most of the abbreviations used in footnotes are avoided in the Bibliography.

The items are arranged here alphabetically as they would appear in the Bibliography of your paper.

Baum, Paull F. Ten Studies in the Poetry of Matthew Arnold. Durham, N.C.: University of North Carolina Press, 1958.

Paley, Morton D. "Tyger of Wrath," <u>Publications</u> <u>of</u>
    <u>the</u> <u>Modern</u> <u>Language</u> <u>Association</u>, LXXXI (Decem-
    ber, 1966), 540-51.

Parkin, Rebecca P. "Mythopoeic Activity in the <u>Rape</u>
    <u>of</u> <u>the</u> <u>Lock</u>," <u>Journal</u> <u>of</u> <u>English</u> <u>Literary</u>
    <u>History</u>, XXI (March, 1954), 30-8.

Pick, John, editor. <u>The</u> <u>Windhover</u>. Columbus, Ohio:
    Charles E. Merrill Publishing Company, 1968.

Prescott, William Hickling. <u>History</u> <u>of</u> <u>the</u> <u>Reign</u> <u>of</u>
    <u>Philip</u> <u>the</u> <u>Second</u>, <u>King</u> <u>of</u> <u>Spain</u>. Edited by
    John Foster Kirk. 3 volumes. Philadelphia: J.B.
    Lippincott and Company, 1871.

Wellek, René and Austin Warren. <u>Theory</u> <u>of</u> <u>Litera-</u>
    <u>ture</u>. New York: Harcourt, Brace & World, Inc.,
    1949.

Woodhouse, A.S.P. "Nature and Grace in <u>The</u> <u>Faerie</u>
    <u>Queene</u>," in <u>Elizabethan</u> <u>Poetry</u>: <u>Modern</u> <u>Essays</u> <u>in</u>
    <u>Criticism</u>. Edited by Paul J. Alpers. New York:
    Oxford University Press, 1967, pp. 345-79.

*If the form for some work that you are using in your paper is not given
in these samples of footnote and bibliography entries, ask your instructor for advice as to the proper form.*

Contents

"... use every man after his desert, and who shall scape whipping?"

Hamlet, II, ii, 513.

Introduction

Nathaniel Hawthorne was born in Salem, Massachusetts, on the Fourth of July, 1804. He was the second child of Nathaniel and Elizabeth Clarke Manning Hathorne. Hawthorne, who changed the spelling of his family name, could trace his lineage back through four generations to Magistrate John Hathorne before whom on March 1, 1692 appeared Tituba, the West Indian slave of the minister of Salem Village, to answer to a charge of witchcraft. This charge touched off a wave of hysteria that culminated, by the following September, in the hanging of nineteen convicted or confessed witches and wizards and the pressing to death of one man who refused to plead either guilty or not guilty to the indictment so that he might pass his fortune on to his descendants by escaping a bill of attainder.

When his son was four years old, Nathaniel Hathorne, a sea captain, died on a voyage at Surinam, Dutch Guiana. Hawthorne continued to live with his mother and sister in Salem. At the age of nine, he injured his foot while playing and remained lame until he was twelve. The enforced inactivity resulting from his lameness and his early love of books combined to produce the habit of reading which stayed with him all his life. The literature he read in his early years reveals a taste for allegory that was to influence his own later writing. His favorite books were Spenser's *Faerie Queene* (years later he named his daughter Una), Thomson's *Castle of Indolence,* and Bunyan's *Pilgrim's Progress.* He counterbalanced these with the plays of Shakespeare.

On his fifteenth birthday, Hawthorne returned to Salem from a three-year sojourn at Raymond, Maine to attend Mr. Archer's school on Marlboro Street. After 1820, Hawthorne left school and began to prepare for college under the tutorial guidance of a Salem lawyer, Benjamin L. Oliver.

In October 1821, Hawthorne entered Bowdoin College in Brunswick, Maine. Latin and English were his best subjects, but he was only slightly better than average in his over-all performance. He graduated 18th in a class of 38 in 1825. At Bowdoin, Hawthorne was a member of

1

the Athenean Society, a literary club. Fellow Atheneans were Horatio
Bridge, who was to become a life-long friend, Franklin Pierce, later
president of the United States through whose influence Hawthorne
received his political appointments, and Jonathan Cilley, later a member of Congress. Hawthorne's membership in the Democratic Party was
fostered in the Athenean Society. (A fellow classmate, Henry Wads-
worth Longfellow, was a member of the rival whig literary club, the
Peucinian Society.)

Hawthorne probably began writing fiction at Bowdoin. Three years
after his graduation, he published *Fanshawe* anonymously at his own
expense, but almost immediately he regretted this act and did everything he could to suppress the book. Similarly, he burned most of the
manuscripts of his first collection of tales. During the period after his
graduation, Hawthorne devoted himself very seriously to preparing
for a literary career by long hours of reading and writing. Randall
Stewart informs us that between 1826 and 1837, 1200 books were with-
drawn in Hawthorne's name from the Salem Athenaeum. After he
burned the manuscripts of his first collection, Hawthorne began
another which he planned to call *Provincial Tales*.[1] E. L. Chandler
gives an account of this project and sets the approximate date for the
writing of "Young Goodman Brown" which was to be included in that
volume:

> His next project was a collection of historical stories, to be called *"Provincial
> Tales"*.... Evidently the first three were written during the spring or fall of
> 1828 or during 1829; Hawthorne seldom could write in the summer. It is
> my belief that four other tales, "Dr. Bullivant," "The Gray Champion,"
> "Young Goodman Brown," and "The May-pole at Merry Mount," pub-
> lished within a few years, were written at this time, or before June, 1830,
> when Hawthorne speaks of the *"Provincial Tales,"* as if completed. There
> must have been a good many destined for that collection, and these seem
> the most likely survivors.[2]

Fannye N. Cherry, writing about the sources of "Young Goodman
Brown," says: ". . . the main source of the tale is, I believe, a story
entitled 'El Coloquico de los Perros' (or 'The Conversation of the
Dogs') by Cervantes."[3] She gives additional information about the
source of the witch ointment in the story: "We can be reasonably sure,

---

[1] See the essay by Richard P. Adams included in this volume.

[2] E. L. Chandler, "A Study of the Sources of the Tales and Romances Written by
Nathaniel Hawthorne before 1853," *Smith College Studies in Modern Languages*,
VII (July, 1926), 12.

[3] Fannye N. Cherry, "The Sources of Hawthorne's 'Young Goodman Brown',"
American Literature, V (1934), 342. See Daniel Hoffman's essay in this volume for
an extension of this topic.

I think, that Hawthorne is indebted to Bacon in the main for the recipe
[for witch ointment] as given in his story. . ."[4] The recipe as found
in Bacon is in *Sylva Sylvarum*, or *A Natural History in Ten Centuries*.
Most critics and biographers of Hawthorne agree that in this ten-
year period of intensive reading and research, Hawthorne became
thoroughly familiar with the events that took place in the Salem witchcraft trials of 1692 through the writings of Cotton Mather, the records
of the trials, and other sources. To give the modern reader of "Young
Goodman Brown" a flavor of the attitudes of that time, I have included in this volume a long excerpt from the writings of Cotton
Mather.[5] Hawthorne was acutely conscious of his ancestors' involvement in the witchcraft trials and, earlier, in the persecution of the
Quakers. In "The Custom House," speaking of his great-great-great-
grandfather, William Hathorne, the first of the family to reach
America, and of his great-great-grandfather, John Hathorne, the magistrate, Hawthorne wrote:

> He [William Hathorne] was a soldier, legislator, judge; he was a ruler in
> the Church; he had all the Puritanic traits, both good and evil. He was
> likewise a bitter persecutor; as witness the Quakers, who have remembered
> him in their histories, and relate an incident of his hard severity towards a
> woman of their sect, which will last longer it is to be feared, than any
> record of his better deeds, although these were many. His son [John
> Hathorne], too, inherited the persecuting spirit, and made himself so
> conspicuous in the martyrdom of the witches, that their blood may fairly
> be said to have left a stain upon him. So deep a stain, indeed, that his old
> dry bones, in the Charter Street burial-ground, must still retain it, if they
> have not crumbled utterly to dust! I know not whether these ancestors of
> mine bethought themselves to repent, and ask pardon of Heaven for their
> cruelties; or whether they are now groaning under the heavy consequences
> of them, in another state of being. At all events, I, the present writer, as
> their representative, hereby take shame upon myself for their sakes, and
> pray that any curse incurred by them—as I have heard, and as the dreary
> and unprosperous condition of the race, for many a long year back, would
> argue to exist—may be now and henceforth removed.

Hawthorne's attitude towards "Young Goodman Brown" (and some
of the other stories intended to be included in the projected collection
Provincial Tales) was strange. The story was published originally in
the *New England Magazine* in April 1835. After he abandoned the
Provincial Tales, he began to gather previously published stories for

---

[4] *Ibid.*, p. 344.
[5] For a good start on further readings about Salem witchcraft trials, I refer
the reader to David Levin's excellent book *What Happened in Salem?* (New York:
Harcourt, Brace & World, Inc., 1960).

Twice-Told Tales which was published in 1837. He rejected "Young Goodman Brown" for that collection, and he chose to exclude it once again when, for the second edition of *Twice-Told Tales* in 1842, he expanded the collection and added a second volume. Finally, in 1846, eleven years after its original publication, he republished the story in *Mosses from an Old Manse*. That Hawthorne was quite sensitive about this story and others in that volume is clear from his prefatory remarks to *Mosses*. He first tried to insist upon his own individuality as distinct from that of his literary creations: "I have appealed to no sentiment or sensibilities save such as are diffused among us all. So far as I am a man of really individual attributes, I veil my face, nor am I, nor have I ever been, one of those supremely hospitable people who serve up their own heart delicately fried, with brain sauce, as a tidbit for their beloved public." After making this disclaimer, however, he was still uneasy about "Young Goodman Brown" and some of the other older pieces in the collection:

> With these idle weeds and withering blossoms I have intermixed some
> that were produced long ago—old, faded things, reminding me of flowers
> pressed between the leaves of a book—and now offer the bouquet, such as
> it is, to any whom it may please. These fitful sketches, with so little of
> external life about them, yet claiming no profundity of purpose, so reserved
> even while they sometimes seem so frank, often but half in earnest, and
> never, when most so, expressing satisfactorily the thoughts which they
> profess to image,—such trifles, I truly feel, afford no solid base for a literary
> reputation.... Unless I could do better, I have done enough in this kind.[6]

Hawthorne is not, of course, the first author to have underestimated his own literary products only to have generations of readers overrule his estimate. *Mosses from an Old Manse* contains some of Hawthorne's best stories: "The Birthmark," "Young Goodman Brown," "Rappaccini's Daughter," "Roger Malvin's Burial."

Some of his contemporaries shared Hawthorne's uneasiness about "Young Goodman Brown." Poe dismissed this story almost with contempt:

> He is infinitely too fond of allegory, and can never hope for popularity
> so long as he persists in it. This he will not do, for allegory is at war with
> the whole tone of his nature, which disports itself never so well as when
> escaping from the mysticism of his Goodman Browns and White Old
> Maids into the hearty, genial, but still Indian-summer sunshine of his

---

[6] See Neal F. Doubleday, "Hawthorne's Estimate of His Early Work," *American Literature*, XXVII (1966) for a good discussion of Hawthorne's views of his own work.

Wakefields and Little Annie's Rambles. Indeed, *his* spirit of "metaphor run-mad" is clearly imbibed from the phalanx and phalanstery atmosphere in which he has been so long struggling for breath.

It is curious that Poe should prefer "Wakefield" to "Young Goodman Brown," for his preference matches that of Hawthorne. Though both stories were printed in 1835 in the *New England Magazine* and both deal with figures who, "by stepping aside for a moment" from their normal ways of life lose their places forever, Hawthorne reprinted "Wakefield" at the first opportunity in *Twice-Told Tales* while passing over "Young Goodman Brown." Yet, of the two stories, "Young Goodman Brown" is more artistic, more subtle in the development of this theme and less openly didactic in pointing its moral.

Henry James shared Poe's scorn of allegory, and, after quoting the final paragraph of "Young Goodman Brown," airily put it aside with these words, "There is imagination in that, and in many another passage that I might quote; but as a general thing I should characterize the more metaphysical of our author's short stories as graceful and felicitous conceits. They seem to me to be qualified in this manner by the very fact that they belong to the province of allegory." Earlier in his book, James treated Hawthorne's obsession with sin as something superficial, something added for artistic embellishment rather than something that arose from deep within the man: "Nothing is more curious and interesting than this almost exclusively imported character of the sense of sin in Hawthorne's mind; it seems to exist there merely for an artistic or literary purpose."[7] Both these critics stand at the opposite pole from such modern critics as Hoffman and Crews whose essays are included in this book. It was only Melville who, among Hawthorne's major contemporaries, saw depth in this story of Goodman Brown. In "Hawthorne and His Mosses," Melville wrote:

> But with whatever motive, playful or profound, Nathaniel Hawthorne has chosen to entitle his pieces in the manner he has, it is certain that some of them are directly calculated to deceive—egregiously deceive—the super-

---

[7] In contrast to Henry James stands the modern critic Newton Arvin (*Hawthorne*, New York: 1961, p. 61) who not only fixes the sense of sin deep in Hawthorne's personality, but also sees it as affecting his "imaginative sanity": "How far had Hawthorne wandered from imaginative sanity when he became capable of viewing all human personality as tainted and corrupt because all men have unuttered and unacted impulses to crime! And can one doubt for a moment that this unwholesome creative mood the product of his own unnaturally prolonged silence, his own abnormal inaction? Out of the very depths of that mood, and lit up by it with as lurid an imaginative glare as Hawthorne was never again to light, sprang that beautiful evil fancy, 'Young Goodman Brown'."

ficial skimmer of pages.... "who in the name of thunder," would anticipate
any marvel in a piece entitled "Young Goodman Brown"? You would of
course suppose that it was a simple little tale, intended as a supplement to
"Goody Two—Shoes." Whereas it is deep as Dante . . .

Over the years, the essays in this volume will testify, critics have come
to agree with Melville and not with Poe and James.

One can no longer deny the sexual implications of the story.
Although many critics speak of the story as allegory, no extended
attempt has been made to discuss thè complete significance of the
allegory. For an allegory to be completely successful, it should exist
simultaneously and exactly on two levels. This is one of the chief
defects of "Rappaccini's Daughter" as an allegory. One can carry out
the Garden of Eden theme just so far, and then one bumps one's
analytical nose up against ambivalent symbols or missing naturalistic
parallels. Or one can read *Billy Budd* and *Light in August* as Christian
allegories and tick off the equivalents for the virgin birth, the Christ-
like silence, the need for one to be sacrificed for the salvation of the
many, but then one trips over the fact that in the real worlds of the
British Navy or the American South, the Christ figure must be in some
sense "guilty" (Billy remains morally innocent; Joe loses control of
his will and is driven by forces he can no longer control) of a crime
that merits the death penalty. "Young Goodman Brown" appears to me
to come as close as a story can to being a "perfect" allegory. It exists
at all points on two levels at once without any failure on either the
naturalistic or the allegorical level. I once raised this point in a face-
tious fashion,[8] but I would like now seriously to pursue it further. One
begins by asking oneself the question: "Did Hawthorne believe and
does he want us to believe that Goodman Brown went out to the woods
and actually met the devil?" On the answer to this question depends
the entire allegory. If you think that the answer is, "Yes," then you
need discuss the story on no other level than that of the horror story
or the supernatural tale. If the answer is, "No," however, you then are
pushed into discussing it as an allegory or as some other form of literature. If he did not actually meet the devil, the devil must then be
symbolic of something else, and, given Hawthorne's Christian orienta-
tion, what else could he be symbolic of but some sort of sin? One does
not go out to meet the devil; one meets him through sin. If one does
not meet the devil face to face in this world, but meets him through
giving oneself to sin, what sin was it that Goodman Brown intended

---

[8] Thomas E. Connolly, "How Young Goodman Brown Became Old Badman
Brown," *College English*, XXIV (November, 1962).

to commit, for no man commits sin in the abstract. As I have lightly argued elsewhere, the "only sin that begs for recognition is that of sexual infidelity." If my original thesis is right (see my essay in this volume), and if my theory about the nature of the sin that Goodman Brown intends to commit is right, then the story exists on two distinct levels and is a perfect allegory. At the risk of reducing the problem to a too rigid frame (and with the intention of stimulating discussion) let me formulate the allegory schematically.

People and Things	*Theological Level*	*Naturalistic (sexual) Level*
Young Goodman Brown	A Calvinist convinced that he is one of the Elect	A smug young husband off for one last fling
Faith	Calvinism with its doctrine of Election for the select few and damnation for the great mass of men	A pretty, young, apparently innocent wife, who is subject to the same physical passions as her husband
The marriage	Young Goodman Brown's Conversion to Grace (the conviction that he is one of the Elect)	The actual marriage
The devil	Sin in the abstract	Sexual infidelity
The forest	Nature, the source of evil for Calvinists (both human nature and Nature —see Cotton Mather)	The passions in general and specifically the trysting place
The pink ribbons	The attractive and illusory aspect of Calvinism; the idea that it is a re-	Faith's divided human nature: apparently sexually innocent and faithful, but potentially subject to her

People and Things	*Theological Level*	*Naturalistic (sexual) Level*
	ligion of salvation rather than one that argues justifiable damnation for all but the Elect	passions and capable of infidelity
Goody Cloyse (Deacon Gookin, etc.)	The catechist and those who teach the real doctrine of Calvinism, the depravity of all men	Those who plant the thought of Faith's potential infidelity in Brown's mind
Old Badman Brown	Still a firm believer in Calvinism, who now believes he is one of the damned and *not* one of the Elect.	A husband who has himself been tempted to infidelity, and who is then shaken to the core by the thought that his pretty wife may be subject to the same temptation

The key to the allegorical interpretation of this story is the marriage. Unless we can reconcile the three-month-old marriage to Faith with Brown's identification of his ancestors' Christianity, the allegory breaks down. To make allegorical sense, the marriage must represent the Conversion to Grace, that moment at which a devout Calvinist becomes convinced that he is one of the Elect. It is helpful to recall Jonathan Edward's account of his acceptance of the doctrine of election and his own Conversion to Grace in the *Personal Narrative:*

> I scarce ever have found so much as the rising of an objection against it, in the most absolute sense, in God's shewing mercy to whom he will shew mercy, and hardening whom he will. God's absolute sovereignty and justice, with respect to salvation and damnation, is what my mind seems to rest assured of, as much as of any thing that I see with my eyes; at least it is so at times. But I have often, since that first conviction, had quite another kind of sense of God's sovereignty than I had then. I have often since had not only a conviction, but a delightful conviction. The doctrine has very often appeared exceeding pleasant, bright and sweet.

For such a doctrine to appear "exceeding pleasant, bright and sweet," the one who so contemplates that doctrine must be pretty certain that he is one of the sheep and not one of the goats. Once one is convinced of one's election, strange transformations of personality are likely to take place. Witness Holy Willie. Once more, for convenience, we can call upon Jonathan Edwards to testify to the change that he felt within himself once he was convinced that he was chosen to receive God's Free Grace of salvation rather than the dread sentence of damnation. Again the source is the *Personal Narrative*.

> And scarce any thing, among all the works of nature, was so delightful to me as thunder and lightning; formerly, nothing had been so terrible to me. Before, I used to be uncommonly terrified with thunder, and to be struck with terror when I saw a thunder storm rising; but now, on the contrary, it rejoiced me. I felt God, so to speak, at the first appearance of a thunder storm; and used to take the opportunity, at such times, to fix myself in order to view the clouds, and see the lightnings play, and hear the majestic and awful voice of God's thunder, which oftentimes was exceedingly entertaining, leading me to sweet contemplations of my great and glorious God.

If these are the feelings of a man who is convinced of his Conversion of Grace, what must the feelings be of the man who, as thoroughly convinced of the doctrines of God's sovereignty and Election as was Jonathan Edwards, becomes convinced that he is not really of the Elect but one of the universal damned?

After Goodman Brown refuses to comply with Faith's plea to "sleep in your own bed tonight," and marches off to his tryst which never takes place, he has a twinge of doubt that prepares him for the descent of the pink ribbons. "Methought as she spoke there was trouble in her face, as if a dream had warned her what work is to be done tonight." Pink is a color produced by blending red (or scarlet) and white, two colors which Hawthorne, as well as many other writers, have used to symbolize illicit passion and purity. The deceptive thing about Calvinism and Faith Brown is that both, on the surface, appear to be attractive and pleasant, one a doctrine that guides people to heaven and the other an innocent, passive wife in a man's world of the double standard. But when one turns out really to condemn all mankind to a deserved eternal damnation and the other demonstrates that marital infidelity is a game at which two can play, the effect is catastrophic, and on both levels Goodman Brown is destroyed. ". . . they carved no hopeful verse upon his tombstone, for his dying hour was gloom."

Young Goodman Brown

Young Goodman Brown came forth at sunset into the street at Salem village; but put his head back, after crossing the threshold, to exchange a parting kiss with his young wife. And Faith, as the wife was aptly named, thrust her own pretty head into the street, letting the wind play with the pink ribbons of her cap while she called to Goodman Brown.

"Dearest heart," whispered she, softly and rather sadly, when her lips were close to his ear, "prithee put off your journey until sunrise and sleep in your own bed tonight. A lone woman is troubled with such dreams and such thoughts that she's afeard of herself sometimes. Pray tarry with me this night, dear husband, of all nights in the year."

"My love and my Faith," replied young Goodman Brown, "of all nights in the year, this one night must I tarry away from thee. My journey, as thou callest it, forth and back again, must needs be done 'twixt now and sunrise. What, my sweet, pretty wife, dost thou doubt me already, and we but three months married?"

"Then God bless you!" said Faith, with the pink ribbons; "and may you find all well when you come back."

"Amen!" cried Goodman Brown. "Say thy prayers, dear Faith, and go to bed at dusk, and no harm will come to thee."

So they parted; and the young man pursued his way until, being about to turn the corner by the meeting house, he looked back and saw the head of Faith still peeping after him with a melancholy air, in spite of her pink ribbons.

"Poor little Faith!" thought he, for his heart smote him. "What a wretch am I to leave her on such an errand! She talks of dreams, too. Methought as she spoke there was trouble in her face, as if a dream had warned her what work is to be done tonight. But no, no; 'twould kill her to think it. Well, she's a blessed angel on earth; and after this one night I'll cling to her skirts and follow her to heaven."

With this excellent resolve for the future, Goodman Brown felt himself justified in making more haste on his present evil purpose. He had taken a dreary road, darkened by all the gloomiest trees of the forest, which barely stood aside to let the narrow path creep through, and closed immediately behind. It was all as lonely as could be; and there

---

* The text printed here is that of the 1900 Riverside edition with modernized spelling and punctuation.

is this peculiarity in such a solitude, that the traveller knows not who may be concealed by the innumerable trunks and the thick boughs overhead; so that with lonely footsteps he may yet be passing through an unseen multitude.

"There may be a devilish Indian behind every tree," said Goodman Brown to himself; and he glanced fearfully behind him as he added, "What if the devil himself should be at my very elbow!"

His head being turned back, he passed a crook of the road, and, looking forward again, beheld the figure of a man, in grave and decent attire, seated at the foot of an old tree. He arose at Goodman Brown's approach and walked onward side by side with him.

"You are late, Goodman Brown," said he. "The clock of the Old South was striking as I came through Boston, and that is full fifteen minutes agone."

"Faith kept me back a while," replied the young man, with a tremor in his voice, caused by the sudden appearance of his companion, though not wholly unexpected.

It was now deep dusk in the forest, and deepest in that part of it where these two were journeying. As nearly as could be discerned, the second traveller was about fifty years old, apparently in the same rank of life as Goodman Brown, and bearing a considerable resemblance to him, though perhaps more in expression than features. Still they might have been taken for father and son. And yet, though the elder person was as simply clad as the younger, and as simple in manner too, he had an indescribable air of one who knew the world, and who[1] would not have felt abashed at the governor's dinner table or in King William's court, were it possible that his affairs should call him thither. But the only thing about him that could be fixed upon as remarkable was his staff, which bore the likeness of a great black snake, so curiously wrought that it might almost be seen to twist and wriggle itself like a living serpent. This, of course, must have been an ocular deception, assisted by the uncertain light.

"Come, Goodman Brown," cried his fellow traveller, "this is a dull pace for the beginning of a journey. Take my staff, if you are so soon weary."

"Friend," said the other, exchanging his slow pace for a full stop, "having kept convenant by meeting thee here, it is my purpose now to return whence I came. I have scruples touching the matter thou wot'st of."

---

[1] In the 1835 version of this story that appeared in *The New England Magazine* (April 1835), p. 250, the word *who* does not appear here; nor does it appear in the first edition (1846) of *Mosses from an Old Manse*, p. 71.

"Sayest thou so?" replied he of the serpent, smiling apart. "Let us walk on, nevertheless, reasoning as we go; and if I convince thee not thou shalt turn back. We are but a little way in the forest yet."

"Too far! too far!" exclaimed the goodman, unconsciously resuming his walk. "My father never went into the woods on such an errand, nor his father before him. We have been a race of honest men and good Christians since the days of the martyrs; and shall I be the first of the name of Brown that ever took this path and kept"—

"Such company, thou wouldst say," observed the elder person, interpreting[2] his pause. "Well said, Goodman Brown! I have been as well acquainted with your family as with ever a one among the Puritans; and that's no trifle to say. I helped your grandfather, the constable, when he lashed the Quaker women so smartly through the streets of Salem; and it was I that brought your father a pitch-pine knot, kindled at my own hearth, to set fire to an Indian village, in King Philip's war. They were my good friends, both; and many a pleasant walk have we had along this path, and returned merrily after midnight. I would fain be friends with you for their sake."

"If it be as thou sayest," replied Goodman Brown, "I marvel they never spoke of these matters; or, verily, I marvel not, seeing that the least rumor of the sort would have driven them from New England. We are a people of prayer, and good works to boot, and abide no such wickedness."

"Wickedness or not," said the traveller with the twisted staff, "I have a very general acquaintance here in New England. The deacons of many a church have drunk the communion wine with me; the selectmen of divers towns make me their chairman; and a majority of the Great and General Court are firm supporters of my interest. The governor and I, too—But these are state secrets."

"Can this be so?" cried Goodman Brown, with a stare of amazement at his undisturbed companion. "Howbeit, I have nothing to do with the governor and council; they have their own ways, and are no rule for a simple husbandman like me. But, were I to go on with thee, how should I meet the eye of that good old man, our minister, at Salem village? Oh, his voice would make me tremble both Sabbath day and lecture day."

Thus far the elder traveller had listened with due gravity; but now burst into a fit of irrepressible mirth, shaking himself so violently that his snakelike staff actually seemed to wriggle in sympathy.

---

[2] In the 1835 version, this word is printed as here (*interpreting*), but in *Mosses from an Old Manse* (1846), p. 72, it appeared as *interrupting*. *Quaker women* appeared as *Quaker woman* in the 1835 version.

"Ha! ha! ha!" shouted he again and again; then composing himself, "Well, go on, Goodman Brown, go on; but, prithee, don't kill me with laughing."

"Well, then, to end the matter at once," said Goodman Brown, considerably nettled, "there is my wife, Faith. It would break her dear little heart; and I'd rather break my own."

"Nay, if that be the case," answered the other, "e'en go thy ways, Goodman Brown. I would not for twenty old women like the one hobbling before us that Faith should come to any harm."

As he spoke he pointed his staff at a female figure on the path, in whom Goodman Brown recognized a very pious and exemplary dame, who had taught him his catechism in youth, and was still his moral and spiritual adviser, jointly with the minister and Deacon Gookin.

"A marvel, truly, that Goody Cloyse should be so far in the wilderness at nightfall," said he. "But with your leave, friend, I shall take a cut through the woods until we have left this Christian woman behind. Being a stranger to you, she might ask whom I was consorting with and whither I was going."

"Be it so," said his fellow traveller. "Betake you to the woods, and let me keep the path."

Accordingly the young man turned aside, but took care to watch his companion, who advanced softly along the road until he had come within a staff's length of the old dame. She, meanwhile, was making the best of her way, with singular speed for so aged a woman, and mumbling some indistinct words—a prayer, doubtless—as she went. The traveller put forth his staff, and touched her withered neck with what seemed the serpent's tail.

"The devil!" screamed the pious old lady.

"Then Goody Cloyse knows her old friend?" observed the traveller, confronting her and leaning on his writhing stick.

"Ah, forsooth, and is it your worship, indeed?" cried the good dame. "Yea, truly, is it, and in the very image of my old gossip, Goodman Brown, the grandfather of the silly fellow that now is. But—would your worship believe it?—my broomstick hath strangely disappeared, stolen, as I suspect, by that unhanged witch, Goody Cory, and that, too, when I was all anointed with the juice of smallage, and cinquefoil, and wolf's bane"—

"Mingled with fine wheat and the fat of a newborn babe," said the shape of old Goodman Brown.

"Ah, your worship knows the recipe," cried the old lady, cackling aloud. "So, as I was saying, being all ready for the meeting, and no horse to ride on, I made up my mind to foot it; for they tell me there is a nice young man to be taken into communion tonight. But now your good worship will lend me your arm, and we shall be there in a twinkling."

"That can hardly be," answered her friend. "I may not spare you my arm, Goody Cloyse; but here is my staff, if you will."

So saying, he threw it down at her feet, where, perhaps, it assumed life, being one of the rods which its owner had formerly lent to the Egyptian magi. Of this fact, however, Goodman Brown could not take cognizance. He had cast up his eyes in astonishment, and, looking down again, beheld neither Goody Cloyse nor the serpentine staff, but his fellow traveller alone, who waited for him as calmly as if nothing had happened.

"That old woman taught me my catechism," said the young man; and there was a world of meaning in this simple comment.

They continued to walk onward, while the elder traveller exhorted his companion to make good speed and persevere in the path, discoursing so aptly that his arguments seemed rather to spring up in the bosom of his auditor than to be suggested by himself. As they went, he plucked a branch of maple to serve for a walking stick, and began to strip it of the twigs and little boughs, which were wet with evening dew. The moment his fingers touched them they became strangely withered and dried up as with a week's sunshine. Thus the pair proceeded, at a good free pace, until suddenly, in a gloomy hollow of the road, Goodman Brown sat himself down on the stump of a tree and refused to go any farther.

"Friend," said he stubbornly, "my mind is made up. Not another step will I budge on this errand. What if a wretched old woman do choose to go to the devil when I thought she was going to heaven: is that any reason why I should quit my dear Faith and go after her?"

"You will think better of this by and by," said his acquaintance composedly. "Sit here and rest yourself a while; and when you feel like moving again, there is my staff to help you along."

Without more words, he threw his companion the maple stick, and was as speedily out of sight as if he had vanished into the deepening gloom. The young man sat a few moments by the roadside, applauding himself greatly, and thinking with how clear a conscience he should meet the minister in his morning walk, nor shrink from the eye of good old Deacon Gookin. And what calm sleep would be his that very night, which was to have been spent so wickedly, but so[3] purely and sweetly now, in the arms of Faith! Amidst these pleasant and praiseworthy meditations, Goodman Brown heard the tramp of horses along

---

[3] This *so* was introduced after the 1835 and 1846 versions of the story.

the road, and deemed it advisable to conceal himself within the verge of the forest, conscious of the guilty purpose that had brought him thither, though now so happily turned from it.

On came the hoof tramps and the voices of the riders, two grave old voices, conversing soberly as they drew near. These mingled sounds appeared to pass along the road, within a few yards of the young man's hiding place; but, owing doubtless to the depth of the gloom at that particular spot, neither the travellers nor their steeds were visible. Though their figures brushed the small boughs by the wayside, it could not be seen that they intercepted, even for a moment, the faint gleam from the strip of bright sky athwart which they must have passed. Goodman Brown alternately crouched and stood on tiptoe, pulling aside the branches and thrusting forth his head as far as he durst without discerning so much as a shadow. It vexed him the more, because he could have sworn, were such a thing possible, that he recognized the voices of the minister and Deacon Gookin, jogging along quietly, as they were wont to do, when bound to some ordination or ecclesiastical council. While yet within hearing, one of the riders stopped to pluck a switch.

"Of the two, reverend sir," said the voice like the deacon's, "I had rather miss an ordination dinner than tonight's meeting. They tell me that some of our community are to be here from Falmouth and beyond, and others from Connecticut and Rhode Island, besides several of the Indian powwows, who, after their fashion, know almost as much deviltry as the best of us. Moreover, there is a goodly young woman to be taken into communion."

"Mighty well, Deacon Gookin!" replied the solemn old tones of the minister. "Spur up, or we shall be late. Nothing can be done, you know, until I get on the ground."

The hoofs clattered again; and the voices, talking so strangely in the empty air, passed on through the forest, where no church had ever been gathered or solitary Christian prayed. Whither, then, could these holy men be journeying so deep into the heathen wilderness? Young Goodman Brown caught hold of a tree for support, being ready to sink down on the ground, faint and overburdened with the heavy sickness of his heart. He looked up to the sky, doubting whether there really was a heaven above him. Yet there was the blue arch, and the stars brightening in it.

"With heaven above and Faith below, I will yet stand firm against the devil!" cried Goodman Brown.

While he still gazed upward into the deep arch of the firmament and had lifted his hands to pray, a cloud, though no wind was stirring, hurried across the zenith and hid the brightening stars. The blue sky was still visible, except directly overhead, where this black mass of cloud was sweeping swiftly northward. Aloft in the air, as if from the depths of the cloud, came a confused and doubtful sound of voices. Once the listener fancied that he could distinguish the accents of towns-people of his own, men and women both pious and ungodly, many of whom he had met at the communion table, and had seen others rioting at the tavern. The next moment, so indistinct were the sounds, he doubted whether he had heard aught but the murmur of the old forest, whispering without a wind. Then came a stronger swell of those familiar tones, heard daily in the sunshine at Salem village, but never until now from a cloud of night. There was one voice, of a young woman, uttering lamentations, yet with an uncertain sorrow, and entreating for some favor, which, perhaps, it would grieve her to ob-tain; and all the unseen multitude, both saints and sinners, seemed to encourage her onward.

"Faith!" shouted Goodman Brown, in a voice of agony and despera-tion; and the echoes of the forest mocked him, crying, "Faith! Faith!" as if bewildered wretches were seeking her all through the wilderness.

The cry of grief, rage, and terror was yet piercing the night, when the unhappy husband held his breath for a response. There was a scream, drowned immediately in a louder murmur of voices, fading into far off laughter, as the dark cloud swept away, leaving the clear and silent sky above Goodman Brown. But something fluttered lightly down through the air and caught on the branch of a tree. The young man seized it, and beheld a pink ribbon.

"My Faith is gone!" cried he, after one stupefied moment. "There is no good on earth; and sin is but a name. Come, devil; for to thee is this world given."

And, maddened with despair, so that he laughed loud and long, did Goodman Brown grasp his staff and set forth again, at such a rate that he seemed to fly along the forest path rather than to walk or run. The road grew wilder and drearier and more faintly traced, and vanished at length, leaving him in the heart of the dark wilderness, still rushing onward with the instinct that guides mortal man to evil. The whole forest was peopled with frightful sounds—the creaking of the trees, the howling of wild beasts, and the yell of Indians; while sometimes the wind tolled like a distant church bell, and sometimes gave a broad roar around the traveller, as if all Nature were laughing him to scorn. But he was himself the chief horror of the scene, and shrank not from its other horrors.

"Ha! ha! ha!" roared Goodman Brown when the wind laughed at him. "Let us hear which will laugh loudest. Think not to frighten me with your deviltry. Come witch, come wizard, come Indian powwow, come devil himself, and here comes Goodman Brown. You may as well fear him as he fear you."

In truth, all through the haunted forest there could be nothing more frightful than the figure of Goodman Brown. On he flew among the black pines, brandishing his staff with frenzied gestures, now giving vent to an inspiration of horrid blasphemy, and now shouting forth such laughter as set all the echoes of the forest laughing like demons around him. The fiend in his own shape is less hideous than when he rages in the breast of man. Thus sped the demoniac on his course, until, quivering among the trees, he saw a red light before him, as when the felled trunks and branches of a clearing have been set on fire, and throw up their lurid blaze against the sky, at the hour of midnight. He paused, in a lull of the tempest that had driven him onward, and heard the swell of what seemed a hymn, rolling solemnly from a distance with the weight of many voices. He knew the tune; it was a familiar one in the choir of the village meeting house. The verse died heavily away, and was lengthened by a chorus, not of human voices, but of all the sounds of the benighted wilderness pealing in awful harmony together. Goodman Brown cried out, and his cry was lost to his own ear by its unison with the cry of the desert.

In the interval of silence he stole forward until the light glared full upon his eyes. At one extremity of an open space, hemmed in by the dark wall of the forest, arose a rock, bearing some rude, natural resemblance either to an altar or a pulpit, and surrounded by four blazing pines, their tops aflame, their stems untouched, like candles at an evening meeting. The mass of foliage that had overgrown the summit of the rock was all on fire, blazing high into the night and fitfully illuminating the whole field. Each pendent twig and leafy festoon was in a blaze. As the red light arose and fell, a numerous congregation alternately shone forth, then disappeared in shadow, and again grew, as it were, out of the darkness, peopling the heart of the solitary wood at once.

"A grave and dark-clad company," quoth Goodman Brown.

In truth they were such. Among them, quivering to and fro between gloom and splendor, appeared faces that would be seen next day at the council board of the province, and others which, Sabbath after Sabbath, looked devoutly heavenward, and benignantly over the crowded pews, from the holiest pulpits in the land. Some affirm that the lady of the governor was there. At least there were high dames well known to her, and wives of honored husbands, and widows, a great multitude, and ancient maidens, all of excellent repute, and fair young girls, who trembled lest their mothers should espy them. Either the sudden gleams of light flashing over the obscure field bedazzled Goodman Brown, or he recognized a score of the church members of Salem village famous for their especial sanctity. Good old Deacon Gookin had arrived, and waited at the skirts of that venerable saint, his revered[4] pastor. But, irreverently consorting with these grave, reputable, and pious people, these elders of the church, these chaste dames and dewy virgins, there were men of dissolute lives and women of spotted fame, wretches given over to all mean and filthy vice, and suspected even of horrid crimes. It was strange to see that the good shrank not from the wicked, nor were the sinners abashed by the saints. Scattered also among their pale-faced enemies were the Indian priests, or powwows, who had often scared their native forest with more hideous incantations than any known to English witchcraft.

"But where is Faith?" thought Goodman Brown; and, as hope came into his heart, he trembled.

Another verse of the hymn arose, a slow and mournful strain, such as the pious love, but joined to words which expressed all that our nature can conceive of sin, and darkly hinted at far more. Unfathomable to mere mortals is the lore of fiends. Verse after verse was sung; and still the chorus of the desert swelled between like the deepest tone of a mighty organ; and with the final peal of that dreadful anthem there came a sound, as if the roaring wind, the rushing streams, the howling beasts, and every other voice of the unconcerted[5] wilderness were mingling and according with the voice of guilty man in homage to the prince of all. The four blazing pines threw up a loftier flame, and obscurely discovered shapes and visages of horror on the smoke wreaths above the impious assembly. At the same moment the fire on the rock shot redly forth and formed a glowing arch above its base, where now appeared a figure. With reverence be it spoken, the figure[6] bore no slight similitude, both in garb and manner, to some grave divine of the New England churches.

"Bring forth the converts!" cried a voice that echoed through the field and rolled into the forest.

At the word, Goodman Brown stepped forth from the shadow of the trees and approached the congregation, with whom he felt a loath-

---

[4] In the 1835 version of this story the phrase "revered pastor" appears. In 1846 it appears as "reverend pastor."

[5] In all versions of this story that appeared during Hawthorne's life this word appeared as *unconverted*. See the next paragraph: "Bring forth the converts!"

[6] See David Levin's essay below, p. 98, fn. 9.

ful brotherhood by the sympathy of all that was wicked in his heart. He could have wellnigh sworn that the shape of his own dead father beckoned him to advance, looking downward from a smoke wreath, while a woman, with dim features of despair, threw out her hand to warn him back. Was it his mother? But he had no power to retreat one step, nor to resist, even in thought, when the minister and good old Deacon Gookin seized his arms and led him to the blazing rock. Thither came also the slender form of a veiled female, led between Goody Cloyse, that pious teacher of the catechism, and Martha Carrier, who had received the devil's promise to be queen of hell. A rampant hag was she. And there stood the proselytes beneath the canopy of fire.

"Welcome, my children," said the dark figure, "to the communion of your race.[7] Ye have found thus young your nature and your destiny. My children, look behind you!"

They turned; and flashing forth, as it were, in a sheet of flame, the fiend worshippers were seen; the smile of welcome gleamed darkly on every visage.

"There," resumed the sable form, "are all whom ye have reverenced from youth. Ye deemed them holier than yourselves, and shrank from your own sin, contrasting it with their lives of righteousness and prayerful aspirations heavenward. Yet here are they all in my worshipping assembly. This night it shall be granted you to know their secret deeds: how hoary bearded elders of the church have whispered wanton words to the young maids of their households; how many a woman, eager for widows' weeds, has given her husband a drink at bedtime and let him sleep his last sleep in her bosom; how beardless youths have made haste to inherit their fathers' wealth; and how fair damsels—blush not, sweet ones—have dug little graves in the garden, and bidden me, the sole guest, to an infant's funeral. By the sympathy of your human hearts for sin ye shall scent out all the places—whether in church, bedchamber, street, field, or forest—where crime has been committed, and shall exult to behold the whole earth one stain of guilt, one mighty blood spot. Far more than this. It shall be yours to penetrate, in every bosom, the deep mystery of sin, the fountain of all wicked arts, and which inexhaustibly supplies more evil impulses than human power— than my power at its utmost—can make manifest in deeds. And now, my children, look upon each other."

---

[7] In the original version (1835), this sentence read: " 'Welcome, my children', said the dark figure, 'to the communion of your grave!' " The change from *grave* to *race* extends the meaning of the earlier sentence: "We have been a race of honest men and good Christians since the days of the martyrs. . ."

They did so; and, by the blaze of the hellkindled torches, the wretched man beheld his Faith, and the wife her husband, trembling before that unhallowed altar.

"Lo, there ye stand, my children," said the figure, in a deep and solemn tone, almost sad with its despairing awfulness, as if his once angelic nature could yet mourn for our miserable race. "Depending upon one another's hearts, ye had still hoped that virtue were not all a dream. Now are ye undeceived. Evil is the nature of mankind. Evil must be your only happiness. Welcome again, my children, to the communion of your race."

"Welcome," repeated the fiend worshippers, in one cry of despair and triumph.

And there they stood, the only pair, as it seemed, who were yet hesitating on the verge of wickedness in this dark world. A basin was hollowed, naturally, in the rock. Did it contain water, reddened by the lurid light? or was it blood? or, perchance, a liquid flame? Herein did the shape of evil dip his hand and prepare to lay the mark of baptism upon their foreheads, that they might be partakers of the mystery of sin, more conscious of the secret guilt of others, both in deed and thought, than they could now be of their own. The husband cast one look at his pale wife, and Faith at him. What polluted wretches would the next glance show them to each other, shuddering alike at what they disclosed and what they saw!

"Faith! Faith!" cried the husband, "look up to heaven, and resist the wicked one. "

Whether Faith obeyed he knew not. Hardly had he spoken when he found himself amid calm night and solitude, listening to a roar of the wind which died heavily away through the forest. He staggered against the rock, and felt it chill and damp; while a hanging twig, that had been all on fire, besprinkled his cheek with the coldest dew.

The next morning young Goodman Brown came slowly into the street of Salem village, staring around him like a bewildered man. The good old minister was taking a walk along the graveyard to get an appetite for breakfast and meditate his sermon, and bestowed a blessing, as he passed, on Goodman Brown. He shrank from the venerable saint as if to avoid an anathema. Old Deacon Gookin was at domestic worship, and the holy words of his prayer were heard through the open window. "What God doth the wizard pray to?" quoth Goodman Brown. Goody Cloyse, that excellent old Christian, stood in the early sunshine at her own lattice, catechizing a little girl who had brought her a pint of morning's milk. Goodman Brown snatched away the child as from the grasp of the fiend himself. Turning the corner by the meeting house, he spied the head of Faith, with the pink ribbons, gazing anxiously forth, and bursting into such joy at sight of him that she skipped along the street and almost kissed her husband before the whole village. But Goodman Brown looked sternly and sadly into her face, and passed on without a greeting.

Had Goodman Brown fallen asleep in the forest and only dreamed a wild dream of a witch meeting?

Be it so if you will; but, alas! it was a dream of evil omen for young Goodman Brown. A stern, a sad, a darkly meditative, a distrustful, if not a desperate man did he become from the night of that fearful dream. On the Sabbath day, when the congregation were singing a holy psalm, he could not listen because an anthem of sin rushed loudly upon his ear and drowned all the blessed strain. When the minister spoke from the pulpit with power and fervid eloquence, and, with his hand on the open Bible, of the sacred truths of our religion, and of saintlike lives and triumphant deaths, and of future bliss or misery unutterable,—then did Goodman Brown turn pale, dreading lest the roof should thunder down upon the gray blasphemer and his hearers. Often, awaking suddenly at midnight, he shrank from the bosom of Faith; and at morning or eventide, when the family knelt down at prayer, he scowled and muttered to himself, and gazed sternly at his wife, and turned away. And when he had lived long, and was borne to his grave a hoary corpse, followed by Faith, an aged woman, and children and grandchildren, a goodly procession, besides neighbors not a few, they carved no hopeful verse upon his tombstone, for his dying hour was gloom.

Cotton Mather

From "Enchantments Encountered"*

II. The *New Englanders* are a people of God settled in those, which were once the *Devil's* territories; and it may easily be supposed that the Devil was exceedingly disturbed, when he perceived such a people here accomplishing the promise of old made unto our Blessed Jesus, *That He should have the utmost parts of the earth for his possession.* There was not a greater uproar among the Ephesians, when the Gospel was first brought among them, than there was among, *The Powers of the Air* (after whom those *Ephesians* walked) when first the *silver trumpets* of the Gospel here made the *joyful sound.* The Devil thus irritated, immediately tried all sorts of methods to overturn this poor plantation: and so much of the Church, as was *fled into this wilderness,* immediately found, *the serpent cast out of his mouth a flood for the carrying of it away.* I believe, that never were more *Santanical devices* used for the unsettling of any people under the sun, that what have been employed for the extirpation of the *vine* which God has here *planted, casting out the heathen, and preparing a room before it, and causing it to take deep root, and fill the land, so that it sent its boughs unto the* Atlantic *Sea* eastward, *and its branches unto the* Connecticut *River* westward, *and the hills were covered with the shadow thereof.* But, all those attempts of hell, have hitherto been abortive, many an *Ebenezer* has been erected unto the praise of God, by his poor people here; and, *having obtained help from God, we continue to this day.* Wherefore the Devil is now making one attempt more upon us; an attempt more difficult, more surprizing, more snarled with unintelligible circumstances than any that we have hitherto encountered; an

---

* Cotton Mather, *The Wonders of the Invisible World* (Boston, 1693). Spelling and capitalization have been modernized.

22

attempt so *critical,* that if we get well through, we shall soon enjoy *halcyon* days with all the *vultures* of hell *trodden under our feet.* He has wanted his *incarnate legions* to persecute us, as the people of God have in the other hemisphere been persecuted: he has therefore drawn forth his more *spiritual* ones to make an attack upon us. We have been advised by some credible Christians yet alive, that a malefactor, accused of *witchcraft* as well as *murder,* and executed in this place more than forty years ago, did then give notice of, *an horrible plot against the country by witchcraft, and a foundation of witchcraft then laid, which if it were not seasonably discovered, would probably blow up, and pull down all the churches in the country.* And we have now with horror seen the *discovery* of such a *witchcraft!* An army of *Devils* is horribly broke in upon the place which is the *center,* and after a sort, the *first-born* of our *English* settlements: and the houses of the good people there are filled with the doleful shrieks of their children and servants, tormented by invisible hands, with tortures altogether preternatural. After the mischiefs there endeavored, and since in part conquered, the terrible plague, of *evil angels,* has made its progress into some other places, where other persons have been in like manner diabolically handled. These our poor afflicted neighbors, quickly after they become *infected* and *infested* with these *demons,* arrive to a capacity of discerning those which they conceive the *shapes* of their troublers; and notwithstanding the great and just suspicion, that the *demons* might impose the *shapes* of innocent persons in their *spectral exhibitions* upon the sufferers, (which may perhaps prove no small part of the *witch-plot* in the issue) yet many of the persons thus represented, being examined, several of them have been convicted of a very damnable *witchcraft*: yea, more than one *twenty* have confessed, that they have signed unto a *book,* which the Devil showed them, and engaged in his hellish design of *bewitching,* and *ruining* our land. *We* know not, at least *I* know not, how far the *delusions* of Satan may be interwoven into some circumstances of the *confessions*; but one would think, all the rules of understanding humane affairs are at an end, if after so many most voluntary harmonious *confessions,* made by intelligent persons of all ages, in sundry towns, at several times, we must not believe the *main strokes* wherein those *confessions* all agree: especially when we have a thousand preternatural things every day before our eyes, wherein the *confessors* do acknowledge their concernment, and give demonstration of their being so concerned. If the Devils now can strike the minds of men with any *poisons* of so fine a composition and operation, that scores of innocent people shall unite, in *confessions* of a crime, which we see actually committed, it is a thing prodigious, beyond the wonders of the former ages, and it threatens no less than a sort of a dissolution upon the world. Now, by these *confessions* it is agreed, *that* the Devil has made a dreadful knot of *witches* in the country, and by the help of *witches* has dreadfully increased that knot: that these *witches* have driven a trade of commissioning their *confederate spirits,* to do all sorts of mischiefs to the neighbors, whereupon there have ensued such mischievous consequences upon the bodies and estates of the neighborhood, as could not otherwise be accounted for: yea, *that* at prodigious *witch-meetings,* the wretches have proceeded so far, as to concert and consult the methods of rooting out the Christian religion from this country, and setting up instead of it, perhaps a more gross *diabolism,* than ever the world saw before. And yet it will be a thing little short of *miracle,* if in so *spread* a business as this, the Devil should not get in some of his juggles, to confound the discovery of all the rest.

. . . . .

IV. But I do not believe, that the progress of *witchcraft* among us, is all the plot which the Devil is managing in the *witchcraft* now upon us. It is judged, that the Devil raised the storm, whereof we read in the eighth chapter of *Matthew,* on purpose to overset the little vessel wherein the disciples of Our Lord were embarked with Him. And it may be feared, that in the *horrible tempest* which is now upon ourselves, the design of the Devil is to sink that happy settlement of government, wherewith almighty God has graciously inclined their majesties to favor us. We are blessed with a governor, than whom no man can be more willing to serve their majesties, or this their province: He is continually venturing his *all* to do it: and were not the interests of his prince dearer to him than his own, he could not but soon be weary of the *helm,* whereat he sits. We are under the influence of a lieutenant governor, who not only by being admirably accomplished both with natural and acquired endowments, is fitted for the service of their majesties, but also with an unspotted fidelity applies himself to that service. Our councilors are some of our most eminent persons, and as loyal subjects to the crown, as hearty lovers of their country. Our constitution also is attended with singular privileges; all which things are by the Devil exceedingly *envied* unto us. And the Devil will doubtless take this occasion for the raising of such complaints and clamors, as may be of pernicious consequence unto some part of our present settlement, if he can so far *impose.* But that which most of all threatens us, in our present circumstances, is the *misunderstanding,* and so the *animosity,* whereinto the *witchcraft* now raging, has enchanted us.

The embroiling, first, of our *spirits*, and then of our *affairs*, is evidently as considerable a branch of the hellish intrigue which now vexes us as any one thing whatsoever. The Devil has made us like a *troubled sea*, and the *mire* and *mud* begins now also to heave up apace. Even good and wise men suffer themselves to fall into their *paroxysms*; and the shake which the Devil is now giving us, fetches up the *dirt* which before lay still at the bottom of our sinful hearts. If we allow the mad dogs of hell to poison us by biting us, we shall imagine that we see nothing but such things about us, and like such things fly upon all that we see. Were it not for what is IN US, for my part, I should not fear a thousand legions of devils: it is by our quarrels that we spoil our prayers; and if our humble, zealous, and united prayers are once hindred: Alas, the *Philistines*, of hell have cut our locks for us; they will then blind us, mock us, ruin us: In truth, I cannot altogether blame it, if people are a little transported, when they conceive all the secular interests of themselves and their families at the stake; and yet at the sight of these heart-burnings, I cannot forbear the exclamation of the sweet-spirited *Austin*, in his pacificatory Epistle to *Jerom*, on the contest with *Ruffin*, *O misera & miseranda conditio!* O condition, truly miserable! But what shall be done to cure these distractions? It is wonderfully necessary, that some healing attempts be made at this time: And I must needs confess (if I may speak so much) like a *Nazianzen*, I am so desirous of a share in them, that if, being thrown overboard, were needful to allay the *storm*, I should think dying a trifle to be undergone, for so great a blessedness.

V. I would most importunately in the first place, entreat every man to maintain an holy jealousy over his soul at this time, and think; may not the Devil make me, though ignorantly and unwillingly, to be an instrument of doing something that would he have to be done? For my part, I freely own my suspicion, lest something of enchantment, have reached more persons and spirits among us, than we are well aware of. But then, let us more generally agree to maintain a kind opinion one of another. That charity without which, even our giving our bodies to be burned would profit nothing, uses to proceed by this rule; it is kind, it is not easily provoked, it thinks no evil, it believes all things, hopes all things. But if we disregard this rule of charity, we shall indeed give our body politic to be burned. I have heard it affirmed, that in the late great flood upon *Connecticut*, those creatures which could not but have quarrelled at another time, yet now being driven together, very agreeably stood by one another. I am sure we shall be worse than *Brutes* if we fly upon one another at a time when the floods of Belial make us afraid. On the one side; [alas, my pen, must thou write

the word, *side* in the business?] There are very worthy men, who
having been called by God, when and where this witchcraft first appeared upon the stage to encounter it, are earnestly desirous to have it
sifted unto the bottom of it. And I pray, which of us all that should
live under the continual impressions of the tortures, outcries, and
havocs which Devils confessedly commissioned by witches make
among their distressed neighbors, would not have a bias that way
beyond other men? Persons this way disposed have been men eminent
for wisdom and virtue, and men acted by a noble principle of conscience: had not conscience (of duty to God) prevailed above other
considerations with them, they would not for all they are worth in
the world have medled in this thorny business. Have there been any
disputed methods used in discovering the works of darkness? It may
be none but what have had great precedents in other parts of the
world; which may, though not altogether justify, yet much alleviate
a mistake in us if there should happen to be found any such mistake
in so dark a matter. They have done what they have done, with mul-
tiplied addresses to God for his guidance, and have not been insensible
how much they have exposed themselves in what they have done. Yea,
they would gladly contrive and receive an expedient, how the shedding
of blood, might be spared, by the recovery of witches, not gone beyond
the reach of pardon. And after all, they invite all good men, in terms
to this purpose, "Being amazed at the number and quality of those
accused of late, we do not know but Satan by his wiles may have en-
wrapped some innocent persons; and therefore should earnestly and
humbly desire the most critical enquiry upon the place, to find out the
fallacy; that there may be none of the servants of the Lord, with the
worshippers of Baal." I may also add, that whereas, if once a witch
do ingeniously confess among us, no more *spectres* do in their shapes
after this, trouble the vicinage; if any guilty creatures will accordingly
to so good purpose confess their crime to any minister of God, and
get out of the snare of the Devil, as no minister will discover such a
conscientious confession, so I believe none in the authority will press
him to discover it; but rejoiced in a soul saved from Death. On the
other side [if I must again use the word *side*, which yet I hope to live to
blot out] there are very worthy men, who are not a little dissatisfied at
the proceedings in the prosecution of this witchcraft. And why? Not
because they would have any such abominable thing, defended from
the strokes of impartial justice. No, those reverend persons who gave in
this advice unto the honorable council; "That presumptions, whereupon persons may be committed, and much more convictions, whereupon persons may be condemned, as guilty of witchcrafts, ought

certainly to be more considerable, than barely the accused persons being represented by a *spectre* unto the afflicted; nor are alterations made in the sufferers, by a look or touch of the accused, to be esteemed an infallible evidence of guilt; but frequently liable to be abused by the Devil's legerdemains": I say, those very men of God most conscientiously subjoined this article to that advice, —"Nevertheless we cannot but humbly recommend unto the government, the speedy and vigorous prosecution of such as have rendered themselves obnoxious; according to the best directions given in the laws of God, and the wholesome statutes of the *English* nation for the detection of witchcraft." Only it is a most commendable cautiousness, in those gracious men, to be very shy lest the Devil get so far into our faith, as that for the sake of many truths which we find he tells us, we come at length to believe any lies, wherewith he may abuse us: whereupon, what a desolation of names would soon ensue, besides a thousand other pernicious consequences? and lest there should be any such principles taken up, as when put into practice must unavoidably cause the *righteous to perish with the wicked*; or procure the bloodshed of any persons, like the *Gibeonites,* whom some learned men suppose to be under a false notion of witches, by *Saul* exterminated.

They would have all due steps taken for the extinction of witches; but they would fain have them to be sure ones; nor is it from any thing, but the real and hearty goodness of such men, that they are loth to surmise ill of other men, till there be the fullest evidence for the surmises. As for the honorable judges that have been hitherto in the commission, they are above my consideration: wherefore I will only say thus much of them, that such of them as I have the honor of a personal acquaintance with, are men of an excellent spirit; and as at first they went about the work for which they were commissioned, with a very great aversion, so they have still been under heartbreaking solicitudes, how they might therein best serve both God and man. In fine, have there been faults on any side fallen into? Surely, they have at worst been but the faults of a well-meaning ignorance. On every side then, why should not we endeavor with amicable correspondencies, to help one another out of the snares wherein the Devil would involve us? To wrangle the Devil out of the country, will be truly a new experiment: Alas! we are not aware of the Devil, if we do not think, that he aims at inflaming us one against another; and shall we suffer ourselves to be Devilridden? or by any unadvisableness contribute unto the widening of our breaches?

To say no more, there is a published and credible relation; which affirms, that very lately in a part of *England,* where some of the neighborhood were quarrelling, a *Raven* from the top of a tree very articulately and unaccountably cried out, *Read the third of Colossians and the fifteenth!* Were I myself to choose what sort of bird I would be transferred into, I would say, *O that I had wings like a dove!* Nevertheless, I will for once do the office, which as it seems, heaven sent that *raven* upon; even to beg, *that the peace of God may rule in our hearts.*

. . . . .

VII. I was going to make one venture more; that is, to offer some safe rules, for the finding out of the witches, which are at this day our accursed troublers: but this were a venture too *presumptuous* and *Icarian* for me to make; I leave that unto those excellent and judicious persons, with whom I am not worthy to be numbered: All that I shall do, shall be to lay before my readers, a brief *Synopsis* of what has been written on that subject. . . . I will begin with,

AN ABSTRACT OF MR. PERKINS'S WAY FOR THE DISCOVERY OF WITCHES.

I. There *are* presumptions, *which do at least probably and conjecturally note one to be a witch. These give occasion to examine, yet they are no sufficient causes of conviction.*

II. *If any man or woman be notoriously defamed for a witch, this yields a strong suspicion. Yet the judge ought carefully to look, that the report be made by men of honesty and credit.*

III. *If a fellow witch, or magician, give testimony of any person to be a witch; this indeed is not sufficient for condemnation; but it is a fit presumption to cause a strait examination.*

IV. *If after cursing there follow death, or at least some mischief: for witches are wont to practice their mischievous facts, by cursing and banning: this also is a sufficient matter of examination, though not of conviction.*

V. *If after enmity, quarrelling, or threatening, a present mischief does follow; that also is a great presumption.*

VI. *If the party suspected be the son or daughter, the manservant or maidservant, the familiar friend, near neighbor, or old companion, of a known and convicted witch; this may be likewise a presumption; for witchcraft is an art that may be learned, and conveyed from man to man.*

VII. *Some add this for a presumption: if the party suspected be found to have the Devil's mark; for it is commonly thought, when* the Devil makes his covenant with them, he always leaves his mark behind them, whereby he knows them for his own:—a mark whereof no evident reason in nature can be given.

VIII. Lastly, if the party examined be unconstant, or contrary to himself, in his deliberate answers, it argues a guilty conscience, which stops the freedom of utterance. And yet there are causes of astonishment, which may befall the good, as well as the bad.

IX. But then there is a conviction, discovering the witch, which must proceed from just and sufficient proofs, and not from bare presumptions.

X. Scratching of the suspected party, and recovery thereupon, with several other such weak proofs; as also, the fleeting of the suspected party, thrown upon the water; these proofs are so far from being sufficient, that some of them are, after a sort, practices of witchcraft.

XI. The testimony of some wizard, though offering to show the witch's face in a glass: This, I grant, may be a good presumption, to cause a strait examination; but a sufficient proof of conviction it cannot be. If the Devil tell the grand jury, that the person in question is a witch, and offers withal to confirm the same by oath, should the inquest receive his oath or accusation to condemn the man? Assuredly no. And yet, that is as much as the testimony of another wizard, who only by the Devil's help reveals the witch.

XII. If a man, being dangerously sick, and like to die, upon suspicion, will take it on his death, that such a one has bewitched him, it is an allegation of the same nature, which may move the judge to examine the party, but it is of no moment for conviction.

XIII. Among the sufficient means of conviction, the first is, the free and voluntary confession of the crime, made by the party suspected and accused, after examination. I say not, that a bare confession is sufficient, but a confession after due examination, taken upon pregnant presumptions. What needs now more witness or further inquiry?

XIV. There is a second sufficient conviction, by the testimony of two witnesses, of good and honest report, avouching before the magistrate, upon their own knowledge, these two things: either that the party accused has made a league with the Devil, or has done some known practice of witchcraft. And, all arguments that do necessarily prove either of these, being brought by two sufficient witnesses, are of force fully to convince the party suspected.

XV. If it can be proved, that the party suspected has called upon the Devil, or desired his help, this is a pregnant proof of a league formerly made between them.

XVI. *If it can be proved, that the party has entertained a familiar spirit, and had conference with it, in the likeness of some visible creatures; here is evidence of witchcraft.*

XVII. *If the witnesses affirm upon oath, that the suspected person has done any action or work which necessarily infers a covenant made, as, that he has used enchantments, divined things before they come to pass, and that peremptorily, raised tempests, caused the form of a dead man to appear; it proves sufficiently, that he or she is a witch.* This is the substance of Mr. *Perkins.*

Richard H. Fogle

Ambiguity and Clarity
in Hawthorne's
"Young Goodman Brown"*

"Young Goodman Brown" is generally felt to be one of Hawthorne's
more difficult tales, from the ambiguity of the conclusions which may
be drawn from it. Its hero, a naïve young man who accepts both society
in general and his fellow-men as individuals at their own valuation, is
in one terrible night presented with the vision of human Evil, and is
ever afterwards "A stern, a sad, a darkly meditative, a distrustful, if
not a desperate man . . . ," whose "dying hour was gloom." So far we
are clear enough, but there are confusing factors. In the first place, are
the events of the night merely subjective, a dream; or do they actually
occur? Again, at the crucial point in his ordeal Goodman Brown sum-
mons the strength to cry to his wife Faith, "look up to heaven, and
resist the evil one." It would appear from this that he has successfully
resisted the supreme temptation—but evidently he is not therefore
saved. Henceforth, "On the Sabbath day, when the congregation were
singing a holy psalm, he could not listen because an anthem of sin
rushed loudly upon his ear and drowned all the blessed strain." On
the other hand, he is not wholly lost, for in the sequel he is only
at intervals estranged from "the bosom of Faith." Has Hawthorne
himself failed to control the implications of his allegory?

I should say rather that these ambiguities of meaning are inten-
tional, an integral part of his purpose. Hawthorne wishes to propose,
not flatly that man is primarily evil, but instead the gnawing doubt
lest this should indeed be true. "Come, devil; for to thee is this world
given," exclaims Goodman Brown at the height of his agony, but he
finds strength to resist the devil, and in the ambiguous conclusion he

---

* Richard H. Fogle, "Ambiguity and Clarity in Hawthorne's 'Young Goodman
Brown'," *New England Quarterly*, XVIII (December, 1945), 448–465. Reprinted by
permission of the journal and of the author.

does not entirely reject his former faith. His trial, then, comes not
from the certainty but the dread of Evil. Hawthorne poses the dangerous question of /449/ the relations of Good and Evil in man, but
withholds his answer. Nor does he permit himself to settle whether the
events of the night of trial are real or the mere figment of a dream.

These ambiguities he conveys and fortifies by what Yvor Winters
has called "the formula of alternative possibilities,"[1] and F. O. Matthiessen "the device of multiple choice,"[2] in which are suggested two
or more interpretations of a single action or event. Perhaps the most
striking instance of the use of this device in "Young Goodman Brown"
is the final word on the reality of the hero's night experience:

> "Had Goodman Brown fallen asleep in the forest and only dreamed a
> wild dream of a witch-meeting?"
>
> "*Be it so if you will;*[3] but alas! it was a dream of evil omen for young
> Goodman Brown."

This device of multiple choice, or ambiguity, is the very essence
of Hawthorne's tale. Nowhere does he permit us a simple meaning,
a merely single interpretation. At the outset, young Goodman Brown
leaves the arms of his wife Faith and the safe limits of Salem town to
keep a mysterious appointment in the forest. Soon he encounters his
conductor, a man "in grave and decent attire," commonplace enough
save for an indefinable air of acquaintanceship with the great world.
". . . the only thing about him that could be fixed upon as remarkable
was his staff, which bore the likeness of a great black snake, so curiously wrought that it might almost be seen to twist and wriggle itself
like a living serpent. *This of course, must have been an ocular deception, assisted by the uncertain light.*"[4] /450/

This man is, of course, the Devil, who seeks to lure the still-reluctant
goodman to a witch-meeting. In the process he progressively under-
mines the young man's faith in the institutions and the men whom he
has heretofore revered. First Goody Cloyse, "a very pious and ex-

---

[1] *Maule's Curse* (Norfolk, Connecticut, 1938), p. 18. Mr. Winters limits his discussion of the device to Hawthorne's novels.

[2] *American Renaissance* (New York, 1941), p. 276.

[3] These and all subsequent italics are mine.

[4] Hawthorne may have taken this suggestion from the serpent-staff of Mercury.
He later uses it for lighter purposes on at least two occasions in *A Wonder Book.*
Mercury's staff is described by Epimetheus as "like two serpents twisting around a
stick, and . . . carved so naturally that I, at first, thought the serpents were alive"
("The Paradise of Children"). Again, in "The Miraculous Pitcher," "Two snakes,
carved in the wood, were represented as twining themselves about the staff, and were
so very skilfully executed that old Philemon (whose eyes, you know, were getting
rather dim) almost thought them alive, and that he could see them wriggling and
twisting."

emplary dame, who had taught him his catechism in youth, and was still his moral and spiritual adviser," is shown to have more than casual acquaintance with the Devil—to be, in fact, a witch. Goodman Brown is shaken, but still minded to turn back and save himself. He is then faced with a still harder test. Just as he is about to return home, filled with self-applause, he hears the tramp of horses along the road:

> On came the hoof tramps and the voices of the riders, two grave old voices, conversing soberly as they drew near. These mingled sounds appeared to pass along the road, within a few yards of the young man's hiding-place; *but, owing doubtless to the depth of the gloom at that particular spot, neither the travellers nor their steeds were visible. Though their figures brushed the small boughs by the wayside, it could not be seen that they intercepted, even for a moment, the faint gleam from the strip of bright sky athwart which they must have passed.* It vexed him the more, because he could have sworn, *were such a thing possible,* that he recognized the voices of the minister and Deacon Gookin, jogging along quietly, as they were wont to do, when bound to some ordination or ecclesiastical council.

The conversation of the minister and the deacon makes it only too clear that they also are in league with the evil one. Yet Goodman Brown, although now even more deeply dismayed, still resolves to stand firm, heartened by the blue arch of the sky and the stars brightening in it.[5] At that moment a cloud, "though no wind was stirring," hides the stars, and he hears a confused babble of voices. *"Once the listener fancied that he could distinguish* the accents of townspeople of his own . . . . /451/ The next moment, so indistinct were the sounds, *he doubted whether he had heard aught* but the murmur of the old forest, whispering without a wind." But to his horror he believes that he hears the voice of his wife Faith, uttering only weak and insincere objections as she is borne through the air to the witch-meeting.

Now comes a circumstance which at first sight would appear to break the chain of ambiguities, for his suspicions seem concretely verified. A pink ribbon, which he remembers having seen in his wife's hair, comes fluttering down into his grasp. This ribbon, an apparently solid object like the fatal handkerchief in *Othello,* seems out of keeping with the atmosphere of doubt which has enveloped the preceding incidents.[6] Two considerations, however, make it possible to defend it.

---

5 Cf. Bosola to the Duchess at a comparably tragic moment in Webster's *Duchess of Malfi*: "Look you, the stars shine still."

6 "As long as what Brown saw is left wholly in the realm of hallucination, Hawthorne's created illusion is compelling . . . . Only the literal insistence on that damaging pink ribbon obtrudes the labels of a confining allegory, and short-circuits the range of association." Matthiessen, *American Renaissance*, p. 284.

One is that if Goodman Brown is dreaming, the ribbon like the rest may be taken as part-and-parcel of his dream. It is to be noted that this pink ribbon appears in his wife's hair once more as she meets him at his return to Salem in the morning. The other is that for the moment the ribbon vanishes from the story, melting into its shadowy background. Its impact is merely temporary.

Be it as you will, as Hawthorne would say. At any rate the effect on Goodman Brown is instantaneous and devastating. Casting aside all further scruples, he rages through the wild forest to the meeting of witches, for the time at least fully accepting the domination of Evil. He soon comes upon a "numerous congregation," alternately shadowy and clear in the flickering red light of four blazing pines above a central rock.

> Among them, *quivering to and fro between gloom and splendor,* appeared faces that would be seen next day at the council board of the province, and others which, Sabbath after Sabbath, looked devoutly heavenward, and benignantly over the crowded pews, from the holiest pulpits in the land. *Some affirm that* the lady of /452/ the governor was there. . . . *Either the sudden gleams of light flashing over the obscure field bedazzled Goodman Brown, or he recognized* a score of the church members of Salem village famous for their especial sanctity.

Before this company steps out a presiding figure who bears "With reverence be it spoken . . . *no slight similitude,* both in garb and manner, to some grave divine of the New England churches," and calls forth the "converts." At the word young Goodman Brown comes forward. "*He could have well-nigh sworn* that the shape of his own dead father beckoned him to advance, looking downward from a smoke wreath, while a woman, with dim features of despair, threw out her hand to warn him back. *Was it his mother?*" But he is quickly seized and led to the rock, along with a veiled woman whom he dimly discerns to be his wife Faith. The two are welcomed by the dark and ambiguous leader into the fraternity of Evil, and the final, irretrievable step is prepared.

> A basin was hollowed, naturally, in the rock. *Did it contain water, reddened by the lurid light? or was it blood? or, perchance, a liquid flame?* Herein did the shape of evil dip his hand and prepare to lay the mark of baptism upon their foreheads, that they might be partakers of the mystery of sin, more conscious of the secret guilt of others, both in deed and thought, than they could now be of their own. The husband cast one look at his pale wife, and Faith at him. What polluted wretches would the next glance show them to each other, shuddering alike at what they disclosed and what they saw!

"Faith! Faith!" cried the husband, "look up to heaven, and resist the wicked one."

Whether Faith obeyed he knew not.

Hawthorne then concludes with the central ambiguity, which we have already noticed, whether the events of the night were actual or a dream? The uses of this device, if so it may be called, are multiple in consonance with its nature. Primarily it offers opportunity for freedom and richness of suggestion. By /453/ it Hawthorne is able to suggest something of the density and incalculability of life, the difficulties which clog the interpretation of even the simplest incidents, the impossibility of achieving a single and certain insight into the actions and motives of others. This ambiguity adds depth and tone to Hawthorne's thin and delicate fabric. It covers the bareness of allegory, imparting to its one-to-one equivalence of object and idea a wider range of allusiveness, a hint of rich meaning still untapped. By means of it the thesis of "Young Goodman Brown" is made to inhere firmly in the situation, whence the reader himself must extract it to interpret. Hawthorne the artist refuses to limit himself to a single and doctrinaire conclusion,[7] proceeding instead by indirection. Further, it permits him to make free with the two opposed worlds of actuality and of imagination without incongruity or the need to commit himself entirely to either; while avoiding a frontal attack upon the reader's feeling for everyday verisimilitude, it affords the author licence of fancy. It allows him to draw upon sources of legend and superstition which still strike a responsive chord in us, possessing something of the validity of universal symbols.[8] Hawthorne's own definition of Romance may very aptly be applied to his use of ambiguity: it gives him scope "so [to] manage his atmospherical medium as to bring out or mellow the lights and deepen and enrich the shadows of the picture."[9]

These scanty observations must suffice here for the general importance of Hawthorne's characteristic ambiguity. It remains to describe its immediate significance in "Young Goodman Brown." Above all,

---

[7] "For Hawthorne its value consisted in the variety of explanations to which it gave rise." *American Renaissance*, p. 277. The extent of my indebtedness to Mr. Matthiessen is only inadequately indicated in my documentation.

[8] "It is only by . . . symbols that have numberless meanings beside the one or two the writer lays an emphasis upon, or the half-score he knows of, that any highly subjective art can escape from the barrenness and shallowness of a too conscious arrangement, into the abundance and depth of nature . . . ." W. B. Yeats, "The Philosophy of Shelley's Poetry," *Ideas of Good and Evil* (London, 1914), p. 90. Thus Hawthorne by drawing upon Puritan superstition and demonology is able to add another dimension to his story.

[9] Preface, *The House of the Seven Gables*.

the separate instances of this "multiple choice device" organically cohere to reproduce in the reader's mind the feel of the central ambiguity of theme, the horror of the hero's doubt. Goodman Brown, a simple and pious nature, is wrecked as a result of the disappearance of the fixed poles of his belief. His orderly cosmos dissolves into chaos as church and state, the twin pillars of his society, are hinted to be rotten, with their foundations undermined.[10] The yearning for certainty is basic to his spirit—and he is left without the comfort even of a firm reliance in the Devil.[11] His better qualities avail him in his desperation little more than the inner evil which prompted him to court tempation, for they prevent him from seeking the only remaining refuge—the confraternity of Sin. Henceforth he is fated to a dubious battle with shadows, to struggle with limed feet toward a redemption which must forever elude him, since he has lost the vision of Good while rejecting the proffered opportunity to embrace Evil fully. Individual instances of ambiguity, then, merge and coalesce in the theme itself to produce an all-pervading atmosphere of uneasiness and anguished doubt.

Ambiguity alone, however, is not a satisfactory aesthetic principle. Flexibility, suggestiveness, allusiveness, variety—all these are without meaning if there is no pattern from which to vary, no center from which to flee outwards. And, indeed, ambiguity of itself will not adequately account for the individual phenomenon of "Young Goodman Brown." The deliberate haziness and multiple implications of its meaning are counter-balanced by the firm clarity of its technique, in structure and in style. /455/

This clarity is embodied in the lucid simplicity of the basic action; in the skilful foreshadowing by which the plot is bound together; in balance of episode and scene; in the continuous use of contrast; in the firmness and selectivity of Hawthorne's pictorial composition; in the carefully arranged climactic order of incident and tone; in the detachment and irony of Hawthone's attitude; and finally in the purity, the grave formality, and the rhetorical balance of the style. His amalgamation of these elements achieves an effect of totality, of exquisite crafts-

---

[10] Goodman Brown is disillusioned with the church in the persons of Goody Cloyse, the minister, and Deacon Gookin, and it will be recalled that the figure of Satan at the meeting "bore no slight similitude . . . to some grave divine of the New England churches." As to the secular power, the devil tells Brown that ". . . the selectmen of divers towns make me their chairman; and a majority of the Great and General Court are firm supporters of my interest. The governor and I, too— But these are state secrets."

[11] The story could conceivably be read as intellectual satire, showing the pitfalls that lie in wait for a too-shallow and unquestioning faith. Tone and emphasis clearly show, however, a more tragic intention.

manship, of consummate artistic economy in fitting the means to the attempted ends.

The general framework of the story has a large simplicity. Goodman Brown leaves his wife Faith and the safe confines of Salem town at sunset, spends the night in the forest, and at dawn returns a changed man. Within this simple pattern plot and allegory unfold symmetrically and simultaneously. The movement of "Young Goodman Brown" is the single revolution of a wheel, which turns full-circle upon itself. As by this basic structure, the action is likewise given form by the device of foreshadowing, through which the entire development of the plot is already implicit in the opening paragraph. Thus Faith is troubled by her husband's expedition, and begs him to put it off till sunrise. "A lone woman is troubled with such dreams and such thoughts that she's afeard of herself sometimes," says she, hinting the ominous sequel of her own baptism in sin. " 'My love and my Faith,' replied young Goodman Brown, 'of all nights in the year, this one night must I tarry away from thee. My journey . . . forth and back again, must needs be done 'twixt now and sunrise.' " They part, but Brown looking back sees "the head of Faith still peeping after him with a melancholy air, in spite of her pink ribbons."

> "Poor little Faith!" thought he, for his heart smote him. "What a wretch am I to leave her on such an errand! She talks of dreams, too. Methought as she spoke there was trouble in her face, as if a dream had warned her what work is to be done to-night. But no, /456/ no; 'twould kill her to think of it. Well, she's a blessed angel on earth; and after this one night I'll cling to her skirts and follow her to heaven."

This speech, it must be confessed, is in several respects clumsy, obvious, and melodramatic;[12] but beneath the surface lurks a deeper layer. The pervasive ambiguity of the story is foreshadowed in the subtle emphasizing of the dream-motif, which paves the way for the ultimate uncertainty whether the incidents of the night are dream or reality; and in his simple-minded aspiration to "cling to her skirts and follow her to heaven," Goodman Brown is laying an ironic foundation for his later horror of doubt. A broader irony is apparent, in the light of future events, in the general emphasis upon Faith's angelic goodness.

Hawthorne's seemingly casual references to Faith's pink ribbons, which are mentioned three times in the opening paragraphs, are like-

---

12 It has the earmarks of the set dramatic soliloquy, serving in this case to provide both information about the plot and revelation of character. Mr. Matthiessen attributes Hawthorne's general use of theatrical devices to the influence of Scott, who leads in turn to Shakespeare. *American Renaissance*, p. 203.

wise far from artless. These ribbons, as we have seen, are an important factor in the plot; and as an emblem of heavenly Faith their color gradually deepens into the liquid flame or blood of the baptism into sin.[13]

Another instance of Hawthorne's careful workmanship is his architectural balance of episodes or scenes. The encounter with Goody Cloyse, the female hypocrite and sinner, is set off against the conversation of the minister and Deacon Gookin immediately afterward. The exact correspondence of the two episodes is brought into high relief by two balancing speeches. Goody Cloyse has lost her broomstick, and must perforce walk to the witch-meeting—a sacrifice she is willing to make since "they /457/ tell me there is a nice young man to be taken into communion to-night." A few minutes later Deacon Gookin, in high anticipation remarks that "there is a goodly young woman to be taken into comunion." A still more significant example of this balance is contained in the full swing of the wheel—in the departure at sunset and the return at sunrise. At the beginning of the story Brown takes leave of "Faith with the pink ribbons," turns the corner by the meeting-house and leaves the town; in the conclusion

> . . . Young Goodman Brown came slowly into the street of Salem village, staring around him like a bewildered man. The good old minister was taking a walk along the graveyard to get an appetite for breakfast and meditate his sermon, and bestowed a blessing, as he passed, on Goodman Brown. He shrank from the venerable saint as if to avoid an anathema. Old Deacon Gookin was at domestic worship, and the holy words of his prayer were heard through the open window. "What God doth the wizard pray to?" quoth Goodman Brown. Goody Cloyse, that excellent old Christian, stood in the early sunshine at her own lattice, catechizing a little girl who had brought her a pint of morning's milk.[14] Goodman Brown snatched the child away as from the grasp of the fiend himself. Turning the corner by the meeting-house, he spied the head of Faith, with the pink ribbons, gazing anxiously forth, and bursting into such joy at the sight of him that she skipped along the street and almost kissed her husband before the whole village. But Goodman Brown looked sternly and sadly into her face, and passed on without a greeting.

---

[13] Further, in welcoming the two candidates to the communion of Evil, the Devil says, "By the sympathy of your human hearts for sin ye shall scent out all the places . . . where crime has been committed, and shall exult to behold the whole earth one stain of guilt, *one mighty blood spot.*" For this discussion of the pink ribbons I am largely indebted to Leland Schubert, *Hawthorne, the Artist* (Chapel Hill, 1944), p. 79–80.

[14] This touch takes on an ironic and ominous significance if it is noticed that Goody Cloyse has that night been Faith's sponsor, along with the "rampant hag" Martha Carrier, at the baptism into sin by blood and flame.

The exact parallel between the earlier and the later situation serves to dramatize intensely the change which the real or fancied happenings of the night have brought about in Goodman Brown.[15] /458/

Contrast, a form balance, is still more prominent in "Young Goodman Brown" than the kind of analogy of scene and episode which I have mentioned. The broad antitheses of day against night, the town against the forest, which signify in general a sharp dualism of Good and Evil, are supplemented by a color-contrast of red-and-black at the witch-meeting, by the swift transition of the forest scene from leaping flame to damp and chill, and by the consistent cleavage between outward decorum and inner corruption in the characters.[16]

The symbols of Day and Night, of Town and Forest, are almost indistinguishable in meaning. Goodman Brown leaves the limits of Salem at dusk and reënters them at sunrise; the night he spends in the forest. Day and the Town are clearly emblematic of Good, of the seemly outward appearance of human convention and society. They stand for the safety of an unquestioning and unspeculative faith. Oddly enough, Goodman Brown in the daylight of the Salem streets is a young man too simple and straightforward to be interesting, and a little distasteful in his boundless reverence for such unspectacular worthies as the minister, the deacon, and Goody Cloyse. Night and the Forest are the domains of the Evil One, symbols of doubt and wandering, where the dark subterraneous forces of the human spirit riot unchecked.[17] By the dramatic necessities of the plot Brown is a larger figure in the Forest of Evil,[18] and as a chief actor at the witch-meeting, than within the safe bounds of the town. /459/

---

[15] Here we may anticipate a little in order to point out the steady and premeditated irony arising from the locutions "good old minister," "venerable saint," and "excellent old Christian"; and the climactic effect produced by the balance and repetition of the encounters, which are duplicated in the sentence structure and the repetition of "Goodman Brown."

[16] Epitomized by Brown's description of the assemblage at the meeting as "a grave and dark-clad company."

[17] "The conception of the dark and evil-haunted wilderness came to him [Hawthorne] from the days of Cotton Mather, who held that 'the New Englanders are a people of God settled in those which were once the devil's territories.' " Matthiessen, *American Renaissance*, pp. 282–283. See also Matthiessen's remark of *The Scarlet Letter* that "... the forest itself, with its straggling path, images to Hester 'the moral wilderness in which she had so long been wandering'; and while describing it Hawthorne may have taken a glance back at Spenser's Wood of Errour." *American Renaissance* pp. 279–280. This reference to Spenser may as fitly be applied to the path of Young Goodman Brown, "darkened by all the gloomiest trees of the forest, which barely stood aside to let the narrow path creep through, and closed immediately behind."

[18] "But he was himself the chief horror of the scene, and shrank not from its other horrors."

The contrast of the red of fire and blood against the black of night and the forest at the witch-meeting has a different import. As the flames rise and fall, the faces of the worshippers of Evil are alternately seen in clear outline and deep shadow, and all the details of the scene are at one moment revealed, the next obscured. It seems, then, that the red is Sin or Evil, plain and unequivocal; the black is that doubt of the reality either of Evil or Good which tortures Goodman Brown and is the central ambiguity of Hawthorne's story.[19]

A further contrast follows in the swift transformation of scene when young Goodman Brown finds himself "amid calm night and solitude . . . . He staggered against the rock, and felt it chill and damp; while a hanging twig, that had been all on fire, besprinkled his cheek with the coldest dew."[20]

Most pervasive of the contrasts in "Young Goodman Brown" is the consistent discrepancy between appearance and reality,[21] which helps to produce its heavy atmosphere of doubt and shadow. The church is represented by the highly respectable figures of Goody Cloyse, the minister, and Deacon Gookin, who in the forest are witch and wizards. The devil appears to Brown in the guise of his grandfather, "in grave and decent attire." As the goodman approaches the meeting, his ears are greeted by "the swell of what seemed a hymn, rolling solemnly from a distance with the weight of many voices. He knew the tune; it was a familiar one in the choir of the village meeting-house." The Communion of Sin is, in fact, the faithful counterpart of a grave and pious ceremony at a Puritan meeting-house. "At one extremity of an open space, hemmed in by the dark wall of the forest, arose a rock, bearing some rude, natural resemblance either to an altar or a pulpit, and surrounded by four blazing /460/ pines, their tops aflame, their stems untouched, like candles at an evening meeting." The worshippers are "a numerous congregation," Satan resembles some grave divine, and the initiation into sin takes the form of a baptism.[22]

Along with this steady use of contrast at the Sabbath should be noticed its firmly composed pictorial quality. The rock, the center of the picture, is lighted by the blazing pines. The chief actors are as it

---

[19] Hawthorne not infrequently uses color for symbol. See such familiar instances as *The Scarlet Letter* and "The Minister's Black Veil."

[20] See Schubert, *Hawthorne, the Artist*, p. 63. One would presume this device to be traditional in the story of the supernatural, where a return to actuality must eventually be made. An obvious example is the vanishing at cockcrow of the Ghost in *Hamlet*. See also the conclusion of Hawthorne's own "Ethan Brand."

[21] Evil must provisionally be taken for reality during the night in the forest, in spite of the ambiguity of the ending.

[22] The hint of the perverse desecration of the Black Mass adds powerfully here to the connotative scope of the allegory.

were spotlighted in turn as they advance to the rock, while the congregation is generalized in the dimmer light at the outer edges. The whole composition is simple and definite, in contrast with the ambiguity occasioned by the rise and fall of the flame, in which the mass of the worshippers alternately shines forth and disappears in shadow.[23]

The clarity and simple structural solidity of "Young Goodman Brown" evinces itself in its tight dramatic framework. Within the basic form of the turning wheel it further divides into four separate scenes, the first and last of which, of course, are the balancing departure from and return to Salem. The night in the forest falls naturally into two parts: the temptation by the Devil and the witch-meeting. These two scenes, particularly the first, make full and careful use of the dramatic devices of suspense and climactic arrangement; and Hawthorne so manipulates his materials as to divide them as sharply as by a dropped curtain.

The temptation at first has the stylized and abstract delicacy of Restoration Comedy, or of the formalized seductions of Molière's *Don Juan*. The simple goodman, half-eager and half-reluctant, is wholly at the mercy of Satan, who leads him step by step to the inevitable end. The tone of the earlier part of this scene is lightly ironic: an irony reinforced by the inherent irony /461/ of the situation, which elicits a double meaning at every turn.

"Come, Goodman Brown," cried his fellow-traveller, "this is a dull pace for the beginning of a journey. Take my staff, if you are so soon weary."

"Friend," said the other, exchanging his slow pace for a full stop, "having kept covenant by meeting thee here, it is my purpose now to return whence I came. I have scruples touching the matter thou wot'st of."

"Sayest thou so?" replied he of the serpent, smiling apart. "Let us walk on, nevertheless, reasoning as we go; and if I convince thee not thou shalt turn back. We are but a little way in the forest yet."

Then begins a skilful and relentless attack upon all the values which Goodman Brown has lived by. His reverence for his Puritan ancestors, "a people of prayer, and good works to boot," is speedily turned against him as the Devil claims them for tried and dear companions. Next comes the episode of Goody Cloyse, who taught the young man his catechism. Brown is sorely cast down, but at length sturdily concludes:

---

23 The general effect is very like that of the famous Balinese Monkey Dance, which is performed at night, usually in a clearing of the forest, by the light of a single torch. The chief figures, the Monkey King and the King of the Demons, advance in turn to this central torch, while the chorus of dancers remains in the semi-obscurity of the background. This dance is allegorical, the Monkeys, as helpers of the Balinese, representing Good against the Evil of the Demons.

"What if a wretched old woman do choose to go to the devil when I thought she was going to heaven: is that any reason why I should quit my dear Faith and go after her?" But no sooner has he rallied from this blow when he is beset by another, still more shrewdly placed: he hears the voices of the minister and Deacon Gookin, and from their conversation gathers that they are bound for the meeting, and eagerly anticipating it. This is nearly final, but he still holds out. " 'With heaven above, and Faith below, I will yet stand firm against the devil!' cried Goodman Brown"; only to be utterly overthrown by the sound of his wife's voice in the air, and the crushing evidence of the fatal pink ribbon.

The style has gradually deepened and intensified along with the carefully graduated intensity of the action, and now Hawthorne calls upon all his resources to seize and represent the immense significance of the moment. Nature itself is made at once to sympathize with and to mock the anguished chaos of /462/ the young man's breast; in his rage he is both at one with and opposed to the forest and the wind.[24] The symphony of sound, which began with the confused babble of voices in the sky as Faith and her witch-attendants swept overhead, rises to a wild crescendo.[25]

> And, maddened with despair, so that he laughed loud and long, did Goodman Brown grasp his staff and set forth again, at such a rate that he seemed to fly along the forest path rather than to walk or run. The road grew wilder and drearier and more faintly traced, and vanished at length, leaving him in the heart of the dark wilderness, still rushing onward with the instinct that guides mortal man to evil. The whole forest was peopled with frightful sounds—the creaking of the trees, the howling of wild beasts, and the yell of Indians; while sometimes the wind tolled like a distant church bell, and sometimes gave a broad roar around the traveller, as if all Nature were laughing him to scorn. But he was himself the chief horror of the scene, and shrank not from its other horrors.

After ascending to this climax, Hawthorne disengages himself and separates his scenes with the definiteness of the dropping of a curtain —by the simple expedient of shifting his view from the hero to his

---

[24] "The intensity of the situation is sustained by all the devices Hawthorne had learned from the seventeenth century, for just as the heavens groaned in Milton's fall of the angels, the winds are made to whisper sadly at the loss of this man's faith." Matthiessen, *American Renaissance*, p. 284. The winds, however, roar rather than "whisper sadly."

[25] Cf. Schubert's account of the sound-effects in "Young Goodman Brown," *Hawthorne, the Artist*, pp. 114–117. Mr. Schubert distorts the effect and purpose of Hawthorne's use of sound in the story by comparing it to "the last movement of Beethoven's Ninth Symphony"—description of sound is not the sound itself—but his perception is extremely valuable.

surroundings. Goodman Brown coming upon the witch-meeting is a mere onlooker until the moment comes for him to step forward for his baptism into sin. Up to that moment Satan usurps the stage. The eye is first directed to the central rock-altar, then to the four blazing pines which light it. Next there is the sense of a numerous assembly, vaguely seen in the fitful firelight. Finally the figure of Satan appears at the base of the rock, framed in an arch of flame. Only when he is summoned are we once more fully aware of Goodman Brown, /463/ as he stands at the altar by his wife Faith. Then, a moment later, comes the second crashing climax when Brown calls upon his wife to "look up to heaven, and resist the wicked one"—cut off abruptly by anticlimax as the meeting vanishes in a roaring wind, and Brown leaning against the rock finds it chill and damp to his touch.

The satisfaction one feels in the clean line of the structure of the story is enhanced by Hawthorne's steady detachment from his materials: an attitude which deepens the impression of classic balance, which in turn stands against the painful ambiguity of the theme. Even the full tone of the intensest scenes, as Goodman Brown rushing through the forest, is tempered by restraint. The participant is overweighted by the calm, impartial (though not unfeeling) spectator; Hawthorne does not permit himself to become identified with his hero. He displays young Goodman Brown not in and for himself, but always in relation to the whole situation and set of circumstances. This detachment of attitude is plainest in the almost continuous irony, unemphatic but nonetheless relentless: an irony organically related to the ever-present ambiguities of the situation, but most evident in sustained tone. Thus, after recording Goodman Brown's aspiration to "cling to Faith's skirts and follow her to heaven," the author adds with deadly calm, "With this excellent resolve for the future, Goodman Brown felt himself justified in making more haste on his present evil purpose."

This detachment is implicit in the quiet, the abstractness, and the exquisite gravity of Hawthorne's style, everywhere formal and exactly though subtly cadenced. It throws a light and idealizing veil over the action,[26] and as it were maintains an /464/ aesthetic distance from it, while hinting at the ugliness it mercifully covers. The difference be-

---

[26] Hawthorne's notion of the ideality which art should lend to nature is apparent in his comment in the introductory essay to *Mosses from an Old Manse* upon the reflection of a natural scene in water: "Each tree and rock, and every blade of grass, is distinctly imaged, and however unsightly in reality, assumes ideal beauty in the reflection." And a few pages later—"Of all this scene, the slumbering river has a dream picture in its bosom. Which, after all was the most real—the picture, or the original? the objects palpable to our grosser senses, or their apotheosis in the stream beneath? Surely the disembodied images stand in closer relation to the soul."

tween the saying and the thing said, at times provides dramatic tension
and a kind of ironic fillip. Note, for example, the grave decorum and
eighteenth-century stateliness, the perverted courtliness, of Satan's
welcome to young Brown and Faith:

> This night it shall be granted you to know their secret deeds: how hoary-
> bearded elders of the church have whispered wanton words to the young
> maids of their households; how many a woman, eager for widows' weeds,
> has given her husband a drink at bedtime and let him sleep his last sleep
> in her bosom; how beardless youths have made haste to inherit their fathers'
> wealth; and how fair damsels—blush not, sweet ones—have dug little graves
> in the garden, and bidden me, the sole guest, to an infant's funeral.

The steady procession of measured, ceremonious generalizations—
"hoary-bearded elders," "wanton words," "beardless youths," and
"fair damsels," is in radical contrast with the implication of the meaning; and the grisly archness of "blush not, sweet ones" is deeply
suggestive in its incongruity.[27]

In "Young Goodman Brown," then, Hawthorne has achieved that
reconciliation of opposites which Coleridge deemed the highest art.
The combination of clarity of technique, embodied in simplicity and
balance of structure, in firm pictorial composition, in contrast and
climactic arrangement, in irony and detachment, with ambiguity of
meaning as signalized by the "device of multiple choice," in its inter-
relationships produces the story's characteristic effect. By means of
these two elements Hawthorne reconciles oneness of action with mul-
/465/ tiplicity of suggestion, and enriches the bareness of systematic
allegory. Contrarily, by them he holds in check the danger of lapsing
into mere speculation without substance or form. The phantasmagoric
light-and-shadow of the rising and falling fire, obscuring and softening
the clear, hard outline of the witch-meeting, is an image which will
stand for the essential effect of the story itself, compact of ambiguity
and clarity harmoniously interfused.

---

[27] I would not be understood to affirm that this adaptation of the eighteenth-
century mock-heroic is the sole effect of Hawthorne's style in "Young Goodman
Brown." The seventeenth century plays its part too. The agony of the goodman
in the forest, and the sympathy of the elements, is Miltonic. And in this same scene
of the witch-meeting Hawthorne twice touches upon Miltonic tenderness and sub-
limity: " 'Lo, there ye stand, my children,' said the figure, in a deep and solemn
tone, almost sad with its despairing awfulness, as if his once angelic nature could
yet mourn for our miserable race . . . . And there they stood, the only pair, as it
seemed, who were yet hesitating on the verge of wickedness in this dark world."

D. M. McKeithan

Hawthorne's "Young Goodman Brown": An Interpretation*

The majority of Hawthorne critics feel that "Young Goodman Brown"[1] is one of the very best of Hawthorne's tales, but there is somewhat less certainty as to its meaning. The theme of the story has been variously stated as the reality of sin, the pervasiveness of evil, the secret sin and hypocrisy of all persons, the hypocrisy of Puritanism, the results of doubt or disbelief, the devastating effects of moral scepticism, or the demoralizing effects of the discovery that all men are sinners and hypocrites.[2]

Mark Van Doren, in the fullest and most recent criticism, gives a thorough analysis of the tale both as to its artistry and as to its meaning. I quote briefly from his discussion of its meaning:

> "Young Goodman Brown" means exactly what it says, namely that its hero left his pretty young wife one evening . . . to walk by himself in the primitive New England woods, the Devil's territory, . . . and either to dream or actually to experience (Hawthorne will not say) the discovery that evil exists in every human heart. . . . Brown is changed. He thinks there is no good on earth. . . . Brown, waking from his dream, if it was

---

* D. M. McKeithan, "Hawthorne's 'Young Goodman Brown': An Interpretation," *Modern Language Notes*, LXVII (February, 1952), 93–6. Reprinted by permission of the journal and of the author.

[1] Published in *The New England Magazine* for April, 1835, and collected in *Mosses from an Old Manse* in 1846.

[2] See, among others, George Parsons Lathrop, *A Study of Hawthorne* (Boston, 1876, p. 203; George E. Woodberry, *Nathaniel Hawthorne* (Boston and New York, 1902), p. 146; Frank Preston Stearns, *The Life and Genius of Nathaniel Hawthorne* (Boston, 1906), p. 181; Newton Arvin, *Hawthorne* (Boston, 1929), pp. 61–62; Austin Warren, *Nathaniel Hawthorne: Representative Selections* (New York, 1934), pp. xxviii, lxix, 362; Randall Stewart, *Nathaniel Hawthorne: A Biography* (New Haven, 1948), p. 262.

a dream, . . . sees evil even where it is not. . . . He had stumbled upon
that "mystery of sin" which, rightly understood, provides the only sane
and cheerful view of life there is. Understood in Brown's fashion, it darkens
and sours the world, withering hope and charity, and perverting whatever is
truly good until it looks like evil at its worst: like blasphemy and hypocrisy.[3]

   This survey of critical opinion is not complete, but it is all I have
space for in this brief note. All of these interpretations are plau- /94/
sible, and a good case might be made for each. Some of them agree
essentially, and the interpretation which I present below partly coin-
cides with some of them, though it points out certain truths so obvious
that I marvel at the critics' neglect of them.

   At the end of Chapter VIII of *The House of the Seven Gables* Hawthorne discusses the effects on various types of mind of the discovery or
suspicion that "judges, clergymen, and other characters of that
eminent stamp and respectability, could really, in any single instance,
be otherwise than just and upright men." But to those critics who think
they have discovered in this or in similar passages the theme of
"Young Goodman Brown" I would suggest that it would be more
logical to look for the theme of "Young Goodman Brown" in "Young
Goodman Brown" itself. One should carefully guard against reading
into the story what is not there. Moreover, elsewhere Hawthorne frequently said that there is evil in every human heart (though evil
impulses or desires may not lead to evil deeds), but he does not, in
his own person, say so in this story, and that is not, I think, its meaning.
The theme is Hawthorne's favorite one: sin and its blighting effects.
Goodman Brown's sin is not identified, but its horrible effects are most
impressively described. At the end of the story he is full of cynicism
and moral scepticism; they are not his sin but merely its effects. The
distinction, it seems to me, is essential to a correct interpretation of
the story.

   Goodman Brown is everyman of average intelligence who is striving
to live the good life. For three months he had been married to a lovely
young woman symbolizing religious faith. He was not loyal to Faith,
though he fully expected to be loyal after just one more indulgence
in sin. At some earlier time he had met Satan and had promised to
meet him in the forest at night. It is doubtful that he recognized Satan
at first, but he knew that his journey was an evil one, and his conscience hurt him because of his disloyalty to Faith. He had confidence
in his ability to indulge in the sin—whatever it was—once more and

[3] Mark Van Doren, *Nathaniel Hawthorne* (New York, 1949), pp. 77–79.

then resist all future temptations. He did not know in advance how far into the forest he would be persuaded to go or what the results would be.

Faith urged him to postpone his journey until the next day, but he said it had to be made between sunset and sunrise. His heart smote him and he called himself a wretch to leave her on such an /95/ errand; he believed it would kill her to know what work was to be done that night—and it would have appalled him too if he had known. He thought of her as a blessed angel on earth and said, "After this one night I'll cling to her skirts and follow her to heaven." This "excellent resolve" did not prevent his making haste "on his present evil purpose." It is clear that before Brown had any suspicions concerning the sincerity of supposedly pious people—that is, before he had entered the forest—he was himself deliberately and knowingly indulging in sin, though with the intention of reforming soon.

In the body of the story Satan is the main speaker. In two disguises—first as the man with the serpent staff and second as the priest who presides at the meeting of sinners—Satan poisons the mind of Brown and destroys his belief in virtue and piety. But the reader should not make Brown's mistake: he should not suppose that Satan always speaks the truth—nor need he suppose that Satan always expresses Hawthorne's own opinions.

Satan denies the existence of virtue and piety in the world. It is a consequence and a punishment of Brown's sin that he believes Satan and thus becomes cynical. Hawthorne himself believed that evil impulses visit every human heart, but he did not believe that most men are mainly evil or that most men convert any considerable proportion of their evil impulses into evil deeds. In *Fancy's Show-Box* he said:

> It is not until the crime is accomplished that guilt clinches its grip upon the guilty heart, and claims it for its own. . . . In truth, there is no such thing in man's nature as a settled and full resolve, either for good or evil, except at the very moment of execution.[4]

In short, Hawthorne himself does not share the black pessimism that finally came to Goodman Brown as a result of his sin. Hawthorne greatly admired many people with whom he was personally acquainted, and many good characters are pictured in his tales and romances.

Goodman Brown became cynical as a result of his sin and thought he saw evil even where none existed. This is not a story of the dis-

---

[4] See Austin Warren, *op. cit.*, p. 62.

illusionment that comes to a person when he discovers that many
supposedly religious and virtuous people are really sinful; it is, /96/
rather, a story of a man whose sin led him to consider all other people
sinful. Brown came eventually to judge others by himself: he thought
them sinful and hypocritical because he was sinful and hypocritical
himself. He did not judge them accurately: he misjudged them. The
minister of Salem village, Deacon Gookin, Goody Cloyse, and Faith
were all good in spite of what Goodman Brown eventually came to
think of them.

Moreover, it is not necessary to choose between interpreting the
story literally and taking it as a dream. "Young Goodman Brown" is an
allegory—which is what Hawthorne meant when he suggested that it
might have been a dream—and an allegory is a fictitious story designed
to teach an abstract truth. In reality, Brown did not go into a forest at
night nor did he dream that he did. What Brown did was to indulge
in sin (represented by the journey into the forest at night—and of
course the indulgence might have lasted much longer than a night:
weeks, months, even years) under the mistaken notion that he could
break off whenever he wanted to. Instead of breaking off promptly, he
continued to indulge in sin longer than he had expected and suffered
the consequences, which were the loss of religious faith and faith in all
other human beings.

What Brown's sin was at the beginning of the story Hawthorne does
not say, but it was not cynicism: at that time he was not cynical,
although he was already engaged in evil dealings with Satan. Cynicism
was merely the result of the sin and came later and gradually. By not
identifying the sin Hawthorne gives the story a wider application.
Which sin it was does not greatly matter: what Hawthorne puts the
stress on is the idea that this sin had evil consequences.

Thomas E. Connolly

Hawthorne's "Young Goodman Brown": An Attack on Puritanic Calvinism*

It is surprising, in a way, to discover how few of the many critics who have discussed "Young Goodman Brown" agree on any aspect of the work except that it is an excellent short story. D. M. /371/ McKeithan says that its theme is "sin and its blighting effects."[1] Richard H. Fogle observes, "Hawthorne the artist refuses to limit himself to a single and doctrinaire conclusion, proceeding instead by indirection,"[2] implying, presumably, that it is inartistic to say something which can be clearly understood by the readers. Gordon and Tate assert, "Hawthorne is dealing with his favorite theme: the unhappiness which the human heart suffers as a result of its innate depravity."[3] Austin Warren says, "His point is the devastating effect of moral scepticism."[4] Almost all critics agree, however, that young Goodman Brown lost his faith. Their conclusions are based, perhaps, upon the statement, "My Faith is gone!" made by Brown when he recognizes his wife's voice and ribbon. I should like to examine the story once more to show that young Goodman Brown did not lose his faith at all. In fact, not only did he retain his faith, but during his horrible experience he actually discovered the full and frightening significance of his faith.

* Thomas E. Connolly, "Hawthorne's 'Young Goodman Brown': An Attack on Puritanic Calvinism," *American Literature*, XXVIII (November, 1956), 370–5. Reprinted by permission of the journal.

1 D. M. McKeithan, "Hawthorne's 'Young Goodman Brown': An Interpretation," *Modern Language Notes*, LXVII, 94 (Feb., 1952).

2 Richard H. Fogle, "Ambiguity and Clarity in Hawthorne's 'Young Goodman Brown,'" *New England Quarterly*, XVIII, 453 (Dec., 1945).

3 Caroline Gordon and Allen Tate (eds.), *The House of Fiction* (New York, 1950), p. 38.

4 Austin Warren, *Nathaniel Hawthorne* (New York, 1934), p. 362.

Mrs. Leavis comes closest to the truth in her discussion of this story in the *Sewanee Review* in which she says: "Hawthorne has imaginatively recreated for the reader that Calvinist sense of sin, that theory which did in actuality shape the early social and spiritual history of New England:"[5] But Mrs. Leavis seems to miss the critical implications of the story, for she goes on to say: "But in Hawthorne, by a wonderful feat of transmutation, it has no religious significance, it is a psychological state that is explored. Young Goodman Brown's Faith is not faith in Christ but faith in human beings, and losing it he is doomed to isolation forever."[6] Those who persist in reading this story as a study of the effects of sin on Brown come roughly to this conclusion: "Goodman Brown became evil as a result of sin and thought he saw evil *where none existed*."[7] Hawthorne's message is far more depressing and horrifying than this. The story is obviously an individual tragedy, and those who treat it as such are /372/ right, of course; but, far beyond the personal plane, it has universal implications.

Young Goodman Brown, as a staunch Calvinist, is seen at the beginning of this allegory to be quite confident that he is going to heaven. The errand on which he is going is presented mysteriously and is usually interpreted to be a deliberate quest of sin. This may or may not be true; what is important is that he is going out to meet the devil by prearrangement. We are told by the narrator that his purpose in going is evil. When the devil meets him, he refers to the "beginning of a journey." Brown admits that he "kept convenant" by meeting the devil and hints at the evil purpose of the meeting.

Though his family has been Christian for generations, the point is made early in the story that young Goodman Brown has been married to his Faith for only three months. Either the allegory breaks down at this point or the marriage to Faith must be looked upon as the moment of conversion to grace in which he became fairly sure of his election to heaven. That Goodman Brown is convinced he is of the elect is made clear at the beginning: ". . . and after this one night I'll cling to her skirts and follow her to heaven." In other words, at the start of his adventure, young Goodman Brown is certain that his faith will help man get to heaven. It is in this concept that his disillusionment will come. The irony of this illusion is brought out when he explains to the devil the reason for his tardiness: "Faith kept me

[5] Q. D. Leavis, "Hawthorne as Poet," *Sewanee Review*, LIX, 197–89 (Spring, 1951).

[6] *Ibid.*

[7] McKeithan, *op. cit.*, p. 95. Italics mine.

back awhile." That is what he thinks! By the time he gets to the meeting place he finds that his Faith is already there. Goodman Brown's disillusionment in his belief begins quickly after meeting the devil. He has asserted proudly that his ancestors "have been a race of honest men and good Christians since the days of the martyrs," and the devil turns his own words on him smartly:

> Well said, Goodman Brown! I have been as well acquainted with your family as with ever a one among the Puritans; and that's no trifle to say. I helped your grandfather, the constable, when he lashed the Quaker woman so smartly through the streets of Salem; and it was I that brought your father a pitch-pine knot, kindled at my own hearth, to set fire to an Indian village, in King Philip's war. They were my good friends, both; and many a pleasant walk have we had along this path, and /373/ returned merrily after midnight. I would fain be friends with you for their sake.

Goodman Brown manages to shrug off this identification of his parental and grandparental Puritanism with the devil, but the reader should not overlook the sharp tone of criticism in Hawthorne's presentation of this speech.

When the devil presents his next argument, Brown is a little more shaken. The devil has shown him that Goody Cloyse is of his company and Brown responds: "What if a wretched old woman do choose to go to the devil when I thought she was going to heaven: is that any reason why I should quit my dear Faith and go after her?" He still believes at this point that his faith will lead him to heaven. The devil's reply, "You will think better of this by and by," is enigmatic when taken by itself, but a little earlier the narrator had made a comment which throws a great deal of light on this remark by the devil. When he recognized Goody Cloyse, Brown said, "That old woman taught me my catechism," and the narrator added, "and there was a world of meaning in this simple comment." The reader at this point should be fairly well aware of Hawthorne's criticism of Calvinism. The only way there can be a "world of meaning" in Brown's statement is that her catechism teaches the way to the devil and not the way to heaven.

From this point on Brown is rapidly convinced that his original conception about his faith is wrong. Deacon Gookin and the "good old minister," in league with Satan, finally lead the way to his recognition that this faith is diabolic rather than divine. Hawthorne points up this fact by a bit of allegorical symbolism. Immediately after he recognizes the voices of the deacon and the minister, we are told by the narrator that "Young Goodman Brown caught hold of a tree for support, being ready to sink down on the ground, faint and overburdened

with the heavy sickness of his heart. He looked up to the sky, doubting whether there really was a heaven above him. Yet there was a
blue arch, and the stars brightened in it." Here the doubt has begun
to gnaw, but the stars are symbols of the faint hope which he is still
able to cherish, and he is able to say: "With heaven above and Faith
below, I will yet stand firm against the devil." But immediately a
symbolic cloud hides the symbolic stars: "While he still gazed upward into the deep arch of the firmament /374/ and had lifted his
hands to pray, a cloud, though no wind was stirring, hurried across the
zenith and hid the brightening stars." And it is out of this black cloud
of doubt that the voice of his faith reaches him and the pink ribbon
of his Faith falls.[8] It might be worthwhile to discuss Faith's pink
ribbons here, for Hawthorne certainly took great pains to call them
to our attention. The ribbons seem to be symbolic of his initial illusion
about the true significance of his faith, his belief that his faith will
lead him to heaven. The pink ribbons on a Puritan lady's cap, signs of
youth, joy, and happiness, are actually entirely out of keeping with
the severity of the rest of her dress which, if not somber black, is at
least gray. When the ribbon falls from his cloud of doubt, Goodman
Brown cries in agony, "My Faith is gone!" and it is gone in the sense
that it now means not what it once meant. He is quick to apply the
logical, ultimate conclusion of Goody Cloyse's catechizing: "Come,
devil; for to thee is this world given."

Lest the reader miss the ultimate implication of the doctrine of
predestination, Hawthorne has the devil preach a sermon at his communion service: "Welcome, my children . . . to the communion of your
race. Ye have found thus young your nature and your destiny." Calvinism teaches that man is innately depraved and that he can do nothing
to merit salvation. He is saved only by the whim of God who selects
some, through no deserts of their own, for heaven while the great mass
of mankind is destined for hell. The devil concludes his sermon: "Evil
is the nature of mankind. Evil must be your only happiness. Welcome
again, my children, to the communion of your race." It is not at all
insignificant that the word *race* is used several times in this passage,
for it was used earlier by Goodman Brown when he said, "We have
been a race of honest men and good Christians. . . ." After this sermon
by the devil, young Goodman Brown makes one last effort to retain

---

[8] F. O. Matthiessen made entirely too much of the wrong thing of this ribbon. Had
young Goodman Brown returned to Salem Village clutching the ribbon, there might
be some point in what Matthiessen says (*American Renaissance*, New York, 1941, pp.
282–284). As it is, the ribbon presents no more of a problem than do the burning
trees turned suddenly cold again.

the illusion that faith will lead him to heaven; he calls out: "Faith! Faith! . . . look up to heaven, and resist the wicked one." But we are fairly sure that he is unsuccessful, for we are immediately told: "Whether Faith obeyed he knew not." /375/

Young Goodman Brown did not lose his faith (we are even told that his Faith survived him); he learned its full and terrible significance. This story is Hawthorne's criticism of the teachings of Puritanic-Calvinism. His implication is that the doctrine of the elect and damned is not a faith which carries man heavenward on its skirts, as Brown once believed, but, instead, condemns him to hell—bad and good alike indiscriminately—and for all intents and purposes so few escape as to make one man's chance of salvation almost disappear. It is this awakening to the full meaning of his faith which causes young Goodman Brown to look upon his minister as a blasphemer when he teaches "the sacred truths of our religion, and of saint-like lives and triumphant deaths, and of future bliss or misery unutterable," for he has learned that according to the truths of his faith there is probably nothing but "misery unutterable" in store for him and all his congregation; it is this awakening which causes him to turn away from prayer; it is this awakening which makes appropriate the fact that "they carved no hopeful verse upon his tombstone."

Though much is made of the influence of Puritanism on the writings of Hawthorne, he must also be seen to be a critic of the teachings of Puritanism. Between the position of Vernon L. Parrington,[9] who saw Hawthorne as retaining "much of the older Calvinistic view of life and human destiny," and that of Régis Michaud,[10] who saw him as "an anti-puritan and prophet heralding the Freudian gospel," lies the truth about Hawthorne.

---

[9] *Main Currents in American Thought* (New York, 1927), II, 443.

[10] "How Nathaniel Hawthorne Exorcised Hester Prynne," *The American Novel Today* (Boston, 1928), pp. 25–46.

Richard P. Adams

From "Hawthorne's Provincial Tales"*

· · · · ·

"Young Goodman Brown" is generally considered the best of the *Provincial Tales* and one of the best stories Hawthorne ever wrote.[1] It is also important because it contains the germ of nearly all his best work to follow. It would be at least partly true to say that *The Scarlet Letter or The Marble Faun* is only "Young Goodman Brown" grown older and bigger.

The question of maturity for Goodman Brown is put in terms of good and evil. At first it seems a fairly simple choice, but the problem is much more complex than Brown seems ever to realize. He leaves the daylit street of Salem Village, saying goodbye to his wife, Faith, with pink ribbons in her cap, and goes into the darkening forest. There, by appointment, he meets the devil, who tries to persuade him to attend a witch meeting, saying that his father and grandfather have often done so and that the leaders of the Puritan community are generally in attendance. Brown, making his simple choice of good over evil, refuses. His confidence is somewhat shaken when they see old Goody Cloyse on the path ahead and he learns that she, who has taught him his catechism, is on her way to the meeting. But he still refuses, and the devil leaves him. As he is congratulating himself on his moral purity and

---

* Richard P. Adams, "Hawthorne's *Provincial Tales*," *New England Quarterly,* xxx (March, 1957), 39–57. Reprinted by permission of the journal and the author.

[1] For good critical discussions of "Young Goodman Brown," see Henry James, *Hawthorne* (New York, 1879), pp. 56–63; F. O. Matthiessen, *American Renaissance* (New York, 1941), pp. 282–284; and R. H. Fogle, *Hawthorne's Fiction* (Norman, Okla., 1952), pp. 15–32. Melville's "Hawthorne and His Mosses," *Literary World,* vii (Aug. 17 and 24, 1850), pp. 125–127, 145–147, though it has little to say specifically about "Young Goodman Brown," is indirectly very illuminating.

fortitude, he is further disconcerted by hearing the minister and Deacon Gookin riding through the forest on the same errand. His resolution is broken when a heavy cloud goes over and he hears the voices of people he knows in Salem, including that of his /42/ wife. He shouts her name, she screams, and one of her pink ribbons flutters down. At this Brown rejects the good he has chosen and embraces evil, rushing through the forest after the devil, himself more like a devil than a man, until he comes to the firelit clearing where the witch meeting is being held.

In the meeting, especially its setting, evil is associated so closely as practically to identify it with sex. At the end of the clearing is a rock used as an altar or pulpit, "surrounded by four blazing pines, their tops aflame, their stems untouched, like candles at an evening meeting. The mass of foliage that had overgrown the summit of the rock was all on fire. . . ." The imagery of fire is typically used by Hawthorne, both before and after the *Provincial Tales*, to connote intense emotion, especially sexual passion, which is specified if anything too obviously here by the physiological correspondences of the pines and the brush-covered rock. But, almost as often in Hawthorne, fire also connotes the warmth of personal and familial association, as opposed to the cold-ness of isolation. Brown's feelings as he approaches are accordingly mixed. He is surprised to see that the congregation includes many presumably virtuous people, as well as "men of dissolute lives and women of spotted fame," and he finds it "strange to see that the good shrank not from the wicked, nor were the sinners abashed by the saints." But as he steps out into the clearing he too feels the "loatheful brotherhood" between himself and the others "by the sympathy of all that was wicked in his heart." It might be more accurate to say by all that is sexual in his character. A parallel ambiguity is suggested by the fact that, as it seems to him, "the shape of his own dead father beckoned him to advance, looking downward from a smoke wreath, while a woman, with dim features of despair, threw out her hand to warn him back. Was it his mother?" If so, the two play typical roles, the father encouraging the son to become a man, the mother trying to keep him a child as long as possible.

Brown and Faith are led to the altar, where the devil, in the guise of a Puritan minister, proposes to reveal the " 'secret deeds' "—that is, the sexual crimes—of their neighbors: /43/ " 'how hoary-bearded elders of the church have whispered wanton words to the young maids of their households; how many a woman, eager for widows' weeds, has given her husband a drink at bedtime and let him sleep his last sleep in her bosom; how beardless youths have made haste to inherit their

fathers' wealth; and how fair damsels . . . have dug little graves in the
garden, and bidden me, the sole guest, to an infant's funeral.' " As the
congregation welcomes the "converts" to the communion of evil, or of
sexual knowledge and guilt, the setting becomes still more suggestive.
"A basin was hollowed, naturally, in the rock. Did it contain water,
reddened by the lurid light? or was it blood? or, perchance, a liquid
flame? Herein did the shape of evil dip his hand and prepare to lay
the mark of baptism upon their foreheads, that they might be partakers
of the mystery of sin, more conscious of the secret guilt of others, both
in deed and thought, than they could now be of their own."

The prospect is too much for Brown, who at this point makes his
final decision, rejects evil, and commands Faith to " 'look up to heaven,
and resist the wicked one.' " Instantly the congregation, Faith, and
the devil disappear, and Brown is alone, "amid calm night and solitude," while the foliage that has been blazing with fire now sprinkles
him "with the coldest dew." He returns to Salem with his isolation
around him like a cloak, shrinks away from the minister, wonders what
god Deacon Gookin is praying to, snatches a child away from Goody
Cloyse, and passes his wife, Faith, in the street without a word. Through
the rest of his long life, Goodman Brown is "A stern, a sad, a darkly
meditative, a distrustful, if not a desperate man. . . ."

The most immediately apparent reason for this final state of Brown's
mind is that he has been required to face and acknowledge the evil
in himself and others, including his young wife, so as to be able to
recognize the good, and has failed the test. Having refused to look at
evil, he is left in a state of moral uncertainty that is worse, in a way,
than evil itself. His inability to judge between good and evil also
prevents him from /44/ entering into stable social relations or having
any sort of intimate contact with others. He has lost Faith, as he says
at one point in the story, in all the ways that the ambiguities of the
name can be made to mean. For Hawthorne, this condition of moral
and social isolation is the worst evil that can befall a man.

But the more important aspect of Brown's personal disaster is his
failure to grow up, in the sense of becoming emotionally mature. This
is not itself a matter of good and evil, though it is a matter where
good and evil are always potentially present. To reach maturity, Brown
must learn to recognize, control, and constructively use powerful feelings that a grown man has, especially about sex. Those feelings, when
loosed in war or civil riot, are the most dangerous forces we know.
But they are also the most effective forces for good. Civilization is
built and preserved, when it is preserved, by men who love their
wives and children, their homelands, and the human race, and who
will not only risk death for themselves but kill other men, if they

must, for the sake of positive emotional values. Brown does not become such a man. In place of the needed capacity for both love and hate or, in the terms of the story, both evil and good, he develops only a great fear of moral maturity and of the knowledge and responsibility that maturity brings.

.   .   .   .   .

/51/ Even the typical structure of the *Provincial Tales* is dynamic. It consists of a pattern of three or four characters who move in a series of shifting relationships. The protagonist, a naïve young man, is attracted by a woman, who somehow seems to bring him into conflict with an evil man or devil. Sometimes he is helped by a benevolent older man, more often not; but essentially the number of characters is always four because when only three appear the devil-figure has a double function. He both frightens and encourages the youthful candidate. This pattern can be most completely demonstrated in "My Kinsman, Major Molineux." Robin, after briefly meeting the devil-figure without makeup, is attracted by a young woman who pretends to be the Major's housekeeper and who evidently aims to seduce him. Then he meets the devil in full rig, and then the kindly citizen who confirms his maturity and encourages him to stay and make it good.

In the other tales the pattern is less complete, but its meanings are sometimes clearer. The function of the woman, for example, is much more plainly evident in "Roger Malvin's Burial" than it is in "My Kinsman, Major Molineux." Reuben sees Malvin as the friendly foster father until he marries Dorcas. Then Malvin haunts him until he declares himself mature, at which point Malvin again seems to be the benevolent father. In "The Maypole of Merry Mount" Edgar's marriage to Edith brings a gloomy foreboding of trouble to both their minds, even before Endicott interferes. And in "Young Goodman Brown" it seems to be Brown's marriage to Faith that really poses the problem of evil; certainly it is her voice from the cloud that leads him to the witch meeting and his deeper involvement with the devil, who may be only trying to help him after all.

We must remember that this is an abstract pattern, useful only insofar as it helps us to understand the stories. But it is /52/ worth noting that the tales in which it appears most clearly, "My Kinsman, Major Molineux," "Young Goodman Brown," and "The Maypole of Merry Mount," are those which now seem esthetically most satisfactory. "The Gray Champion" is a splendid picture, but the woman does not appear, and the real protagonist is kept in the background, so that the dynamic effect is dampened. In "The Gentle Boy" the pattern is so much distorted that it can hardly be said to exist at all; and "The

Gentle Boy" is one of Hawthorne's weakest works. The same pattern
is awkwardly weighted in "Roger Malvin's Burial," but without some
reference to it that tale can hardly be understood. With these necessary
reservations, I think it is proper to say that the four-character pattern
is normal for Hawthorne in the *Provincial Tales.*

The psychological implications of this pattern, though not its final
or most important values, are too emphatic to be ignored. The young
man's attraction to a sexually potent woman, his struggle to free
himself from dependence on and antagonism toward a fatherly man,
and his achievement of, or his failure to achieve, adult status—these
matters, we cannot help noticing, are precisely those with which
modern psychoanalysis has been most deeply concerned.

To put it simply, Hawthorne, like Freud (and Sophocles, among
many others), was very much interested in what is now called the
Oedipus complex. He recognized, as Freud did later, that the typical
crisis of adolescence, for a boy in our culture, is that which involves
his ambivalent attitude and feelings toward his father. The themes
of incest, parricide, and fear of castration that appear in both men's
work represent the hazards of a boy's normal emotional development
from adolescence to manhood. Which is perhaps only to say that both
men were dealing with human nature: Hawthorne empirically, for
esthetic purposes, and Freud more scientifically, for therapeutic purposes.

Carl Jung's formula for what he calls "individuation," or /53/
"the integration of the personality," is in many ways closer to Hawthorne's pattern than is Freud's theory. The process according to Jung
consists of a series of encounters within the psyche. Unassimilated
elements of the mind or soul are represented to consciousness as
strongly personified figures, symbolic and archetypal. The first to
appear, Jung says, is the Shadow, which is a mirror reflection, or negative double, of the conscious character. For a man, it takes the form of
a terrifying male apparition, or devil. The second figure to appear is
what Jung calls the Anima, who embodies all the feminine elements in
the male personality. She has an ambivalent appeal, and seems both
attractive and dangerous, threatening emotional chaos and at the same
time offering the most valuable kind of occult wisdom. The third
figure is the Old Wise Man, a benevolent sage, master, or teacher. All
these, Jung says, must be faced, absorbed, and assimilated before a
man can become fully mature. The process is difficult and risky. Its
terrors are imaginary and may therefore seem unreal, but Jung maintains that a failure to deal adequately with any of these archetypes

may lead to serious neurotic disorders. Neurosis, in these terms, is the penalty for a failure of the imagination to arrange the symbols of various necessary components of the developing personality in their proper working order and relationship.[2] Jung's terms seem almost exactly the same as Hawthorne's, though they come in a slightly different order, Hawthorne putting the woman ahead of the devil more often than not. But Jung says that "Under so-called normal conditions, the shadow is largely identical with the anima. . . ."[3]

Freud, Jung, and Hawthorne are all three concerned about the same kind of psychological truth; they use very similar formulas to describe the same crisis of development; and they arrive at closely similar conclusions, so far as the facts of experience are concerned. Henry James was if anything too condescending in his remark, "The fine thing in Hawthorne is /54/ that he cared for the deeper psychology, and that, in his way, he tried to become familiar with it."[4] Hawthorne shows in the *Provincial Tales* that he had a more advanced notion of the working of unconscious mental processes, if that is what James meant, than James had, at least in 1879.

The most important values in the *Provincial Tales* are finally esthetic; and, as I have remarked elsewhere,[5] the basic esthetic problem for Hawthorne's generation of American artists was to join themselves and the culture of this country to the romantic movement which had already been so well begun in Europe. Though various people had made beginnings, all rather tentative and none quite successful, before 1830, in Hawthorne's *Provincial Tales* we find the earliest creative work done and published in the United States in which the true positive romantic note is struck and held.

The best evidence in support of this claim is Hawthorne's dynamic use of the pattern of symbolic death and rebirth. The pattern of death and rebirth was not in itself a new device; its history goes back as far as history itself has gone, to early Sumerian times. Among English poets, Milton used it with fine effects, most obviously in "Lycidas" and more massively in *Paradise Lost, Paradise Regained,* and *Samson Agonistes.* But, like other writers in the humanistic tradition, Milton used the pattern in a static way. He began with an intellectual understanding of Christian (or pre-Christian) religious and cultural truth.

---

[2] Carl G. Jung, *The Integration of the Personality* (New York, 1939), pp. 17–24, 69–88.

[3] Jung, *The Integration of the Personality,* pp. 91.

[4] James, *Hawthorne,* p. 63.

[5] See my "Romanticism and the American Renaissance," *AL,* XXIII (Jan. 1952), 421, and "Emerson and the Organic Metaphor," *PMLA,* LXIX (March 1954), 130.

Symbolic death tested this truth in experience and questioned it in
spirit, placing the truth and the protagonist in danger of literal death
and damnation. Finally the truth was vindicated and accepted emotionally, and the esthetic pattern returned full circle. The truth remained the same truth, and the whole effect was to bring the esthetic
pattern into equilibrium, or a state of rest. /55/

The romantics make it dynamic. In works such as *Faust, The Ancient
Mariner*, and *The Prelude* the pattern of death and rebirth ends,
if it can be said to end at all, at a point beyond its beginning. It is
not a matter of doubt and reconciliation, or an emotionally enriched
return to a given formula. It involves the discovery of a new attitude
which enables the protagonist to carry his revolt through to a sort
of open completion; to make it, in fact, not just a revolt against an
old truth but a radical departure from all old concepts of truth as
a static value. The romantic protagonist dies in much the same symbolic
sense as his humanistic predecessor, by withdrawing from the generally
accepted ways of thinking and feeling. But he is reborn in a very
different sense and into a whole new, different world. Instead of re-
turning he goes on indefinitely.

All of which is to say, in a sense, that the typical protagonist in
early romantic literature recapitulated the author's own departure
from the more or less mechanistic humanism, or humanistic mechan-
ism, of the eighteenth century and his regeneration as an exponent of
more or less dynamic nineteenth-century romanticism. That was not a
simple process for those who went through it, and they were not able at
the time to describe it in such baldly simple terms as I have used. What
they could do and did was to embody something of the esthetic and emotional quality of the process in works of poetry and, later, fiction. Their
results are still valuable because, for one thing, our experience is not
so much different from theirs as we might wish. Most people are
still caught in the old irreconcilable dichotomy of humanistic and
mechanistic views, and have to be twice-born in order to be capable
of creative work. The romantic literature of the past, as well as that
of the present, can help to show the way.

Hawthorne handles the romantic theme very well. His unresolved
ambiguities express the conflicts out of which the romantic development comes, and mean something more than just the tough-minded
acceptance of the fact that men are both good and evil. They strongly
imply a transcendence of good and evil as absolute, static values or
concepts, because it /56/ is out of the tension between these opposites
that the power to move onward is generated. Young Goodman Brown is
lost because he rejects one of the necessary elements, and with it his

ability to progress. Like Milton's hero, he ends where he has begun,
but Hawthorne reverses the values, so that Brown returns to Puritan
Salem not with enriched faith but in a state of complete spiritual
impoverishment. He should have fallen, should have let himself be
tempted and damned out of the old dispensation entirely, should
have accepted the devil's destructive knowledge, which was death sure
enough, but which might therefore have led eventually to rebirth. By
refusing he has caught himself in the trap of an absolute and static
moral isolation. To make the point more literally, it is only by exposing himself all the way to the hostile power of evil that he can
move off dead center in his progress toward manhood. Because he
refuses to do so he fails to reach maturity, which is a condition of
being able to move in any direction one wishes and of being willing
to take the consequences of whatever moves one makes. A state, that
is, of freedom with responsibility.

Many readers will have strong moral objections to this interpretation. But the actual weakness of it is its assumption that Brown is a
real person, with a real choice between real courses of action. That is
not the fact. Brown is a fictional character, a symbol, an imaginary
entity in an imaginative tale. Hawthorne tries to suggest the kind of
reality that is involved, and to forestall the wrong kind of criticism,
by asking at the end, "Had Goodman Brown fallen asleep in the forest
and only dreamed a wild dream of a witch-meeting?" His answer is
that it does not matter. "Be it so if you will," he says; "but alas! it
was a dream of evil omen for young Goodman Brown." We are told,
in effect, that this is an imaginary garden with a real toad in it, and
that we are not to let the imaginariness of the garden blind us to the
reality of the toad. At the same time we must not let the reality of
the toad—that is, the seriousness of the moral crisis through which
Brown is imagined as passing—blind us to the equally significant
imaginariness of the garden, /57/ the purely arbitrary symbolic structure of the story. Brown cannot choose. Hawthorne has decided that
he shall refuse the choice, and has created the whole situation accordingly. The story is a highly artistic exploration of the moral problem.

"Young Goodman Brown" is the best of the *Provincial Tales,* partly
because it most powerfully symbolizes the terrors and difficulties at
the crisis of development, and fixes the very moment of that crisis in
an esthetic projection combining the maximum of force with the
maximum of control and finish. Other stories in the group are hardly
less remarkable, however, for the cogency with which they seize the
moment of significant change, and for the beauty with which they
express the tensions out of which development comes. Their uni-

versality lies in the common feeling of young people everywhere in revolt against parental and social authority. Their special appeal is to romantics who are in revolt against all fixed ideas of order and whose need is for a larger freedom than either a humanist or a mechanist can imagine. In rendering that special feeling, out of the experience of his own time and the revolt of his own generation, Hawthorne effectively began to establish himself in *Provincial Tales* as a romantic artist of the highest rank.

Thomas F. Walsh, Jr.

The Bedeviling of Young
Goodman Brown*

> Had Goodman Brown fallen asleep in the forest and
> only dreamed a wild dream of a witch-meeting?[1]

The above question, found in the second to the last paragraph of
Nathaniel Hawthorne's famous short story, "Young Goodman Brown,"
has perhaps inspired more comment than any other sentence of the
author's works. But it is futile to attempt to answer the question,
especially since the author himself has intentionally avoided it.[2] Yet
most commentators have chosen between the two alternatives that
Hawthorne has offered, and their choice determines the meaning they
give to the short story: those who think that Goodman Brown's experience in the forest is not a dream say that he is the victim of an
evil world in which he finds himself (such an interpretation makes
Hawthorne more pessimistic than he is usually thought to be); those

---

* Thomas F. Walsh, Jr., "The Bedeviling of Young Goodman Brown," *Modern
Language Quarterly*, XIX (December, 1958), 331–6. Reprinted by permission of
the journal and the author.

[1] *Complete Works of Nathaniel Hawthorne*, with Introductory Notes by George
Parsons Lathrop, Standard Library Edition (Boston, 1882), II, 105. Subsequent
references to the short story will be made to this text.

[2] Certainly a close examination of Hawthorne's narrative technique—his handling
of the point of view—does not give the answer. The story is told fairly consistently
from the point of view of Goodman Brown; everything that the reader sees and hears
Goodman Brown sees and hears except for one passage: "So saying, he threw it
[the staff] down at her feet, where, perhaps, it assumed life, being one of the rods
which its owner had formerly lent to the Egyptian magi. Of this fact, however, Goodman Brown could not take cognizance." *Works*, II, 95. A complete consistency of
point of view would reinforce an interpretation which stresses the subjective experience of Brown, but what is to be done with this passage?

who think that Brown's experience is a dream put the responsibility for his despair, not on the world, but on him.[3]

It is the purpose of this paper, which is more in agreement with the conclusions of the latter group, to show that Hawthorne's method in "Young Goodman Brown" is such that the tale's full meaning cannot be determined by the narrative itself, which would involve at- /332/ tempting to answer the author's question about Brown's experience in the forest. Rather, the reader must be conscious of a threefold symbolic pattern which objectifies Brown's subjective experience, thereby showing that it is he rather than the world who is responsible for his despair. The reader can never be certain about what actually happened in the forest: he can, however, be certain, not only of the nature and stages of Goodman Brown's despair, but also of its probable cause. And all this can be worked out from the symbolic pattern.

For an understanding of what happens to Goodman Brown the reader should be conscious of three sets of symbols: first, Faith, Brown's wife, represents religious faith and faith in mankind; second, Brown's journey into the forest represents an inward journey into the black, despairing depths of his soul; third, the devil represents Brown's darker, doubting side, which eventually believes that evil is the nature of mankind. The symbolic movement of the forest scenes is from the bosom of Faith to the loss of faith, which involves despair, from the village of belief to the depths of the forest of despair, and from a doubting balance of Brown's personality to the complete submergence of the brighter side into the darker side, which objectifies despair. The three sets of symbols tell the story of a man, young and naïve in the ways of the world, who, finding that men are not all good, became so convinced they are all bad that he could not remove the doubt of universal evil from his mind.

It is difficult to treat each set of symbols separately, so interlaced with each other are they, but first let us consider Faith, who, Haw-

---

[3] Newton Arvin, *Hawthorne* (Boston, 1929), is representative of the first group. He writes that "Young Goodman Brown of Salem makes the horrid discovery that all that he has honored and respected—in the persons of his most virtuous fellow townsmen and even of his pure wife, Faith—is but the cloak for intrinsic wickedness of every atrocious and debasing kind" (pp. 61–62). He finds that the story served the author as a palliative for his incipient morbid "imaginative disease." F. O. Matthiessen, *American Renaissance* (New York, 1941), is representative of the second group. He offers the wet twig which touches Brown's cheek after the revelation in the forest as proof that Brown had dreamed. He writes of "Young Goodman Brown": "Hawthorne's main concern with this material is to use it to develop the theme that mere doubt of the existence of good, the thought that all other men are evil, can become such a corrosive force as to eat out the life of the heart" (pp. 283–84).

thorne tells us, is "aptly named" (p. 89). Faith is symbolic of Brown's faith, which he gradually loses as he doubts more and more the existence of any goodness in man. The physical movement away from Faith, marking his own loss of faith, can be traced through the forest scene to the climax at the witches' gathering. Brown's feelings of guilt about his movement away from his wife help to underscore the psychological turmoil involved in the process. He is conscious of the dangers of the mission but is impelled onward by the thoughts of evil which hold him fascinated until it is too late to turn back to his wife and so to faith.

Tracing this symbol through, we note that as Goodman Brown enters the forest, he salves his guilty conscience with the "excellent resolve" that he will cling to Faith's skirts forever after this night (p. 90). When he meets the devil, he tells him that " 'Faith kept me back awhile' " (p. 91). As he proceeds deeper into the forest, his conscience continues to disturb him: at one point he bemoans the fact that his action will break Faith's heart, while at another point he asks himself why he should quit his Faith (pp. 93, 96). But nevertheless he moves on, going deeper and deeper until his very senses play tricks on him. He tries to reassure himself against overwhelming doubts by looking to the sky; he beguiles himself that he is safe as long as he has the blue heavens and Faith. /333/

But one cannot contemplate such thoughts about evil, which by their very nature undermine all belief, and at the same time keep one's faith. Goodman Brown tries and becomes a man who leans too far over the edge of a pit. Thus the heavens darken and the symbolic pink ribbon makes him cry out in realization, " 'My Faith is gone!' " (p. 99), as truly it is, and he wildly laughs in his despair. The storm in his soul and in the forest rises, and he stumbles into the heart of the forest depths where there is symbolically represented the complete perversion of all that he once held dear. As Richard Harter Fogle points out, all the external manifestations of his faith are turned upside down: "The Communion of Sin is, in fact, the faithful counterpart of a grave and pious ceremony at a Puritan meetinghouse. . . . Satan resembles some grave divine, and the initiation into sin takes the form of baptism."[4] And as the external evidences of his religion are perverted, so, climactically, is his very faith, which is symbolized by his discovering his wife in the unholy communion. He has despaired, believing all men are depraved and religion a sham.

---

[4] Richard Harter Fogle, *Hawthorne's Fiction: The Light and the Dark* (Norman, Okla., 1952), p. 29.

Second, there is the journey into the black depths of Young Goodman Brown's soul, paralleled by his journey into the dark under-
growth of the forest. When he enters the forest, we are told, "He had
taken a dreary road, darkened by all the gloomiest trees of the forest,
which barely stood aside to let the narrow path creep through, and
closed immediately behind. It was all as lonely as could be . . ." (p.
90). This act is symbolic of what he is doing: he is plunging into
the road leading to despair, and the immediate closing of the trees
symbolizes the shutting off of his escape. He is alone, cut off from
humanity with but one companion, the devil, his own evil genius. The
farther he goes, the more hopeless his plight becomes; even Brown
realizes it:

> "Friend," said the other, exchanging his slow pace for a full stop, "having
> kept covenant by meeting thee here, it is my purpose now to *return* whence I
> came. I have scruples touching the matter thou wot'st of."
> "Sayest thou so?" replied he of the serpent, smiling apart. "*Let us walk on*,
> nevertheless, reasoning as we go; and if I convince thee not thou shalt turn
> back. We are but a *little way* in the forest yet."
> "*Too far! too far!*" exclaimed the goodman, *unconsciously resuming* his
> walk (pp. 91–92).

The italics are mine and indicate how the physical journey into the
forest is related to the devil's growing power over Goodman Brown's
soul and to Brown's realization of what he is doing. He knows he
has gone too far, but he does not turn back. In the established pattern, he walks on, and the devil talks persuasively: "They continued
to walk onward, while the elder traveller exhorted his companion to
make good speed and *persevere in the path* . . ." (p. 95).

It is not long until the forest is darkened by the black cloud with
/334/ its attendant voices, symbolizing Brown's doubt-tortured soul as
he cries in despair: " 'Faith!' shouted Goodman Brown, in a voice of
agony and desperation; and the echoes of the forest mocked him, crying, 'Faith! Faith!' as if bewildered wretches were seeking her all
through the wilderness" (p. 98). Then we are told, "The road grew
wilder and drearier and more faintly traced, and vanished at length,
leaving him in the heart of the dark wilderness, *still rushing onward*
with the instinct that guides mortal man to evil" (p. 99).

This scene is Hawthorne's finest bit of writing in the story, making
the following scene in the heart of the forest almost anticlimactic.
The point of view throughout is consistent and clear. It is Brown
who sees and doubts and hears and thinks he hears. We, the readers,
see both him and the innermost depths of his soul.

Third, Young Goodman Brown moves from a state of belief, in which the good and naïve side of his nature predominates, to a state of despair, in which the good side becomes submerged in the dark side, symbolized by the devil.[5] The black man Brown meets in the forest is the dark side of his own nature objectified. What this man suggests and reveals to him are his own thoughts, which gradually possess him completely.

We are told not only that Goodman Brown looks like the devil, but that so too do his father and grandfather. This family identification with the devil, together with the stages by which Goodman Brown comes to believe that his fellow men are evil, becomes most important to an understanding of the beginnings of the dark thoughts which eventually overpower him. The first people who are mentioned with reference to sin are his father and grandfather. Early in his journey Brown protests,

"My father never went into the woods on such an errand, nor his father before him. We have been a race of honest men and good Christians since the days of the martyrs; and shall I be the first of the name of Brown that ever took this path and kept—"

There Brown echoes the good report he might have heard from anyone in the village; but the devil, representing the evil doubts in his mind, rejoins with,

"I helped your grandfather, the constable, when he lashed the Quaker woman so smartly through the streets of Salem; and it was I that brought your father a pitch-pine knot, kindled at my own hearth, to set fire to an Indian village, in King Philip's war" (p. 92).

The facts concerning the persecution of the Quakers and the Indians Goodman Brown must certainly have known before, although in the past he might never have allowed himself to think of them in relation to sin. But what is most interesting, of all those who are /335/ mentioned and revealed by the devil, his father and grandfather have in their history that which would make one suspect that they were of the devil's party. Thus, Goodman Brown, having sinned himself or at least realizing his own potentiality for sin, makes the mistake of identifying himself, as the resemblance of three generations of Browns

---

[5] Neal Frank Doubleday, "Hawthorne's Use of Three Gothic Patterns," *College English*, VII (1946), 256, has noted that "Goodman Brown's guide was his own evil nature," and that the guide's leaving him is a "sign to us that no longer were a good and evil nature contending in Goodman Brown."

to the devil shows, with his ancestors in a sort of heredity of sin. Behind it all we can see the author brooding over his own ancestors, for, like Goodman Brown's father and grandfather, William Hathorne persecuted both Indians and Quakers, leading two hundred of the former into slavery after killing eight and ordering Anne Coleman and four of her Quaker friends whipped through Salem, Boston, and Dedham.

From doubts, then, about himself and his ancestors, who show evidences of being evil, Goodman Brown moves to those whose lives are, on the surface of things, uncorrupt. But in his naïveté he begins to suspect that all men are instrsically evil, even if they are respected members of the community, as were his father and grandfather. Doubts about his ancestors spread, until Goody Cloyse, Deacon Gookin, the parson, and finally Faith herself fall victims to his diseased mind.

The symbolic representation of such increasing doubts is given in the sequence with the devil. The devil is Brown, father, grandfather, all rolled into one, the exact counterpart of Faith, Brown's heavenly side. He is Brown's darker side, which believes that evil is the nature of man. In the forest the dark side of Brown's nature overcomes the good side. We notice that when Brown conjectures about the proximity of the devil, he appears as if he sprang from Brown's very being:

> and he glanced fearfully behind him as he added, "What if the devil himself should be at my very elbow!"
>
> His head being turned back, he passed a crook of the road, and, looking forward again, beheld the figure of a man, in grave and decent attire, seated at the foot of an old tree (p. 90).

The devil not only looks like the Browns, but he is distinguished by a diabolic *laughter* and a *staff*. We are told that the devil discoursed "so aptly that his arguments seemed rather to spring up in the bosom of his auditor than to be suggested by himself" (p. 95). Brown continues on until the ribbon scene. Then the cry of despair —but note its form: "And, maddened with despair, so that he *laughed* loud and long, did Goodman Brown grasp his *staff* and set forth again, at such a rate that he seemed to fly along the forest path rather than to walk or run" (p. 99).

The submergence is now complete: Brown's dark nature has wholly enveloped his good. He is a devil with a devil's *laughter* and a devil's *staff*. If this were not enough, Hawthorne, describing Brown in the forest, tells us, "But he was himself the chief horror of the scene," which stresses the inward symbolic significance of Brown's /336/

experience, thereby emphasizing the fact that the cause of Brown's despair is from within, not from without (p. 99). Such an interpretation is firmly clinched by the following: "The fiend in his own shape is less hideous than when he rages in the breast of man. Thus sped the demoniac on his course . . ." (p. 100). And finally, we are not surprised to hear the devil say, " 'Evil is the nature of mankind' " (p. 104), which is nothing more than an echo, in a forest of echoes, of the demon-like Brown's, " 'There is no good on earth; and sin is but a name. Come, devil; for to thee is this world given' " (p. 99).

What actually happened in the forest must remain, as Hawthorne chose to put it, a question. What happens once Goodman Brown emerges from the forest is clear enough: Goodman Brown lived and died an unhappy, despairing man. These clear facts imply that Brown did enter the forest. The reader, following the narrative line of the story, then asks what happened in the forest. But Hawthorne asks the same question himself, which suggests that it is futile to examine the facts of the narrative to determine the meaning of the story.

The only solution to the problem lies in the tale's complex symbolic pattern. We are sure that on the physical level Goodman Brown emerged from the dark wilderness to live the rest of his dismal life in his community. We are also sure from the threefold symbolic pattern that Brown never emerged from the forest depths of despair. And from the identification of the Brown family with the devil we can reach to the origins of that despair: we see a man who began to doubt, with some reason, the goodness of his own family, which led him to doubt the goodness of all men, until he concluded that, "Evil is the nature of mankind," words uttered by the devil, who represents the dark side of Brown's nature. Hawthorne has shown symbolically not only what happened to a man's soul, but why it happened. His handling of his symbols is expert, subtle, and brilliant enough to dispose the reader to overlook whatever narrative deficiencies there may be.

Paul W. Miller

Hawthorne's "Young Goodman Brown": Cynicism or Meliorism?*

Critics have agreed that Young Goodman Brown, in the course of the Hawthorne story of the same name, moves from a state of simple faith in God and his fellow man to an evil state involving damnation, or at least soul jeopardy.[1] They have also generally implied that as well as being an individual, Young Goodman Brown is in some sense intended to be a type. They have not generally indicated, however, whether they think he is intended to typify all mankind or only one segment of it.[2] The question is important, it seems to me, because on the answer one gives to it depends one's understanding of Hawthorne's view of man when he wrote the story, as well as one's interpretation of this enigmatic but nonetheless fascinating tale.

If, on the one hand, Young Goodman Brown is intended to represent all mankind, Hawthorne himself must be regarded, at the /256/ time of composition of this story, as a totally cynical man, obsessed with the notion that even the best of men are but whited sepulchres, unable either to save themselves or to find salvation through divine

---

* © 1959 by The Regents of the University of California. Reprinted from *Nineteenth-Century Fiction*, XIV (December, 1959), 255–264, by permission of The Regents.

[1] Thomas E. Connolly in "Hawthorne's 'Young Goodman Brown': An Attack on Puritanic Calvinism," *AL*, XXVIII, 370–375, has recently taken exception to this view, however. He writes: "Young Goodman Brown did not lose his faith at all. In fact, not only did he retain his faith, but during his horrible experience he actually discovered the full and frightening significance of his faith." I take further note of Connolly's view later in my article.

[2] Notable exceptions include Newton Arvin (*Hawthorne* [Boston, 1929], pp. 61–62), who concludes that Young Goodman Brown is intended to represent all mankind, and D. M. McKeithan ("Hawthorne's 'Young Goodman Brown': An Interpretation," *MLN*, LXVII [Feb. 1952], 95–96), to whom Young Goodman Brown is "a man whose sin led him [mistakenly] to consider all other people sinful," and who is therefore *not* representative of all mankind.

grace.[3] But if, on the other hand, Young Goodman Brown is intended to represent only a certain segment of mankind, his creator
must be viewed as much less pessimistic than the alternative interpretation would suggest.

If it is concluded that Young Goodman Brown's condition is not
intended to represent that of all mankind, it remains to be considered
whether such men as Brown are doomed by their nature alone to
separation from God and man, or whether the kind of society in
which they live is an important factor in this separation. If the latter—
and if it be granted that in Hawthorne's view, the individuals who
comprise society are in a measure free to alter it[4]—it may be concluded that the story, though pessimistic so far as the fate of Young
Goodman Brown is concerned, need not be so regarded as it relates
to the Young Goodman Browns of the future. On the contrary, it
might be regarded as melioristic in outlook, anticipating the dawning
of a new and better day.

There remains to be considered an alternative to both possibilities
of interpretation mentioned above. It is embodied in Henry James's
conclusion that

> the magnificent little romance of *Young Goodman Brown* [*sic*], for instance,
> evidently means nothing as regards Hawthorne's own state of mind, his
> conviction of human depravity and his consequent melancholy; for the
> simple reason that if it meant anything, it would mean too much.[5]

This is to say, in effect, that the picture of mankind painted in "Young
Goodman Brown" is so dark that it cannot reflect Hawthorne's view
accurately. Consequently it must be viewed simply as an exercise
in the free play of the imagination.

James's interpretation of Hawthorne's tale is convenient. It spares
/257/ the reader the necessity of raising certain disturbing questions,
such as the following: Did Hawthorne mean, in "Young Goodman
Brown," that the most pious-seeming of men, along with the grossest
sinners, are absolutely depraved? If he did, how can his view of
mankind here be squared with the views he expressed in *The Scarlet*

---

[3] Witness, in this connection, Arvin's statement: "How far had Hawthorne
wandered from imaginative sanity when he became capable of viewing all human
personality as tainted and corrupt. . . . Out of the very depths of that mood, and lit up
by it with as lurid an imaginative glare as Hawthorne was ever again to light, sprang
that beautiful evil fancy, 'Young Goodman Brown' [*op. cit.*, p. 61]."

[4] An assumption ably defended by Henry G. Fairbanks in a recent issue of *PMLA*
("Sin, Free Will, and 'Pessimism' in Hawthorne," LXXI [Dec. 1956], 976).

[5] James, *Hawthorne* (New York, 1887), p. 102.

Letter, where the scarlet letter itself becomes a symbol of natural
virtue annealed by human suffering, or in *The House of The Seven
Gables,* where humanity is represented by the virtuous if faltering
Clifford and Hepzibah Pyncheon as well as by that melodramatic
quintessence of evil, the Judge?

At the same time one is impressed with the convenience of James's
approach one is led to question its correctness. For unless a story is
light and frivolous, one expects the critic who finds it difficult to
interpret either to discover a meaning in it, or dispraise it finally as
inferior art. James, however, does neither. He is far from defining
the story's tone as frivolous, he professes himself unable to find a
serious meaning in it, yet he does not dispraise it. Instead he attempts
to remove the story from the realm of serious art by asserting it was
inspired by the "moral picturesqueness" of "the secret that we are
really not by any means so good as a well-regulated society requires
us to appear." James seems to mean here that Hawthorne, in writing
"Young Goodman Brown," was not interested in revealing a truth,
but in achieving a poetic effect based on the paradoxical existence
among men, of evil in the guise of good.

Whether or not James is right here would seem to depend on the
degree of seriousness and conviction one finds in the story. If, after
finishing it, one thinks of Young Goodman Brown only as a shadowy
figment of the imagination, one is perhaps justified in regarding his
story as a hypothetical or speculative tale. But if, like the present
reader, one conceives of Brown as only a little less real than Hamlet
or Othello and much more real than such characters as Hawthorne's
Mrs. Bullfrog[6] or Ethan Brand, if one shudders with Brown at the
impalpable menace of the forest, and if, after finishing the story, one is
drawn to dark speculation on Brown's soul state at death, one /258/
would seem obliged to take the story seriously, to try to pluck out
the heart of its mystery.[7]

Whether or not Young Goodman Brown is intended to represent
all mankind would appear to depend upon whether or not the author
has included in the story a representative sample of mankind, and

---

[6] Hawthorne writes of this story in his *Note-Book* (September 16 [1841]) : ". . . As
to Mrs. Bullfrog, I give her up to the severest reprehension. The story was written
as a mere experiment in that style; it did not come from any depth within me,—
neither my heart nor mind had anything to do with it."

[7] Norman Holmes Pearson (*Hawthorne's Usable Truth* [Canton, N.Y., 1949], p. 11)
is one critic who evidently finds the story much more convincing, as well as more
profound, than James. He writes: "The conclusions [of Young Goodman Brown] are
as indefinable on the part of the reader as of Hawthorne, but the situation obtains for
limitless contemplation."

if so, upon whether Young Goodman Brown is himself representative of that sample. If there were not a fair sample of mankind in the story, Brown would not of course be representative of all mankind, even though everyone else in the story might closely resemble him in essentials.

To put the matter specifically, if it be granted that Young Goodman Brown in the course of the story moves from a state of simple faith to an evil state, and if the story suggests—as Brown himself suspects—that the other characters of the story, as representatives of all mankind, have gone through a similar experience, it will appear that Young Goodman Brown, in the essential matters of the spirit, is representative of all mankind. But if, on the other hand, it be concluded that owing to the Devil's deluding him with false imaginings in the forest, or showing him a sample of mankind which is not truly representative, Young Goodman Brown's suspicions about the world are not justified, then it will follow that Brown himself is not representative of all mankind, but only of some vile, suspicious portion of it.

Among recent critics who conclude that "Young Goodman Brown" views all human nature skeptically, is Richard Fogle. He writes apropos of this tale: "Hawthorne wishes to propose, not flatly that man is primarily evil, but instead the gnawing doubt lest this should indeed be true."[8] In Fogle's view, then, Brown would be representative of all mankind as well as of the other characters in the story.

McKeithan presents a view of the story very different from Fogle's. He writes:

> This is not the story of the disillusionment that comes to a person when he discovers that many supposedly religious and virtuous people are really sinful; /259/ it is, rather, a story of a man whose sin led him to consider all other people sinful. . . . He did not judge them accurately: he misjudged them.[9]

In other words, Young Goodman Brown does not even come near to being a representative of all mankind. Like a mirror with wavy lines in it, he perversely reflects the world as the world is not. In this view, "Young Goodman Brown" is the story of a warped and twisted psyche atypical of mankind in general.

One may be drawn to a conclusion very like McKeithan's without accepting all the evidence he adduces to support it. One may agree,

---

8 Fogle, "Ambiguity and Clarity in Hawthorne's 'Young Goodman Brown,' " *NEQ*, XVIII (Dec. 1945), 448.

9 McKeithan, *op. cit.*, pp. 95–96.

for example, that Faith retains her virtue in the story. Even Goodman Brown, suspicious as he is, has no proof to the contrary, as
the narrator makes clear: "Whether Faith obeyed [Goodman Brown's
plea to 'look up to heaven, and resist the wicked one'] he knew not."
And the narrator's description of Faith the next morning, "bursting
into such joy at sight of him [Brown] that she skipped along the
street and almost kissed her husband before the whole village," would
certainly suggest that she had summoned the strength to heed her
husband's plea. Joy such as Faith showed that morning would seem to
be a more natural consequence of resisting temptation than yielding
to it, especially with the stakes so high.

There may be some doubt in one's mind, though, whether Brown
was as wrong in his judgments concerning the minister of Salem
village, Deacon Gookin, and Goody Cloyse, as he was about Faith.
For it appears from the story that all three, in contrast to Faith, were
of Satan's party even before the forest meeting. Only Faith and Brown
himself are referred to as "the converts." It is at this point that an
important ambiguity arises, not of the both/and, but of the either/or
variety. How do we know whether the figures Young Goodman Brown
sees in the forest—the figures of the minister, the deacon, the other
citizens of Salem village and of the state of Massachusetts, and Faith
herself—are genuine witches,[10] or merely specters of truly virtuous
townspeople conjured up by the Devil?[11] They can- /260/ not be
both at the same time. The same sort of problem faced Hamlet when
confronted by his father's ghost, but Brown, unlike Hamlet, simply
ignores the problem, leaving it to haunt his interpreters.

In the absence of any final answer to this problem, I conclude that
the witches Goodman Brown saw were genuine. Even Faith was a

---

[10] By "genuine" witches, I mean persons dedicated to, or sorely tempted to dedi-
cate themselves to, evil.

[11] As was brought out in the Salem witch trials, the Devil was commonly credited
with the power of employing specters to counterfeit the shape of innocent persons.
Such manifestations of Satan's power were according to the best authorities quite
rare, however. See in this connection Cotton Mather, *Wonders of the Invisible World*
(1693 ed.), p. 19: "But that which makes this Descent [of the Devil] the more
formidable, is the *multitude* and *quality* of Persons accused of an Interest in this
Witchcraft, by Efficacy of the *Spectres* which take their Name and Shape upon
them. . . . That the Devils have obtain'd the power, to take on them the likeness of
harmless people." See also David Levin, *What Happened at Salem?* (n.p., 1952),
p. 16. That Hawthorne was well aware of this conventional attribution of power to
the Devil is attested not only by his general familiarity with New England witchcraft,
but by the following sentence in his "Alice Doane's Appeal" (*Tales, Sketches and
Other Papers* [Boston, 1883], XII, 291): "The whole miserable multitude, both sinful
souls and false spectres of good men, groaned horribly and gnashed their teeth, as
they looked upward to the calm loveliness of the midnight sky, and beheld those
homes of bliss where they must never dwell."

witch, in terms of my footnote definition of the word. She had been tempted by Satan; then, yielding initially to temptation much as Brown himself had done, suffered herself to be conveyed to the Witches' Sabbath to conclude her pact. Faith's pink ribbon which Goodman Brown sees fluttering down in the forest is the confession of her initial yielding. But Faith's confession also serves as a means of grace. Openly signifying that she still delights in the beautiful things of this world, that she is still vain of her appearance, that the whiteness of her angelism is still mixed with the crimson of her passion for Young Goodman Brown, the pink ribbons keep Faith humble and honest, and thus contribute to her ultimate preservation from the Evil One. Even so, for the duration of her stay in the forest, Faith remains a "witch."

Why do I conclude that the other figures Goodman Brown saw in the forest were also "real" witches? Principally because none of them had ever made any public confession of sin, failure to do which is a dangerous sign in any human being. The proof that they had never admitted to human frailty was Brown's trauma on discovering their guilt. In public the minister "mediate[d] his sermon," Deacon Gookin prayed "holy words," and Goody Cloyse "catechiz[ed]." None of them showed any signs of frailty corresponding to the pink ribbons of Faith, those efficacious talismans that confess one is still earthbound even though one's aspiration is heavenward.[12] Nor did /261/ any of them confess, as Faith confessed, to "being troubled with such dreams and such thoughts that she's afeard of herself sometimes." The minister, Deacon Gookin, and Goody Cloyse were the "unco' guid, or the rigidly righteous" of Salem village, and as such were likely candidates for Satan's party.

In other terms, they were pharisees, and their pharisaism led them to hypocrisy. Obeying the letter of the law, they kept from others, and perhaps themselves as well, the sobering fact that, being human, they were unable to follow perfectly the spirit of the law. They fell far short of the ideal expressed elsewhere by Hawthorne: "Be true! Be true! Be true! Show freely to the world, if not your worst, yet some trait whereby the worst may be inferred."[13]

---

[12] Connolly rightly observes that the pink ribbons are out of keeping with the severity of Puritan dress, but then concludes not that Faith is atypical of the Puritans, but that the pink ribbons represent Young Goodman Brown's "initial illusion about the true significance of his faith" (p. 374). However Connolly fails to explain why if this is true, near the end of the story when Goodman Brown's illusion is presumably shattered, Faith still sports the pink ribbons. Regarded in their proper light, the ribbons are not a reflection of Brown's misguided view of Faith, but an adjunct of Faith herself.

[13] Hawthorne, *The Scarlet Letter* (London, 1906), p. 313.

To summarize, then, although one might reject some of the evidence on which McKeithan's conclusions are based, one might accept at least part of his evidence and conclusion: namely that Faith retains her virtue finally, and that Brown is consequently wrong in continuing to view that part of humanity which Faith represents with suspicion. In this view, Brown, as McKeithan asserts, is not representative of all mankind, and consequently the story is not totally pessimistic.

In apologizing for Brown's misanthropic view of mankind, one might argue that it was an easy step from the observation that all but one at the Witches' Sabbath were corrupt, to the conclusion that all at the Witches' Sabbath, indeed all mankind, were corrupt. And it would be especially easy for Brown, after discovering that some he had regarded as at least as virtuous as Faith had made a pact with the Devil, to come to the conclusion that Faith also had fallen.

At the same time one understands why Brown came to these conclusions, one must recognize that there was no valid reason for his coming to them. As long as his wife Faith gave signs of being faithful, Brown should not have despaired. Even if Faith herself had yielded to the Devil (I speak of Faith now as his wife rather than as a personified abstraction), Brown should have cast his net more /262/ widely in Salem village and beyond it in his search for virtue. He should have reckoned with the possibility that somewhere in Salem village, or at least beyond its narrow confines, there might be men neither "famous for their especial sanctity" nor "given over to all mean and filthy vice, and suspected even of horrid crimes." For it is worth noting that all of those Brown observes at the Witches' Sabbath fall into one or the other of these categories. Brown should have considered the possibility that the man who confesses his virtue is mixed with vice may possess not only humility, but true virtue as well, insofar as virtue is a plant that grows on mortal ground.

Having concluded that Brown's misanthropic view of all mankind is unjustified, and consequently that Brown, in his own devotion to evil, is not representative of all mankind, one may ask what portion of mankind he does represent.

The answer, I think, is that he represents those weaker members of a puritanical society who are traumatized, arrested in their spiritual development, and finally destroyed by the discovery that their society is full of "whited sepulchres." Others in such a society, with more strength but less moral sensitivity than Brown, recognize the power of hypocrisy to give the appearance of virtue (the *sine qua non* of success), and capitalize on this discovery to rise to the highest positions of secular and religious authority. Then there are those few hardy souls, who, like Faith, with difficulty preserve their virtue by letting a tincture of their vice be displayed on their breastplate of righteousness.

Hawthorne stands in this story, then, as an analyst and critic of the society that demands so much of a man that he can achieve what is demanded only through hypocrisy, and that blinds itself so thoroughly to the power of sin in the lives of even its best men that it denies them the ritual and balm of public confession.[14] /263/

Other critics have noted Hawthorne's concern with the moral rigorism of Puritanism. Vladimir Astrov, for example, comparing Hawthorne with Dostoevski writes:

... Hawthorne and Dostoevski ... stressed the power of the irrational and the abysmal in soul and life. ... [15]

Puritan rigorists had always to protect their integrity and their peace with blinds of inflexible dogmas from the impact of reality. This was the ostrich way to remain "pure" and "consistent." The security thus achieved was, of course, an illusory one. ... [16]

The result was, inevitably, perpetual moral conflicts, remorse, feelings of sin and guilt.[17]

---

[14] Connolly regards "Young Goodman Brown" not as an attack on the rigorism and hypocrisy of Puritan society, but on Puritanic-Calvinistic theology, specifically on the doctrine of election, faith in which Connolly—and presumably Hawthorne—somewhat oversimply regards as the Puritan way of salvation. But there is surely nothing peculiarly Puritanic-Calvinistic in Goodman Brown's resolve to "cling to her [Faith's] skirts and follow her to heaven"; any orthodox Christian who believed in salvation by faith might make the same resolve. Moreover, I see nothing in Hawthorne's presentation of Faith to justify identifying her with faith in election rather than with the more orthodox faith in Christ's sacrifice.

One other Hawthorne critic besides Connolly, Frank Preston Stearns, in *The Life and Genius of Nathaniel Hawthorne* (Boston, 1906), p. 181, has suggested that Hawthorne may be chiefly concerned with Puritanism in "Young Goodman Brown." He writes: "He [Hawthorne] may have intended this for an exposure of the inconsistency, and consequent hypocrisy, of Puritanism; but the name of Goodman Brown's wife is Faith, and this suggests that Brown may have been himself intended for an incarnation of doubt, or *disbelief* carried to a logical extreme. Whatever may have been Hawthorne's design, the effect is decidedly unpleasant." But Stearns fails to clarify or follow up this suggestion.

[15] Astrov, "Hawthorne and Dostoevski as Explorers of the Human Conscience," *NEQ*, XV (June, 1942), 296.

[16] Astrov, p. 304.

[17] Astrov, p. 302.

Herbert Schneider, similarly emphasizing Hawthorne's concern
with the blind, malevolent side of human nature, which no display
of virtue can eradicate, writes:

> For him [Hawthorne] sin is an obvious and conspicuous fact, to deny which
> is foolish. Its consequences are inevitable and to seek escape from them is
> childish. The only relief from sin comes from public confession. Anything
> private or concealed works internally until it destroys the sinner's soul.[18]

These words shed light on the soul state of the minister of Salem,
Deacon Gookin, Goody Cloyse, and Goodman Brown, as well as on
that of Hester Prynne, in connection with whom they were written.
And Arthur Miller, attempting in his preface to *The Crucible* to
establish a connection, long since denied by G. L. Kittredge,[19] between
the outburst of witchcraft at Salem and Puritanism, has this to say:

> The witch hunt was not, however, a mere repression. It was also, and as
> importantly, a long overdue opportunity for everyone so inclined to express
> publicly his guilt and sins, under the cover of accusations against the vic-
> tims. . . . These people had no ritual for the washing away of sins. It is
> another trait we inherited from them, and it has helped to discipline us as
> well as to breed hypocrisy among us.[20] /264/

Finally, Hawthorne himself has in another work made his criticism
of Puritanism explicit:

> In truth, when the first novelty and stir of spirit had subsided,—when the
> new settlement [Salem] . . . had actually become a little town . . . its rigidity
> could not fail to cause distortions of the moral nature. Such a life was sinister
> to the intellect and sinister to the heart; especially when one generation
> had bequeathed its religious gloom and the counterfeit of its religious ardor,
> to the next; for these characteristics, as was inevitable, assumed the form
> both of hypocrisy and exaggeration, by being inherited from the example
> and precept of other human beings, and not from an original and spiritual
> source.[21]

---

[18] Schneider, *The Puritan Mind* (New York, 1930), p. 260.

[19] Kittredge, *Witchcraft in Old and New England* (Cambridge, Mass., 1929), pp.
372–373. But Schneider, quoted above, differs, arguing that the epidemic of witchcraft
at Salem was a product of Puritanism (p. 42).

[20] Miller, *The Crucible* (New York, 1953), pp. 7, 20.

[21] Hawthorne, "Main Street" in *The Snow Image*, III (Boston, 1900), 89–90.
Quotations from "Young Goodman Brown" are also from this edition, in *Mosses
From An Old Manse*, I, 102–124.

What better anatomy than this could be found of the kind of society that produced Young Goodman Brown?

In "Young Goodman Brown," then, Hawthorne, as well as "explaining" the Salem witch trials, is pleading that what survives of Puritan rigorism in society be sloughed off, and replaced by a striving for virtue starting from the confession of common human weakness. Such a society would be based upon the firm foundation of humility and honesty rather than upon the sinking sands of human pride and the hypocrisy that accompanies it. In such a society, the soul of even a Goodman Brown might prosper. "Young Goodman Brown" is not so much the story of Brown's view of society as it is the story of the impact of a certain type of society on a man such as Brown.

Daniel Hoffman

Just Married!-In the Village of Witches*

ONE

Another of Hawthorne's newly married couples never had known carefree bliss as Lord and Lady of the May. For Young Goodman Brown, after a proper Puritan upbringing by his father, the deacon, the minister, and Goodwife Cloyse who taught him the catechism, was wedded in Salem village to pretty Faith, with pink ribbons on her cap. Young Goodman has a rendezvous to keep with a stranger in the forest, and although Faith importunes him to 'tarry with me this night . . . of all nights in the year,' he leaves her behind, dissembling his 'evil purpose.' Goodman's 'covenant' is kept with a dark-clad stranger whose staff 'might almost be seen to twist and wriggle itself like a living serpent.' Walking together, they 'might have been taken for father and son.' Reluctantly the youth penetrates the dreary forest where, though 'It was all as lonely as could be . . . the traveller knows not who may be concealed . . . he may yet be passing through an unseen multitude.'

They overtake old Goody Cloyse, who greets the stranger familiarly: 'And is it your worship indeed . . . in the very image of my old gossip, Goodman Brown, the grandfather of the silly fellow that now is.' Her broomstick has been stolen but she's off to the meeting afoot, 'for they tell me there is a nice young man to be taken into communion tonight.' She disappears on the stranger's 'writhing stick,' and a moment later the deacon and /149/ minister ride by. 'There is a goodly young woman to be taken into communion,' says the deacon; the minister urges him to 'Spur up,' for 'Nothing can be done, you know,

* Daniel Hoffman, *Form and Fable in American Fiction* (New York: Oxford University Press, 1965), pp. 149–67. © 1961 by Daniel G. Hoffman. Reprinted by permission.

until I get on the ground.' Goodman Brown begins to understand toward what he is 'journeying so deep into the heathen wilderness.'

The rest of the story I shall discuss below, with closer attention to certain details. Brown's destination is a Witches' Sabbath—'of all nights in the year' this must be October 31, All Saints' Eve, and he finds, at a rock altar flanked by blazing pines, all the worthies of Salem in the coven of the Prince of Darkness. At the call, 'Bring forth the converts!' Brown steps forward—'he was himself the chief horror of the scene, and shrank not from its other horrors.' 'Thither came also the slender form of a veiled female.' The Devil addresses them: 'Depending upon one another's hearts, ye still had hoped that virtue were not all a dream. Now are ye undeceived. Evil is the nature of mankind. Evil must be your only happiness. Welcome again, my children, to the communion of your race.' At a natural basin in the rock, 'the shape of evil' dipped his hand and prepared 'to lay the mark of baptism upon their foreheads, that they might be partakers of the mystery of sin.' At this eleventh hour Young Goodman Brown cries in agony and terror, 'Faith! Faith! look up to heaven, and resist the wicked one.'

Young Goodman Brown never knew whether Faith obeyed him. The phantasmagoric tableau vanishes, and he finds himself alone in the dark forest. 'A hanging twig, that had been all on fire, besprinkled his cheek with the coldest dew.' Hawthorne's control of his powerfully ambivalent structural metaphors in this story—the synoptic *enjambement* of journey, initiation, and witchcraft—gives him the authority to ask at the end, without diminution of intensity, 'Had Goodman Brown fallen asleep in the forest and only dreamed a wild dream of a witch-meeting?' The author can even say, 'Be it so if you will; but alas! it was a dream of evil omen for young Goodman Brown.' His life henceforth leads not, like Edgar the May Lord's, toward heaven by /150/ a difficult path; his heart has been blighted by this initiation into the coven of evil that binds mankind. 'They carved no hopeful verse upon his tombstone, for his dying hour was gloom.'

This tale is one of Hawthorne's masterpieces, and it has received its share of appreciative comment. Fogle sensitively explicates the delicate balance Hawthorne achieved between ambiguity of implication and clarity of form, while Roy R. Male finds the center of meaning in 'the fact that Faith's ambiguity is the ambiguity of womanhood and ... the dark night in the forest is essentially a sexual experience, though it is also much more.'[1] My concern is to discover what imaginative

---

[1] Fogle, *Hawthorne's Fiction*, pp. 15–32; Male, *Hawthorne's Tragic Vision*, pp. 76–80.

possibilities Hawthorne found in his ancestral *donnée* of Salem witchcraft and how he realized them in 'Young Goodman Brown.'

All readers of course acknowledge that the Witches' Sabbath is
one of Hawthorne's most memorable dramatizations of man's recognition of evil, and it is often remarked that Hawthorne did not forget
that his own great-great-grandfather 'made himself so conspicuous in
the martyrdom of the witches, that their blood may fairly be said
to have left a stain upon him.' To do justice to Hawthorne's achievement we will do well to take as seriously as he did, for artistic purposes,
the role of his Salem forebears in 1692. Speaking of the witch-condemn-
ing magistrate and of an earlier Hathorne who had scourged the
Quakers, Hawthorne writes in the introductory chapter of *The Scarlet
Letter*, 'I, the present writer, as their representative, hereby take
shame upon myself for their sakes, and pray that any curse incurred
by them—as I have heard, and as the dreary and unprosperous condition of the race, for many a long year back, would argue to exist—may
now and henceforth be removed.'

Such a curse was in fact pronounced on Judge Hathorne. 'That
God would take vengeance' was the cry of Goodwife Cary's husband,
who had been forced to see her tortured and taunted by accusers whose
cruelties that magistrate abetted in the names /151/ of piety and
justice.[2] The curse on the one hand identifies these antecedent
Hathornes with the Pyncheons in *The House of the Seven Gables*;
but on the other it identifies Nathaniel Hawthorne's sense of inherited
guilt, of original sin, with their inhumanities.[3]

When a writer is truly prepossessed by the guilt of his pious ancestors
in such affairs, we cannot dismiss the involvement of his fictional
characters with curses and witchcraft as merely the Gothic machinery
of romance, nor as artistic devices for producing ambiguities. Hawthorne *was* thus prepossessed by the part of his paternal forebears
in Salem's season of horror. The zeal of those Puritans to discover
satanism in their neighbors became for their descendant an emblem,
an allegorical 'type,' of their particular tragic flaw—hypocritical pride.
Endicott would serve as 'the Puritan of Puritans' in 'The Maypole,' but
his iron rigidity would be manifested elsewhere in Hawthorne's work

---

[2] Nathaniel Cary's letter was printed by Robert Calef in *More Wonders of the
Invisible World* (1692), reprinted in Burr, *Narratives of the Witchcraft Cases*, p. 351.

[3] The actual curse pronounced upon the Pyncheons, 'God will give you blood to
drink,' were the dying words of Sarah Good to the Rev. Nicholas Noyes of Salem
who was present at her execution. Judge Hathorne had committed Sarah Good's
four-year-old child to prison, where she was fettered in irons. See Calef in *Narratives*,
pp. 345, 358.

in contexts yet more destructive of man's capacity for bliss. When the
Puritans had dealt with Morton's one dissident colony on the neigh-
boring hill and turned instead upon each other, the consequences of
their iron rule blighted both themselves and their posterity. In his
historical sketch 'Main Street' Hawthorne without ambiguity presents
their triumphs against the heretics and witches who threatened the
Puritan commonwealth, and concludes,

> It was impossible for the succeeding race to grow up, in heaven's freedom,
> beneath the discipline which their gloomy energy of character had estab-
> lished; nor, it may be, have we even yet thrown off all the unfavorable
> influences, which, among many good ones, were bequeathed us by our
> Puritan forefathers. Let us thank God for /152/ having given us such
> ancestors; and let each successive generation thank Him, not less fervently,
> for being one step further from them in the march of ages.

The source of that balance between Hawthorne's clarity of design
and ambiguity of meaning, which Fogle justly proposes as the key
to his achievement, lies in his capacity to present the world of his
Puritan forebears through a simultaneous double-exposure. We see
old Salem both as they saw it, accepting their values, and as it appears
from Hawthorne's very different view. Thus the Puritan values function both as absolutes (to the characters) and as one of several possible
choices offered to the reader. Hawthorne so manages this doubleness
that he can criticize Puritanism without destroying our suspension of
disbelief in its premises. One of these which served his purposes
especially well was witchcraft.

'It has also been made a doubt by some,' four New England clergymen wrote in 1689, introducing a book by Cotton Mather which Nathaniel Hawthorne would read, 'whether there are any such things as
Witches, *i.e.*, such as by Contract or Explicit Covenant with the Devil,
improve, or rather are improved by him to the doing of things strange
in themselves and besides their natural Course. But (besides that the
Word of God assures us that there have been such, and gives order
about them) no Age passes without some apparent Demonstration of
it.'[4] Puritanism was perhaps as close to the Manichean as any Christian
sect has come; the Power of Evil was acknowledged with the same
fervor as the Power of Light. Indeed, it was a faith more pessimistic
than that of the ancient dualists, for it made no provision for the
goodness of man. The terrifying insecurity of each soul that it was not

---

4 *Memorable Providences, Relating to Witchcrafts and Possessions*, reprinted in
Narratives, p. 95.

among the Elect produced those psychological tensions in Puritan culture which set the New England background apart from the heritage of the other colonies. One of those tensions reached the breaking-point in Salem, /153/ where upright, pious citizens like John Hathorne condemned their neighbors to death on evidence no stronger than this:

> These ten ... did vehemently accuse [Goodwife Cory] of Afflicting them, by Biting, Pinching, Strangling, etc. And they said, they did in their Fits see her likeness coming to them, and bringing a Book for them to Sign; Mr. Hathorne, a Magistrate of Salem, asked her, why she Afflicted those Children? she said, she did not Afflict them; he asked her, who did then? she said, 'I don't know, how should I know?' she said, they were Poor Distracted Creatures, and no heed to be given to what they said; Mr. Hathorn and Mr. Noyes replied that it was the Judgement of all that were there present, that they were bewitched, and only she (the Accused) said they were Distracted; She was Accused by them, that the Black Man whispered to her in her Ear now (while she was upon Examination) and that she had a Yellow Bird, that did use to Suck between her fingers. . . . When the Accused had any motion of their Body, Hands or Mouth, the Accusers would cry out, as when she bit her Lip, they would cry out of being bitten . . . if she stirred her Feet, they would stamp and cry out of Pain there. After the Hearing the said Cory was committed to Salem Prison, and then their crying out of her abated.

The passage is from Calef's *More Wonders of the Invisible World* (1692), a book bitterly critical of the trials.[5] This same woman appears in 'Young Goodman Brown'; Goody Cloyse complains to the Black Man that her broomstick 'hath strangely disappeared, stolen, as I suspect, by that unhanged witch Goody Cory.' (Goody Cloyse, herself indicted for witchcraft, was the sister of two other witches, one whom Mr. Hathorne examined, the other whom he committed.[6])

Hawthorne found two means of taking witchcraft seriously as a way of revealing 'the truths of the human heart.' Accepting the reality of witchcraft as a sin, he would share the Puritans' abhorrence, as unredeemedly damned souls, of all who trafficked /154/ in sortilege and necromancy. In his early story, 'The Hollow of the Three Hills,' a young woman meets a withered witch by such a spot, 'so gray tradition tells,' as was 'once the resort of the Power of Evil and his plighted subjects. . . . in the performance of an impious baptismal

---

[5] Calef, in *Narratives*, p. 344. That Hawthorne read it we infer from the victims named in 'Main Street,' whose sufferings are reported by Calef alone among the chronicles of Salem.

[6] *Ibid.* pp. 346–7.

rite.' But this woman has long since received the Devil's baptism, and the role of the old witch is to bring to life before her the parents she has dishonored, the husband she has driven mad, the child she has killed. In her crimes against the human heart she, like Ethan Brand, is guilty of the Unpardonable Sin; still capable of remorse, she dies, the final victim of her own enormities. Some of the materials for 'Young Goodman Brown' are touched on here, but by the time Hawthorne conceived the later tale he had devised a far more radical means of employing them.

Suppose Hawthorne, for artistic purposes, to have taken witchcraft at exactly the value his great-great-grandsire put upon it; suppose him to have been able to believe that Goody Cory and others like her had really made covenants with the Black Man; suppose such Accusers as Abigail Williams were factually correct in reporting 'That she saw a great number of Persons in the Village at the Administration of a Mock Sacrament.'[7] What were the logical moral consequences of beliefs such as those Judge Hathorne had acted upon? It is obvious that no one was exempt from suspicion, that the hysterical seizures of the accusers might be produced by the 'spirit' of any member of the colony. Mistress Ann Hibbens, the sister of Governor Bellingham himself, had been executed for a witch in 1656. When the line between the damned witches and the accusing Christians became too fine to draw with certainty, even the avid Cotton Mather had to concede 'that some of those that were concerned grew amazed at the number and condition of those that were accused, and feared that Satan, by his wiles, had entrapped innocent persons under the imputation of that crime; and at last, as /155/ was evidently seen, there must be a stop put, or the generation of the kingdom of God would fall under condemnation.'[8]

Suppose, then, that an innocent young Puritan, newly married, as yet unaware of his taint of original sin, should leave his faith just long enough, on one night, to follow the dark stranger into the forest—and find there the Witches' Sabbath where those who took the Devil's communion were all the members of his daylight world of piety. Hawthorne takes witchcraft more seriously, in fact, than had John Hathorne or Cotton Mather, for unlike them he does not flinch to acknowledge the covenant of the fallen nature of all mankind. Magistrate Hathorne seems not to have recanted or repented after the general amnesty, as did a more distinguished judge, Samuel Sewall.

---

7 Calef, in *Narratives*, pp. 345–6.

8 Mather, *Magnalia Christi Americana*, Book VI, chap. lxxxii.

John Hathorne would seem to have made no connection between the
state of his own soul in God's sight and his responsibility, say, for the
sufferings of Giles Cory, whose wife he had committed for witchcraft.
Cory, also accused and seeing that none had been cleared by trial,
'chose to undergo what Death they would put him to . . . [The
sentence was pressing, *peine forte et dure*]. His Tongue being prest
out of his Mouth, the Sheriff with his Cane forced it in again when
he was dying.'[9] No, Nathaniel Hawthorne could accept the guilt of
alleged witches only as their individual share of the guilt of mankind.
He must accept also the guilt of their accusers and tormentors. 'Young
Goodman Brown' is one of his expiations for John Hathorne's guilt,
as well as for his own.

Not only an expiation but a judgment upon his fathers, too. For
what Young Goodman Brown learns at the Witches' Sabbath, while
it is a knowledge more profound than that of the zealots who did the
devil's work in 1692, is still but a partial knowledge. It is too incom-
plete to win him wisdom or happiness. He is so blinded by perception
of evil that his life is ever after blighted. In this he is true to the Puritan
past, as Haw- /156/ thorne envisaged it. In the struggle between jollity
and gloom, Young Goodman Brown would seem to have had no choice.
On his return to Salem he finds his wife Faith 'gazing anxiously forth,
and bursting into such joy at the sight of him that she skipped along
the street and almost kissed her husband before the whole village.'
This would have been, for Brown, but to deepen their 'stain of guilt'
in the eyes of their fellow-hypocrites. 'Goodman Brown looked sternly
and sadly into her face, and passed on without a greeting.'

This tale, like 'The Maypole of Merry Mount,' presents the sym-
bolistic development of details elaborated from within a frame of
allegory. The names of the couple are as allegorical as any in Bunyan:
The Puritan Everyman is the husband of Christian Faith. By the end
of the tale he proves more Puritan than Christian, renouncing her
larger vision for the 'distrustful,' 'desperate,' 'gloom' of his life and
death. Faith, too, had been at the Witches' Sabbath; she can accept
man even with full knowledge of his evil nature. But Goodman lacks
her largesse, her charity, her balance. 'Often, awaking suddenly at
midnight, he shrank from the bosom of Faith; . . . when the family
knelt down at prayer, he scowled and muttered to himself, and gazed
sternly at his wife, and turned away.' Faith remains true to him—
she follows his 'hoary corpse' to the grave, but he has indeed been
damned by his night among the witches.

---

[9] Calef, in *Narratives*, p. 367.

TWO

The singular quality of Young Goodman Brown's adventure is the
intensity with which the dramatic, theological, psychological, and
cultural dimensions of the tale are fused together in the single structural metaphor of his journey into the dark forest and his return to
the daylight world. Traditions of witchcraft served Hawthorne's complex purposes with extraordinary precision in each of these dimensions
of meaning. If 'Young Goodman Brown' is the most profound work of
fiction drawing /157/ on those traditions in American writing,[10] one
reason for this is that Hawthorne knew better than any author of his
century what the traditions signified or could be made to signify. The
interest in Salem witchcraft of James Russell Lowell, for instance, or of
Professor Kittredge, proves to be merely preliminary to an attempt
to exculpate their Puritan ancestors from the opprobrium of history.[11]
Hawthorne, as we have seen, had the courage to recognize the cosmic
irony of the situation in which innocent, charitable Christians were
tortured to death by the ministers and magistrates of God's chosen
people. But it is not only his tragic sense of the family connection
that makes witchcraft a masterful metaphor in Hawthorne's tale.
From his wide study of witchcraft and of the witchcraft trials came
the materials he fused into the multiplex pattern of 'Young Goodman
Brown': from the self-righteous accounts by zealots like Increase and
Cotton Mather, the caustic attack upon them by Robert Calef, the
records in the Essex County Courthouse, as well as from Hawthorne's
awareness of oral traditions concerning witchcraft and of treatments of
the subject in literature by Cervantes, Goethe, and Irving. The peculiar

---

10 For a survey of 'New England Witchcraft in Fiction' see G. H. Orians, *American
Literature*, II (March 1930), 54–71.

11 Lowell, in his essay 'Witchcraft,' occasioned by the publication in 1867 of
Salem Witchcraft by Charles W. Upham, echoes that historian in averring that
"The proceedings of the Salem trials are sometimes spoken of as though they were
exceptionally cruel. But, in fact, if compared with others of the same kind, they
were exceptionally humane . . . it is rather wonderful that no mode of torture other
than mental was tried at Salem. . . . all died protesting their innocence. . . . though
an acknowledgment of guilt would have saved the lives of all [sic]. This martyr
proof of the efficacy of Puritanism in the character and conscience may be allowed
to outweigh a great many sneers at Puritan fanaticism.' Lowell cites the case of
Goody Cary to prove that 'The accused . . . were not abandoned by their friends.
In all the trials of this kind there is nothing so pathetic as the picture of [Nathaniel]
Cary holding up the weary arms of his wife . . . and wiping away the sweat from
her brow and the tears from her face.' Of Mr. Hathorne's retort he says nothing.
Among My Books (Boston, 1882), pp. 146–7.
    See G. L. Kittredge, *Witchcraft in Old and New England* (Cambridge, Mass.,
1922), pp. 362–5.

significances of this story are /158/ rooted in the cultural significances of witchcraft itself. This we can see by examining a schematic statement of the way his structural metaphor served Hawthorne. We can trace the elaboration in his tale of the several kinds of meaning associated by long tradition with witchchaft and the Witches' Sabbath.

Hawthorne's protagonist takes a journey, away from daylight, reality, piety, and Faith. Traveling through darkness he is guided by the Satanic image of his own father (and grandfather) toward an initiation into both forbidden knowledge and a secret cult. The ceremony of initiation is a ritual representing the spiritual inversion of Christianity (the rock 'altar,' the trees ablaze like both 'hell-kindled torches' and 'candles' 'at an evening meeting,' and the 'mark of baptism' which the Devil is about to place on their foreheads). The forbidden knowledge in whose name the Devil-Father welcomes Brown and Faith 'to the communion of your race' is not only knowledge of man's evil nature generally, but knowledge specifically of original sin, represented by the welcoming spirit of Brown's father among the fiends as well as by the Devil's having assumed his father's form. It is also carnal knowledge, sexual sin. As we have seen, however, Faith is in the forest too; in one sense she *is* the forest, and Brown has qualified for admission to the witches' orgy by having carnal knowledge of her. (In another sense, however, which is ever equally valid in the tale, Faith transcends Brown's knowledge of evil with all-encompassing love.) In rejecting her love after his initiation, Brown is guilty of that Manichean prepossession with the dark side of man's nature which Hawthorne presents as the special sin of the Puritans. Each of these suggestions is a characteristic feature of the traditional attitudes toward witchcraft.

In the Salem trial records it is apparent that belief in witches was held on two different levels of conception by the seventeenth-century Puritans in New England.[12] /159/

On the one hand there is the belief of the Accusers. What, in fact, did such witnesses as those who testified against Goody Cory offer as evidence of her guilt? That she affected them, made them sick, caused them to itch or to vomit, afflicted their livestock, caused shipwrecks at sea, wrought havoc with their silverware, invisibly caused solid objects to move, had intercourse with devils, suckled her familiar at a

---

[12] An acquaintance with the British and Continental literature on the subject shows that these two types of belief were characteristic of Christian attitudes toward witchcraft since the Middle Ages. In no way was the experience of Salem uniquely a Colonial American phenomenon; indeed, much has been made by Kittredge and other writers of the comparative mildness of the American epidemic when seen in the context of English, Scottish, French, German, or Scandinavian experience.

hidden teat on her body. Such charges as these recur innumerably in the long annals of witchcraft. They led Professor Kittredge to regard as the basis of witchcraft the belief that human beings can with supernatural powers wreak harm and destruction on their enemies.

The second type of belief in witches is of a different sort. The Black Sabbath in 'Young Goodman Brown' may stand as representative of the more highly organized, conceptual regard for witchcraft as the involvement of the witches in a religious cult which rivals Christianity. Indeed, it is a sect which threatens the Christian commonwealth with destruction. Consequently the witches are not content with the expression of personal malice; nor are they merely individuals who have made solitary compacts with the Devil. They are organized into covens, the Devil or one of his minions is their acknowledged priest and leader, they hold services which are horrible and blasphemous parodies of the Christian Mass, and the working of their will is one of the trials with which God in His Almighty Wisdom has decreed that the Faith of the Christian Commonwealth shall be tried on earth.

This sophisticated intellectual conception is in fact a development of medieval theology, which took for granted the identity of the sorcerers and necromancers mentioned in the Bible with the witches discovered in contemporary Christendom. The /160/ prodigious learning of Increase and Cotton Mather, both of whose works on witchcraft Hawthorne studied, reflects their intimate familiarity with a large corpus of theological literature on witchcraft. The authoritative compendium of orthodox theological opinion on this subject is the *Malleus Maleficarum* of Henricus Institoris (1489). The arguments quoted above in favor of belief in witchcraft, offered exactly two centuries later by Cotton Mather and his four sponsors, are contained in the answer to the first Question in *Malleus*. Kittredge, whose *Witchcraft in Old and New England* lists the prolific theological discussion of the problem on both sides of the Atlantic, concludes that

> the orgies of the Witches' Sabbath [were] systematized in the fourteenth and fifteenth centuries by the scholastic ingenuity of devout theologians and described in confessions innumerable wrung by torture from ignorant and superstitious defendants in response to leading questions framed by inquisitors who had the whole system in mind before the trial began.[13]

To support this theory Kittredge suggests that the Church, from its first concern with witchcraft, regarded the practice as heretical. Since the Church had had long experience with the perpetration of other heresies—Manichaean, Paulician, Catharian, Waldensian—in each

---

[13] *Op. cit.*, p. 243.

instance of which there was a rival religious organization, when the medieval theologians turned their attention to witchcraft their speculation followed long-established dogmatic practice.[14]

In 'Young Goodman Brown' Hawthorne makes effective use /161/ of both sets of beliefs. He employs the theological conceptualization of witchcraft as the Antichrist for the architecture of his tale, and he uses several folk beliefs (not necessarily dependent upon the foregoing) for verisimilitude of detail and for the evocation of wonder, awe, and terror. The compact with the Black Man, the Devil's shapeshifting and his serpentine staff, the transportation of witches by means of magical ointments and broomsticks, their existence as disembodied spirits, the withering of living things at the witches' or Devil's touch, are motifs of folk belief often encountered independently of the Witches' Sabbath. Yet the theological construct had by the late seventeenth century passed into popular tradition, since such notorious cases as the trials of the Lancashire witches in 1612 had been celebrated in unnumbered chapbooks, black-letter ballads, popular narratives, and literary works. Consequently some of the informants (like Abigail Williams) averred that they had witnessed Black Masses and the ceremonial partaking of the evil sacrament by the neighbors they accused.

Hawthorne thus is able to take advantage of the idea—by Puritan times both theological and popular—that witchcraft represents forbidden knowledge, and that its attainment takes the form of an initiatory ceremonial, a Witches' Sabbath. In folklore the two strains of witchcraft and demonology merged in this ceremony, where the witch sold his soul to the Devil. Hawthorne quotes almost verbatim from Cotton Mather's *Wonders of the Invisible World* when he tells us that Faith stepped forward to receive the Devil's baptism beside 'Martha Carrier, who had received the devil's promise to be queen of hell.'[15]

The theological level of 'Young Goodman Brown' is greatly strengthened by the youth's horrified recognition that the form of his father

---

[14] 'In the course of the fourteenth century the papal inquisitors discovered (so they thought) a new heretical sect—the sect of devil-worshipping witches. These, it logically followed, must hold meetings, and such meetings must resemble those of other heretics. . . . The idea of a Sabbath of Witches was neither ancient nor of popular origin. It was a mere transference. What was already established in the inquisitorial mind with regard to the Satanic Synagogue of the Cathari was shifted, as a matter of logical course, to the alleged asemblies of the new heretical sect, the devotees of witchcraft.' *Witchcraft in Old and New England*, p. 246.

[15] Burr, *Narratives*, p. 144.

seems to beckon him toward the unholy communion. This is itself a dreamlike duplication of the first appearance of the Black Man in the forest, for when Goodman walked /162/ beside him 'they might have been taken for father and son.' The paternal image is reduplicated yet again when Goody Cloyse greets 'The devil! . . . Yes, truly it is, and in the very image of my old gossip, Goodman Brown, the grandfather of the silly fellow that now is.' She of course is using *gossip* in its original sense of *God-sib*—'A person spiritually related to another through being a sponsor at a baptism.' This is to say that Goodman Brown's grandfather had taken Goody Cloyse to her first witch meeting. The tripling of generations in Brown's family who have taken the Devil's Mass reinforces the theological conception of witchcraft as one of Satan's entrapments of the human soul. Our original sin makes us vulnerable.

The inference is unmistakeable that Old Brown had had carnal knowledge of Goody Cloyse, and that it was through such carnal knowledge that her initiation was completed. Young Goodman's bitter rejection of Faith after his return to the 'real' world supports the inference that it was through his knowledge of her that he made acquaintance with the Black Man in the first place. He is reliving the Puritan allegory of the Fall, in which woman, as Governor Endicott warned the May Lord, is 'that sex which requireth the stricter discipline.' But if woman is the agent of the Fall, for Young Goodman Brown that Fall is anything but fortunate, for it fails to prepare the way for his salvation.

The forbidden knowledge, then, is sexual knowledge and its attendant guilt. Its possession forces Brown to recognize that all the antecedent generations of his name have also sinned as he has sinned. If the procreative act is sinful, then all mankind is indeed knit together in the Devil's skein: 'Evil is the nature of mankind. Evil must be your only happiness.'

The association of witchcraft itself with sexuality, debauchery, and carnal abandon is an aspect of popular tradition of which Hawthorne shows his empathetic understanding. The evidence of modern anthropological scholarship strongly suggests that witchcraft perpetuated the same fertility cult religion which survived also in the folk rituals observing the seasonal festivals. 'The only /163/ essential difference between these two kinds of rites is that, while the popular fertility rites were carried out publicly with the whole village participating, the witches' sabbaths were carried out in secret, at night, and were participated in only by witches and wizards who were initiated into

the secret art.'[16] In the *Malleus Maleficarum* witches are said to copu-
late with devils, to impair the power of generation, and to deprive
man of his virile member. Such ecclesiastical negation of their influence on fecundity argues that the witches themselves claimed exactly
the contrary power.

Since the association of witchcraft with fertility is rooted in the
rites performed to invoke increase, the connection is maintained most
strongly where witches are thought of as members of a sect perform-
ing communal rituals. Contrarily, when popular belief regards the
witch as merely an individual malefactor, the connection with sexual
abundance withers in the popular mind. The latter is the stage
in which New England tradition for the most part conceived of the
witches. Although there is sporadic mention of witch meetings among
travellers' accounts of the seventeenth century[17] and although some
of the Salem Accusers spoke of witch meetings, the notion of the witch
most generally held was that of the malicious woman who uses the
limitless infernal powers bestowed on her by the prince of Darkness—
to /164/ prevent the farmer's butter or annoy her neighbors' cows.[18]
By the end of the eighteenth century the idea of the coven drops out of
recorded beliefs; oral traditions, as Hawthorne heard them, would
elaborate the simple motifs of transformation, malice, the magic
weapon, and the afflicted crone which he knew from a poem he praised
—'The Country Lovers' (1795) by his friend Thomas Green Fessenden:

> . . . a witch, in shape of owl,
>   Did steal her neighbor's geese, sir,
> And turkeys too, and other fowl,
>   When people did not please her.

---

[16] Runeberg, *Witches, Demons, and Fertility Magic*, p. 241. Runeberg suggests
that witchcraft in its modern form emerged when the pagan magicians and the
Catharian cultists were driven to join forces by inquisitorial persecution.

[17] For example, John Josselyn (1675) reported how Mr. Foxwell, sailing a shallop
off Cape Ann at night, heard 'loud voices from the shore, calling Foxwell, Foxwell,
come a shore . . . upon the Sands they saw a great fire, and Men and Women hand
in hand dancing about it in a ring, after an hour or two they vanished . . .' Landing
by daylight 'he found the footing of Men, Women and Children shod with shoes;
and an infinite number of brand-ends thrown up by the water but neither *Indian* nor
English could be met with on the shore, nor in the woods. . . . *There are many stranger
things in the world, than are to be seen between London and Stanes.*' Quoted in
Dorson, *Jonathan Draws the Long Bow* (Cambridge, 1946), pp. 26–7.

[18] Dorson gives some sixty instances of such witchcraft beliefs in nineteenth-
century New England, *Jonathan Draws the Long Bow*, pp. 33–47. See also Clifton
Johnson, *What They Say in New England* (Boston, 1896), pp. 235–60; John Greenleaf
Whittier, *The Supernaturalism of New England* (London, 1847), pp. 49–55, 62–3.

And how a man, one dismal night,
Shot her with silver bullet,
And then she flew straight out of sight
As fast as she could pull it.

How Widow Wunks was sick next day,
The parson went to view her,
And saw the very place, they say,
Where forsaid ball went through her![19]

Nonetheless in 'Young Goodman Brown' the projection of witch-craft as sexual knowledge is arrestingly clear. It is true that much of the traditional imagery of witchcraft is easily susceptible of carnal interpretation—the serpentine staff, flying, the leaping flames—but Hawthorne manages his descriptions so skillfully that the phallic and psychosexual associations are made /165/ intrinsic to the thematic development of his story. The Puritan focus of the tale brings out with special clarity the inherent sexual character of Young Good-man's quest. Brown's whole experience is described as the penetration of a dark and lonely way through a branched forest—to the Puritans, the Devil's domain. At journey's end is the orgiastic communion amidst the leaping flames. Along the way, when Young Goodman abandons himself to the Devil, he 'grasp[ed] his staff and . . . seemed to fly along the forest path . . . rushing onward with the instinct that guides mortal man to evil.' Where, if in neither the Salem trial records nor in contemporary traditions of witch lore, did Hawthorne find the connection between witchcraft and sexuality that becomes one of the important cruces of his story?

The answer can only be in Hawthorne's reading of European writings which presented witchcraft in a different aspect from his American sources. We know that he was intimately familiar with Goethe's *Faust*,[20] and that he had read *El colloquio de los perros* of Cervantes in the Spanish. These works include two of the most important imaginative treatments of witchcraft. In *Faust*, Part I, after witnessing the disgusting orgies of Walpurgisnacht, Faust is given

---

[19] For folk provenience of the belief that only a silver bullet can kill a witch, see Whittier, *Supernaturalism of New England*, p. 49; Johnson, *What They Say in New England*, p. 240; Dorson, pp. 40–41; for the transference of the wound from the witch's animal to her human form, see Whittier, pp. 52, 63; Johnson, pp. 238, 239, 260; Dorson, pp. 35–6. These references span the entire nineteenth century.

[20] Hawthorne mentions Goethe in 'A Virtuoso's Collection.' His dependence on Goethe for the theme of the Devil's Compact is proposed by William Bysshe Stein, *Hawthorne's Faust* (Gainesville, Fla., 1953).

the witches' potion by Mephistopheles and immediately turns into a
goatish lecher. In Cervantes he found a detailed enumeration of witch
beliefs that extended the moral and theological implications of
Goethe's treatment. The witch Canizares, mistaking one of the dogs
for the son of another witch, pours out to him a long monologue
revealing her own witchcraft. We know Hawthorne to have read this
one of *Los novelas ejemplares*, for when, in 'Young Goodman Brown,'
Goody Cloyse meets the Devil, they exchange a recipe for flying ointment: an application of 'juice of smallage, and cinquefoil, and wolf's
bane—Mingled with fine wheat and the fat of a newborn babe' gives
the witch the gift of flight. It has been observed /166/ that Hawthorne
used this identical recipe a year later (July 1836) in a magazine he
edited, and here he added a comment which shows that he knew
exactly what he was doing with his witches in 'Young Goodman
Brown':

> Cervantes, in one of his tales, seems of the opinion that the ointment
> cast them into a trance, during which they merely dreamt of holding
> intercourse with Satan. If so, witchcraft differs little from nightmare.[21]

But Cervantes provided Hawthorne with more than the recipe for
flying salve and the equating of witchcraft with nightmare, important
as these are in 'Young Goodman Brown.' The old witch in *El colloquio
de los perros* tells the dog,

> We go to meet [our lord and master] in a large field that is a long way
> from here. There we find a huge throng of people, made up of witches and
> wizards . . . we gorge ourselves with food, and other things happen which . . .
> I should not dare tell you as they are so filthy and loathesome that they
> would be an offense to your chaste ears . . . Vice becomes second nature
> and witchcraft is something that enters into our blood and bones. It is
> marked by a great ardor, and at the same time it lays such a chill upon the
> soul as to benumb its faith and cause it to forget its own well-being, so that
> it no longer remembers the terrors with which God threatens it nor the
> glories of Heaven that he holds out to it.

---

[21] 'Witch Ointment,' from *The American Magazine*, reprinted in Arlin Turner,
Hawthorne as Editor (University, La., 1941), p. 253. See Fanny N. Cherry, "The
Sources of Hawthorne's "Young Goodman Brown,"' *American Literature*, V (Jan.
1934), 342–8. Another source of the formula was Bacon, *Sylva Sylvarum* X, 975.
Hawthorne's recipe corresponds roughly to the first of three formulae in Margaret
Murray, *The Witch Cult of Western Europe* (Oxford, 1921), with the addition of
baby fat from the third. Miss Murray had these tested by A. J. Clark, an analytical
chemist, who reported that aconite (wolf's bane) and hemlock (smallage) would
in fact produce the illusion of flight (pp. 100–105, 279–80).

In short, seeing that it is a sin that is concerned with carnal pleasure, it must of necessity deaden, stupefy, and absorb the senses . . . I see and understand everything, but carnal pleasure keeps my will enchained, and I always have been and always shall be evil.[22] /167/

Hawthorne, too, would send his Goodman Brown to a nightmare-meeting of carnal pleasure and universal sexual guilt. The youth's acceptance of fleshly ardor lays a chill upon his soul, benumbs his faith, and alienates him from the glories of Heaven. When the Devil welcomes Goodman and his bride to the communion of the damned, he endows them with the power to know the secret sins of 'all whom ye have reverenced from youth'; and these are sins of sexual passion —adultery, murder of mates, of babes born out of wedlock. To know such sins as these, the Devil tells them, is 'your nature and your destiny.'

The lore of witchcraft thus served Hawthorne well, connecting 'the communion of the race' superstitiously with the Devil's Compact, psychologically with sexual knowledge and guilt, theologically with evil and original sin, and culturally with acceptance of the past. Young Goodman's journey resembles Robin's search for his kinsman, but the fertility rites he celebrates are a bitter parody not only of the Christian sacraments but of the pagan paradise of 'The Maypole of Merry Mount.' His Fall from innocence is unredeemed, as we have seen, by his incapacity to return Faith's love. Like Aylmer in 'The Birthmark,' he had to have perfection—or nothing. In his sense of his own sin, then, Young Goodman is self-deceived. For it is not his implication in sexual sin which damns him, but his Puritan misanthropy, his unforgiving lovelessness, his lack of faith in Faith. She, as both his mortal wife and his *ange blanche*, had, like him, appeared before the Font of Evil. She is in fact the Devil's only antagonist in this tale, for are not all the Puritans—preachers, teachers, catechists and all—roaring about in the orgiastic coven? They have all taken the Black Man's black bread; Faith alone has such faith in man that she can transcend the revelation that he is fallen. But Young Goodman Brown, like his own fathers, like Goody Cloyse and all of Salem, like Hawthorne's distinguished ancestors too, really believed in witches, rather than in men. And so he joylessly became one.

---

[22] Cervantes, *Three Exemplary Novels*, transl. by Samuel Putnam (New York, 1950), pp. 186, 189.

David Levin

Shadows of Doubt: Specter
Evidence in Hawthorne's
"Young Goodman Brown"*

Indeed, all *Jury-men* should be, *Boni Homines*, that is to Say,
Good Men. Our Old Compellation of a Neighbour, by the
Title, of, *Goodman*, was of this Original; As much as to say,
One Qualified to *Serve on a Jury*.

—Cotton Mather

In "Young Goodman Brown," a young Puritan's faith is permanently
damaged when he attends a witches' sabbath in the woods and finds
strong evidence that the best people in his community are devil-
worshippers. Here Hawthorne confronts his protagonist with specters
that are almost literally shadows of doubt. The significance of these
shadows will become clearer if we project them in the light of two
statements written in the autumn of 1692, after twenty Massachusetts
men and women accused of witchcraft had been executed. The first
is by Increase Mather, the second by Thomas Brattle.

. . . the Father of Lies [Mather declared] is never to be believed: He will
utter twenty great truths to make way for one lie: He will accuse twenty
Witches, if he can thereby bring one honest Person into trouble: He mixeth
Truths with Lies, that so those truths giving credit unto lies, Men may
believe both, and so be deceived.[1]

---

* A revised version of David Levin, "Shadows of Doubt: Specter Evidence in
Hawthorne's 'Young Goodman Brown'," *American Literature*, XXXIV (November,
1962), 344–352. Reprinted by permission of the journal and the author.

[1] Increase Mather, *Cases of Conscience Concerning Evil Spirits Personating
Men* (Boston, 1693), reprinted in David Levin, ed., *What Happened in Salem?*
(New York, 1960), p. 122.

Brattle was astonished by the ease with which witnesses avoided a crucial distinction:

> And here I think it observable [he wrote], that often, when the afflicted [witnesses] do mean and intend only the appearance and shape of such an one (say G[oodman]. Proctor) yet they positively swear that G. Proctor did afflict them; and they have been allowed so to do; as tho' there was no real difference between G. Proctor and the shape of G. Proctor.[2]

Hawthorne's Goodman Brown commits the very mistakes that Brattle and Mather belatedly deplored in 1692. He lets the Devil's true statements about the mistreatment of Indians and Quakers prepare him to accept counterfeit evidence, and he fails to insist on the difference between a person and the person's "shape," or specter. Most modern critics who have discussed the story have repeated both these errors, even though Hawthorne clearly identifies the chief witness as the Devil and the setting as the Salem Village of witchcraft days. In the last decade, /345/ several articles have rightly contended that Hawthorne meant to reveal the faultiness of Goodman Brown's judgment;[3] but the first and most cogent of these did not prevent so distinguished a critic as Harry Levin from alluding to "the pharisaical elders" whom Goodman Brown sees "doing the devil's work while professing righteousness."[4] And the cogent article itself insists that "it is not necessary to choose between interpreting the story literally and taking it as a dream"; that Brown neither goes into a forest nor dreams that he goes into a forest. What Brown does, says D. M. McKeithan, is "to indulge in sin (represented by the journey . . .)"[5]

I believe that one must first of all interpret the story literally. The forest cannot effectively represent sin, or the unconscious mind of Goodman Brown, or the heart of the dark moral wilderness, until one has understood the literal statements about the forest in regard to the literal actions that occur therein. Instead of agreeing with one recent critic that "the only solution to the problem" of what happens

---

[2] Letter of Thomas Brattle, dated October 8, 1692, and reprinted in *ibid.*, p. 130. The letter was probably circulated in manuscript; the name of the addressee is unknown.

[3] D. M. McKeithan, "Hawthorne's 'Young Goodman Brown': An Interpretation," *Modern Language Notes*, LXVII (February 1952), 93–96; Thomas F. Walsh, Jr., "The Bedeviling of Young Goodman Brown," *Modern Language Quarterly*, XIX (December 1958), 331–36; Paul W. Miller, "Hawthorne's 'Young Goodman Brown': Cynicism or Meliorism?," *Nineteenth-Century Fiction*, XIV (December 1959), 255–64.

[4] Harry T. Levin, *The Power of Blackness: Hawthorne, Poe, Melville* (New York, 1958), p. 54.

[5] McKeithan, p. 96.

in the forest "lies in the tale's complex symbolic pattern,"[6] let us try
to accept Hawthorne's explicit statements of fact. Instead of inventing
a new definition of the word "witch," as another critic has done,[7] let
us try to read the story in the terms that were available to Hawthorne.
A proper reading of the literal action removes some of the ambiguity
that it is now so fashionable to admire, but it does not clash with a
psychoanalytic reading,[8] and it should leave open a sufficient variety
of interpretations to satisfy those who insist on multiple meanings. It
will also clarify the fine skill with which Hawthorne made the
historical materials dramatize his psychological insights and his
allegory.

Hawthorne knew the facts and lore of the Salem witchcraft "delusion," and he used them liberally in this story as well as others. He
set the story specifically, as the opening line reveals, not in his native
Salem, but in Salem Village, the cantankerous hamlet (now Danvers)
in which the afflictions, the accusations, and the diabolical /346/ sabbaths centered in 1692. Among the supposedly guilty are the minister
of Salem Village and two women who were actually hanged in that
terrible summer. Hawthorne not only cites testimony that Martha
Carrier "had received the Devil's promise to be queen of hell"; he
also quotes Cotton Mather's description of her as a "rampant hag,"
and he even violates Goodman Brown's point of view in order to
introduce another actual rumor of 1692: "Some affirm that the lady
of the governor was there [at the witches' sabbath]." He takes great
care to emphasize the seeming presence at the witches' sabbath of
the best and the worst of the community—noting with superbly appropriate vagueness, just before the climax, that the "figure"[9] who prepares to baptize Goodman Brown "bore no slight similitude, both in

---

[6] Walsh, p. 336.

[7] Miller, p. 259 n. 10.

[8] Two admirable interpretations that emphasize Freudian perceptions and reve-
lations in the story deserve especial recommendation here. See Daniel Hoffman,
Form and Fable in American Fiction (New York, 1961); and Frederick C. Crews,
The Sins of the Fathers: Hawthorne's Psychological Themes (New York, 1966).

[9] The first published versions of the story used the word "apparition" here. See
The New-England Magazine, VIII (April 1835), 257; and *Mosses from an Old Manse*
(New York, 1846), p. 80. The word was changed to "figure" in Hawthorne's last
revision of *Mosses from an Old Manse* (Boston, 1857).

The text of this story has often been erroneously printed. One important change
seems to have been made by George P. Lathrop in the edition he published nineteen
years after Hawthorne's death. Every earlier version that I have seen, including
Hawthorne's last revision, says that "the chorus of the desert" at the spectral meeting
in the forest seemed to include "the roaring wind, the rushing streams, the howling
beasts, and every other voice of the unconverted wilderness. . . ." Lathrop and
almost every editor after him changed the word "unconverted" to "unconcerted." I
have been following Hawthorne's last revision.

garb and manner, to some grave divine of the New England churches."

There can be no doubt that Hawthorne understood clearly the importance of what was called "specter evidence" in the actual trials. This was evidence that a specter, or shape, or apparition, representing Goodman Proctor, for instance, had tormented the witness or had been present at a witches' meeting. Hawthorne knew that there had been a debate about whether the Devil could, as the saying went, "take the shape of an angel of light," and in both "Alice Doane's Appeal" and "Main Street" he explicitly mentioned the Devil's ability to impersonate innocent people.[10] He was well aware that Cotton Mather had warned against putting too much confidence in this sort of evidence; he also knew that after the Mathers and Thomas Brattle had opposed even the admission of /347/ specter evidence (the Mathers on the ground that it was the Devil's testimony), the court had convicted almost no one and not a single convict had been executed. It seems certain, moreover, that Hawthorne had read Cotton Mather's biography of Sir William Phips, in which Mather the historian not only echoes his father's language about truths and lies, but clearly suggests that one of the Devil's purposes had been the traducing of Faith.

> On the other Part [Mather wrote in 1697], there were many persons of great Judgment, Piety and Experience, who from the beginning were very much dissatisfied at these Proceedings; they feared lest the *Devil* would get so far into the *Faith* of the People, that for the sake of many *Truths*, which they might find him telling of them, they would come at length to believe all his *Lies*, whereupon what a Desolation of *Names*, yea, and of *Lives* also, would ensue, a Man might without much *Witchcraft* be able to Prognosticate; and they feared, lest in such an extraordinary Descent of *Wicked Spirits* from their *High Places* upon us, there might such *Principles* be taken up, as, when put into *Practice*, would unavoidably cause the *Righteous to* /348/ *perish with the Wicked*, and procure the Blood-shed of Persons like the *Gibeonites*, whom some learned Men suppose to be under a false Pretence of *Witchcraft*, by *Saul* exterminated.[11]

If we set aside the alternative possibilities for a while and examine the story from the seventeenth-century point of view—the perception

---

[10] Hawthorne even joked casually about this kind of imposture. Of his participation in the experiment at Brook Farm he wrote: "The real me was never an associate of the community; there has been a spectral Appearance there, sounding the horn at daybreak, and milking the cows . . . and doing me the honor to assume my name." Quoted in Randall Stewart, *Nathaniel Hawthorne, A Biography* (New Haven, 1949), p. 60.

[11] Cotton Mather, *Magnalia Christi Americana: or, The Ecclesiastical History of New-England* (London, 1702), Book II, p. 62.

of Goodman Brown through which Hawthorne asks us to see almost all the action—we will find a perfectly clear, consistent portrayal of a spectral adventure into evil. Goodman Brown goes into the forest on an "evil errand," promising himself that after this night he will "cling" to the skirts of his wife, Faith, "and follow her to heaven." Once in the wilderness, he himself conjures the Devil by exclaiming, "What if the Devil himself should be at my very elbow!" Immediately, he beholds "the figure of a man," and this figure quite unambiguously tells him that it has made the trip from Boston to the woods near Salem Village—at least fifteen or twenty miles—in fifteen minutes. Brown refuses the Devil's staff and announces that he is going back to Faith, but the Devil, "smiling apart," suggests that they "walk on, nevertheless, reasoning as we go." /348/

The reasoning proceeds from this point, as the Devil tries to convince Brown that the best men are wholly evil. Most of the argument that follows corresponds to the traditional sophistry of the Devil—the kind of accusation with which Satan nearly discourages Edward Taylor's saint from joining the church in *God's Determinations Touching His Elect*. It is here that the Devil mentions true sins (the mistreatment of Indians and Quakers) in order to induce despair: men are so wicked that nothing can save them.[12] Against this first argument Goodman Brown resists longer than some modern critics have resisted, for he sees that the alleged hypocrisy of elders and statesmen is "no rule for a simple husbandman like me." Foolishly, however, he believes the Devil's testimony—as his neighbors did in 1692—and he frankly tells him that "my wife, Faith," is the foundation of his reluctance to become a witch.

This admission invites the Devil to proceed, and it determines the organization of the rest of his argument. With typical subtlety he pretends to give up at once, because

> ". . . I would not for *twenty* old women like the one hobbling before us that Faith should come to any harm."
> As he spoke he *pointed his staff at a female figure* on the path, *in whom Goodman Brown recognized* a very pious and exemplary old dame. . . .[13]

---

12 Here again we should notice that Cotton Mather had used language very close to Hawthorne's. In a sermon called "The Door of Hope," Mather cautioned against "A sinful and woful Despair." Some men, he said, "rashly conclude" that "because they see no *help* to their Souls in themselves. . . . there is no *hope* for their Souls any where else." And among several "*Reasons* of Despair" to which he offered answers at the end of the sermon, the fifth reads: "I doubt I have committed the *unpardonable Sin*; and then, all my hope is lost forevermore." *Batteries Upon the Kingdom of the Devil* (London, 1695), pp. 100 ff.

13 The italics are mine.

The Devil has of course conjured this "figure," which moves "with' singular speed for so aged a woman," and he appears to it in "the very image"—soon afterward, "the shape"—"of old Goodman Brown, the grandfather of the silly fellow that now is." When the woman's figure has served his purpose, the Devil throws his staff "down at her feet," and she immediately disappears. Brown accepts this evidence without question, for by this time the Devil is "Discoursing so aptly that his arguments [seem] rather to spring up in the bosom of his auditor than to be suggested by himself." /349/

But Goodman Brown holds back once again, and the Devil, assuring him that "You will think better of this by and by," vanishes. Just as Brown is "applauding himself greatly," he is assaulted by another kind of airy evidence: disembodied voices. The "mingled sounds" *appear* to pass "within a few yards," and although the "figures" of the minister and deacon "brushed the small boughs by the wayside, it could not be seen that they intercepted, even for a moment, the faint gleam from the strip of bright sky athwart which they must have passed." Brown cannot see "so much as a shadow," but "he could have sworn"—as witnesses in 1692 did indeed swear—that he recognized the deacon and the minister in "the voices, talking so strangly in the empty air."

Now, as Brown doubts that "there really [is] a heaven above him" the Devil has only to produce evidence that Faith, too, is guilty. Hearing the voice of Faith from a "black mass" of cloud that "hurried" across the sky although no wind is stirring, Brown calls out to her in agony, and the "echoes of the forest"—always under the Devil's control—mock him. Then the Devil sends his final argument, Faith's pink ribbon, as her voice fades into the far-off laughter of fiends. At the end of the story we learn that this evidence, too, was spectral, for Faith wears her ribbons when her husband returns home in the morning; but now, in the forest, Brown is convinced that his "Faith is gone," that the world belongs to the Devil. He takes up the Devil's staff and "seems to fly along the forest path rather than to walk or run, . . . rushing onward with the instinct that guides mortal man to evil."

With beautiful care Hawthorne makes his descriptive language reinforce these meanings through the rest of the horrible experience. "Flying" among the black pines, Brown finally sees the "lurid blaze" of the witch meeting and pauses "in a lull of the tempest that had driven him onward." The verse that he hears is sung "by a chorus, not of human voices, but of all the sounds of the benighted wilderness, pealing in awful harmony together," and his own cry sounds in "unison with the cry of the desert." At the sabbath itself he sees, "quivering

between gloom and splendor," *faces* belonging to the best people of
the colony. A congregation shines forth, then disappears in shadow,
and again grows, "as it were, *out of the darkness, peopling the heart
of the solitary woods /350/ at once.*"[14] Brown believes that he recognizes "a score" of Salem Village church members before he is "well
nigh ready to swear" that he sees "the figure" of the minister, "the
shape of his own dead father," "the dim features" of his mother, and
"the slender form" of his wife. When he stands with the form of
Faith, they are "the only [human] pair, *as it seemed,*" who hesitate
"on the verge of wickedness in this dark world." It is "the shape of
evil" that prepares to baptize them, and the figure that stands beside
Brown is that of his "pale" wife.[15] When he implores her to "look up
to heaven and resist the wicked one," the whole communion disappears, and he cannot learn "whether Faith obeyed."

The clarification that this reading achieves for the story should
remove some of the objections that have been raised against it even
by its admirers. When we recognize that the Devil is consistently
presenting evidence to a prospective convert who is only too willing
to be convinced, we do not need to complain with F. O. Matthiessen
against Hawthorne's "literal insistence on that damaging pink ribbon";
nor need we try, with R. H. Fogle, to explain the ribbon away.[16] One
might insist that even here Hawthorne restricts his language admirably to Brown's perception, for he says that *something* fluttered lightly
down through the air and that Brown, on seizing it, *beheld* a pink
ribbon. Brown's sensory perception of the ribbon is no more literal
or material than his perception of the Devil, his clutching of the staff,
or his hearing of the Devil's statement about the fifteen-minute trip
from Boston to the woods near Salem Village. But such an argument
is really unnecessary. The seventeenth-century Devil could produce
specters, with or without the consent of the people they resembled,

---

14 The italics are mine.

15 Here it might be argued that Hawthorne says Faith was actually present, for
he writes that "the wretched man beheld his Faith, and the wife her husband," and
just before Brown cries out Hawthorne writes, "The husband cast one look at his
pale wife, and Faith at him. What polluted wretches would the next glance show
them to each other ... !" It is more consistent with Hawthorne's practice throughout
the story to read these references to Faith's observation as Goodman Brown's view
of her reaction. All the action has been seen from Brown's point of view, and
Hawthorne has never entered Faith's mind. Surely the exclamation is in Brown's
mind only, for it prompts him to act, and his plea that she look up to heaven
leaves him standing alone. Her specter vanishes with the others.

16 F. O. Matthiessen, *American Renaissance: Art and Expression in the Age of
Emerson and Whitman* (New York, 1941), p. 284; and R. H. Fogle, "Ambiguity and
Clarity in Hawthorne's 'Young Goodman Brown,'" *New England Quarterly*, XVIII
(December 1945), 451.

and he could make cats, birds, and other /351/ familiars seem to materialize before terrified witnesses.[17] For such a being, and with a witness overcome by "grief, rage, and terror," a ribbon posed no great difficulty.

Hawthorne's technique thus gives a clear view of his meaning. When we stop looking for what we may wish to believe about Puritans who whipped Quakers and burned Indian villages, we can recognize just what it is that Goodman Brown sees. Hawthorne does not tell us that none of the people whom Brown comes to suspect is indeed a diabolical agent, but he makes it clear that Brown has no justification for condemning any of them—and no justification for suspecting them, except for the shadowy vista that this experience has opened into his own capacity for evil. Asking whether these people were "really" evil is impertinent, for it leads us beyond the limits of fiction. The story is not about the evil of other people but about Brown's doubt, his discovery of the *possibility* of universal evil. Before reading the Devil's statements here in the light of ideas that Hawthorne suggested elsewhere, we must read them in their immediate context. At the witch meeting, the "shape of evil" invites Goodman Brown to "the communion" of the human "race," the communion of evil, but we have no more right than Brown himself to believe the Father of Lies. Indeed, Hawthorne's brilliant success depends on this distinction. He gives us an irresistible picture of a "crisis of faith and an agony of doubt";[18] we must notice that Brown finally does exorcise the spectral meeting, but that he can never forget his view of the specters or the abandon in which he himself became "the chief horror" in the dark wilderness. He lives the rest of his life in doubt, and the literal doubt depends on his uncertainty about whether his wife and others are really evil. /352/ If he were certain that they had been present in the forest, he would not treat them even so civilly as he does during the rest of his life. It is the spectral quality of the experience—both its uncertainty and its unforgettable impression—that makes the doubt permanent.

The question, then, is not whether Faith and the others were really there, in their own persons, at the witch meeting. When Hawthorne asks whether Goodman Brown had "fallen asleep in the forest and

---

[17] Cf. Cotton Mather, *Magnalia Christi Americana*, Book II, p. 60; and Cotton Mather, in *Memorable Providences, Relating to Witchcraft and Possessions* (Boston, 1689), reprinted in Levin, ed., *What Happened in Salem?*, pp. 96–97: "Other *strange* things are done by them in a way of *Crafty Illusion*. They do craftily make of the *Air*, the *Figures* and *Colors* of things that never can be truly created by them. All men might *see*, but, I believe, no man could *feel* some of the Things which the *Magicians of Egypt*, exhibited of old."

[18] The phrase is Harry Levin's. See *The Power of Blackness*, p. 54.

only dreamed a wild dream of a witch meeting," and replies, "Be it so if you will," he offers an alternative possibility to the nineteenth-century reader who refuses to take devils seriously even in historical fiction. The choice lies between dream and a reality that is unquestionably spectral. Neither Hawthorne nor (at the end) even Goodman Brown suggests that the church members were present in their own persons. Brown's question is whether the Devil, when he took on their shapes, had their permission to represent them. That is why Hawthorne can say, "Be it so if you will." For the meaning remains the same even if Brown, having for some odd reason fallen asleep in the woods before the story begins, has dreamed the entire experience.

By recognizing that Hawthorne built "Young Goodman Brown" firmly on his historical knowledge, we perceive that the tale has a social as well as an allegorical and a psychological dimension. In the judgment of this goodman whose title certified that he was "Qualified to Serve on a Jury," Hawthorne condemns that graceless perversion of true Calvinism which, in universal suspicion, actually led a community to the unjust destruction of twenty men and women. But we ought also to be reminded of some general truths about proper ways to read this wonderfully shrewd writer. We must not underestimate his use of historical materials, even when he is writing allegory; nor should we let an interest in patterns of image and symbol or an awareness that he repeatedly uses the same types of character obscure the clear literal significance of individual stories. Working over an amazingly—some critics have said, an obsessively—narrow range of types and subjects, he nevertheless achieves a remarkable variety of insights into human experience.

E. Arthur Robinson

The Vision of Goodman Brown: A Source and Interpretation*

Students of "Young Goodman Brown" agree in general that its main materials are drawn from Cotton Mather's *The Wonders of the Invisible World*, published the year following the Salem witchcraft trials, in which Mather describes the devil's appearing as a "small black man" to lure people to forest rendezvous where church sacraments were imitated and mocked.[1] Hawthorne, indeed, virtually quotes Mather in placing Martha Carrier among the witches as a "rampant hag" and promised "queen of hell."[2] I have found, however, no comment upon Hawthorne's possible use of a passage from Mather's *Magnalia Christi Americana* (1702) as a secondary source. The Puritan historian recalls Governor Winthrop's 1632 visit with the leaders of the Pilgrim settlement. "But there were at this time in *Plymouth*," relates Mather, "two ministers, leavened so far with the humours of the *rigid separation*, that they insisted vehemently upon the unlawfulness of calling any *unregenerated man* by the name of *good-man such an one*, until by their indiscreet urging of this whimsey, the place began to be disquieted." When asked to intercede, Winthrop applied the distinction between civil and church discipline which stood him in good stead at home. Mather records the defeat of the extreme separatists:

The wiser people being troubled at these trifles, they took the opportunity of governour *Winthrop's* being *there*, to have the thing publicly propounded

* E. Arthur Robinson, "The Vision of Goodman Brown: A Source and Interpretation," *American Literature*, XXXV (May, 1963), 218–225. Reprinted by permission of the journal and the author.
[1] Cited in *Nathaniel Hawthorne, Representative Selections*, ed. Austin Warren (New York, 1934), pp. 361–362.
[2] Cf. Cotton Mather, *The Wonders of the Invisible World* (London, 1862), p. 159.

in the congregation; who in answer thereunto, distinguished between a
theological and a *moral goodness;* adding, that when *Juries* were first used
in *England*, it was usual for the *crier*, after the names of persons fit for that
service were called over, to bid them all, *Attend, good men, and true;* whence
it grew to be a *civil custom* in the *English* /219/ *nation*, for neighbours living
by one another, to call one another *good man such an one:* and it was pity
now to make a stir about a *civil custom*, so innocently introduced. And that
speech of Mr. *Winthrop's* put a lasting stop to the little, idle, whimsical
conceits, then beginning to grow obstreperous.[3]

Obviously, this concern with calling an unregenerate man "goodman"
resembles the ironic overtones in Hawthorne's story of Goodman
Brown.

Without corroborating Winthrop's etymology, the *Oxford English
Dictionary* offers interesting evidence upon connotations of "goodman"
in colonial days. Several citations agree with Winthrop in stressing
the colloquial status of the term, one entry from 1577 explaining that
"goodman" is added to the surnames of yeomen "amongst their
neighbours, . . . not in matters of importance or in lawe." An archaic
meaning may be particularly applicable to Hawthorne's tale. After
defining "goodman" as "the master or male head of a household," the
O.E.D. cites its former application to "a husband" himself or "a
householder in relation to his wife"—quoting a writer of 1593 who asks
the pointed question: "Why is the husband called his wives good-
manne?" Another makes the sly comment: "Little our goodmen knowes
what their wiues thinkes." Hawthorne, of course, would not need
to know these passages to be familiar with traditional connotations
of the word.

Taken together, Mather's account and the *O.E.D.* throw a curious
light upon Hawthorne's tale. Dramatizing as it does a Calvinistic
concept of universal evil in mankind, "Young Goodman Brown" is
clearly ironic in its continued stress upon the protagonist's title.
Similarly the name Faith, given to Brown's wife, is played upon in
such statements as "Faith kept me back a while" and "My Faith is
gone." Nor is it coincidence that Brown and his wife are subjects
of a common irony. Brown once calls himself by title with apparently
self-conscious sarcasm: "Come witch, come wizard, come Indian

---

[3] Cotton Mather, *Magnalia Christi Americana: or, the Ecclesiastical History of
New-England*, 2nd ed. (Hartford, Conn., 1820), I, 117. Under the name of his
Aunt Mary Manning, Hawthorne twice borrowed the *Magnalia* from the Salem
Athenaeum Library, in 1827 and 1828 (Marion L. Kesselring, *Hawthorne's Reading:
1828-1850*, New York, 1949, p. 57).

powwow, come devil himself, and here comes Goodman Brown."[4] Since this heightened realization of evil potential follows /220/ immediately upon the "goodman's" discovery that his wife has an appointment with the devil, their matrimonial situation is pertinent. In the archaic sense of "goodman" the title could mean "Young Husband Brown."[5]

The internal evidence that the "Goodman" of the title refers in part to Brown's marital status may be subsumed briefly under three headings: 1) veiled and overt sexual references in the story, 2) the role of Brown's father and mother, 3) the significance of young Brown's dream or vision.

I

As proselytes for baptism by the devil, the most evident quality which Brown and Faith have in common is the fact that they are "but three months married." Pertinent also is the nature of the temptations presented to the devil's regular communicants. Old Goody Cloyse decided to "foot it" to the meeting, "for they tell me there is a nice young man to be taken into communion tonight." Men are attracted by the converse situation, as Goodman Brown learns upon hearing Deacon Gookin's remark to the minister, "Moreover, there is a goodly young woman to be taken into communion," and the clergyman's reply, "Mighty well, Deacon Gookin!" The dominant motivation for the secret sins revealed in Satan's speech is also sexual:

"This night it shall be granted you to know their secret deeds: how hoary-bearded elders of the church have whispered wanton words to the young maids of their households; how many a woman, eager for widow's weeds, has given her husband a drink at bedtime and let him sleep his last sleep in her bosom; how beardless youths have made haste to inherit their fathers' wealth; and how fair damsels—blush not, sweet ones—have dug little graves in the garden, and bidden me, the sole guest, to an infant's funeral. By the sympathy of your human hearts for sin ye shall scent out all the places—whether in church, bed-chamber, street, field, or forest—where crime has been committed. . . ."

---

[4] All quotations from "Young Goodman Brown" are from *The Works of Nathaniel Hawthorne* (Boston, 1882), II, 89–106.

[5] In recent years several critics have observed that sex figures largely in the background of "Young Goodman Brown," without, however, presenting full analysis of motifs in the story which support this view and give it significance. See Roy R. Male, *Hawthorne's Tragic Vision* (Austin, Texas, 1957), pp. 76–80; and Daniel G. Hoffman, *Form and Fable in American Fiction* (New York, 1961), pp. 149–168.

The devil's exhortation does not imply that sex is the sole origin /221/ of sin,[6] which indeed "inexhaustibly supplies more evil impulses than human power . . . can make manifest in deeds." Satan apparently recognizes that the young couple's situation renders them particularly susceptible to allurements of the flesh. Self-knowledge, however, is not the key, since Brown is already aware of his own sinfulness. Rather, as Satan declares, the converts hitherto have retained a childlike reverence for their elders: "Ye deemed them holier than yourselves, and shrank from your own sin, contrasting it with their lives of righteousness. . . . Yet here are they all in my worshipping assembly." The verbal irony which had disturbed the congregation in Plymouth takes on a more universal cast in the mind of Brown, as one after another his more respected townspeople reveal their predilection for sin.

Clearly the climax of Brown's religious ordeal is a vision of sin in his wife Faith. Reflection suggests that mistrust of Faith is also the origin of that ordeal. For instance, why should this vision overwhelm Brown at just this time, when in his own words he is "but three months married"? The story has an "everyman" atmosphere that makes Brown, with his common name, symbolic of mankind. As a boy he had found tendencies in himself not sanctioned by the society within which he was growing up and he had blamed these upon personal weakness. His marital shock also presupposes early idealization of woman: his Faith is a "blessed angel on earth; and after this one night I'll cling to her skirts and follow her to heaven." Brown's ordeal is to learn that his sinful longings belong to the pattern of his race, and that none are exempt, not even women.

II

The role of Brown's parents subtly reinforces the significance of sex in the story. Neither parent is living, and Brown has succeeded to his father's position. Both have been householders, but as husband, Brown insists, his father "never went into the woods on such an errand, nor his father before him." The emphasis upon succession of generations is ironic because Brown's inherited passions are the cause of these generations. Yet there is desperation in /222/ his

---

6 Yet in Hawthorne's writing the origin of sin is linked closely with sex, as R. H. Fogle has noted in *Hawthorne's Fiction: The Light and the Dark* (Norman, Okla., 1952), p. 105: "the sin of *The Scarlet Letter* is a symbol of the original sin, by which no man is untouched. All mortals commit the sin in one form or another. . . ." See also Male, pp. 8-9.

insistence, for Satan has appeared in a guise resembling Brown so closely that the two "might have been taken for father and son." (In more modern terminology, Brown's quest for universal sin could be regarded as both a search for a father and initiation into Puritan manhood.) Goody Cloyse recognizes Satan simultaneously as the devil and the "image of my old gossip, Goodman Brown, the grandfather of the silly fellow that now is."[7] At the witches' meeting Brown's father, far from censuring him, urges him forward to baptism in evil, "while a woman, with dim features of despair, threw out her hand to warn him back. Was it his mother?" Well may his mother warn him, for here she is, in the devil's company, unable to give her son power "to resist, even in thought," the attraction of evil. Instead she becomes another symbol of that attraction.

III

All these details in "Young Goodman Brown" take on a further dimension upon introduction of the dream motif near the end of the story. As usual Hawthorne leaves the degree of actuality unresolved. Has Brown, he asks, "only dreamed a wild dream of a witch-meeting? Be it so if you will. . . ." If we accept this reading of the story, much that was before objective becomes rather a manifestation of Brown's inner nature: Satan's punctilio in greeting him as "Goodman Brown," his amusement at the youth's trust in his elders, etc. Father and mother now appear only in their son's imagination. Young Brown must be conceived as simultaneously proclaiming his father's righteousness and picturing the devil's approaching him in his parent's lineaments; as revering Goody Cloyse at the same time that he imagines her scorn of him as the "silly fellow that now is" and her recognition of the devil's presence in his more experienced male ancestors. The young man's intuition is shocked by contradictory contrasts between himself and his forebears. The implication is that Brown's marital experience has awakened him to recognition of the universal role of sex, with special relevance to sin.

In short, Goodman Brown has realized that his father was a man like himself and his mother a woman like Faith. His passions /223/ and those of his wife are the product of like passions. Since Brown fights to repress this knowledge, the discovery comes subconsciously at first and then with awful awareness, emerging finally in the form of a vision. His imagination embodies carnal appetites in all the

---

[7] Hoffman goes so far as to state: "The inference is unmistakable that Old Brown had had carnal knowledge of Goody Cloyse" (p. 163).

people he has venerated from childhood—his father, the woman who taught him his catechism, the deacon, the minister, and finally and logically his mother. Against each he tests his new intuition, and in each instance he is startled anew to find that it fits. Subconsciously, the devil's speech is his own also, for the sins recounted are more in keeping with Brown's naïveté than with his image of Satanic sophistication.

The dream-hypothesis forces likewise a reassessment of Faith. The dream ends convincingly but there is no satisfactory point for it to begin, Hawthorne's technique gravitating between the traditional dream-vision and modern expressionism. Brown's opening conversation with his bride may thus be as subjective as the rest of his vision. She begins by warning her husband to sleep in his own bed this night and hints that she, too, has dreams—and yet this may be only Brown's fancy growing out of incipient doubts. The substance of his suspicion could be infidelity, since the deacon in Brown's "dream" evinces interest in Faith's initiation into evil, but the presentation of husband and wife before Satan insinuates a more pervasive doubt. Mutual discovery of guilt tends to presume a common guilt. Brown's suspicion focuses not on Faith's unfaithfulness but on the quality of their shared passion. Faced, in his imagination, with mutual recognition of their common pollution, the young husband appeals to heaven for assistance and calls on his wife to do likewise, but the vision ends before she can respond. The disillusionment is that of a bridegroom. Thereafter Brown cannot accept Faith's kisses without questioning the impulses of her nature, and he thinks of no woman as an angel on earth that will lead him to heaven.

From this point of view Faith's pink ribbons symbolize passion,[8] and also, contrary to some critical comment, the conclusion be- /224/ comes characterized by inevitability and ironic power.[9] In the first place, doubts such as Brown's are by nature unresolved; perhaps the conviction that his wife *can* be tempted by sensuality is enough to disrupt his life. In the second place, Brown's vision ends in com-

---

8 Faith's ribbons have called forth a variety of interpretations. Thomas E. Connolly, reading the story as religious allegory, in "Hawthorne's 'Young Goodman Brown': An Attack on Puritanic Calvanism," *American Literature*, XXVIII, 374 (Nov., 1956), sees the ribbons as symbolic of Brown's "initial illusion . . . that his faith will lead him to heaven." At an opposite extreme Male regards the ribbons as a specifically feminine symbol: "the pink ribbons blend with the serpentine staff in what becomes a fiery orgy of lust" (p. 77).

9 The usual charge is that Hawthorne's conclusion is "anticlimactic." See Caroline Gordon and Allen Tate, *The House of Fiction* (New York, 1950), p. 38; and Wallace and Mary Stegner, eds., *Great American Short Stories* (New York, 1957), p. 14.

promise. Through a long lifetime he shrinks at midnight "from the bosom of Faith" and scowls upon her at family prayers, but this aversion does not prevent their producing numerous offspring. Thus Brown, a middle-class Puritan yeoman, becomes no ascetic or hermit.

The significance of Brown's vision is shown in sharper relief when we see that in essence the symbolism of Faith's pink ribbons is repeated in "The Birthmark" and "Rappaccini's Daughter," first in Georgiana's flaw of complexion and then in Beatrice's poisonous plant, both of these being crimson or purple and both representative of woman's physical nature.[10] Like Brown, Aylmer and Giovanni allow feminine imperfection to become an obsession, the one shortly after and the other shortly before marriage. Georgiana even regards her defect as one of her natural charms before her union with the idealistic Aylmer, and allegorically Hawthorne makes the servant Aminadab, who mutters, "If she were my wife, I'd never part with that birthmark," represent "man's physical nature" and Aylmer a "type of the spiritual element" in man.[11] Similarly Beatrice, ironically named for Dante's spiritual guide, is a paradoxical combination of a poisonous body and a soul which as "God's creature" craves "loves as its daily food."[12] Her spirit could lead Giovanni upward, as Brown thought to follow Faith, but her physical beauty, which resembles the gorgeous but fatal plant, is deadly unless he can assimilate sufficient poison to join her upon equal terms. The moral is old and complex: woman, albeit of finer spiritual quality than man, possesses physical attributes that lure man to evil, al- /225/ though the evil may not be within her power or will. Beatrice's unanswered question is whose fault it is. "Oh, was there not," she asks Giovanni (speaking for her sisterhood in many Hawthorne tales), "from the first, more poison in thy nature than in mine?"

The two later stories resolve a portion of Brown's dilemma by making it clear that since woman's imperfection is physical, her spirit may triumph over "the gross fatality of earth"[13] in heaven. Hawthorne interrupts the story of "Rappaccini's Daughter" to point out that

---

10 First published in 1835, "Young Goodman Brown" was passed over in *Twice-Told Tales* (1837, 1842) and received book publication with "The Birthmark" (1843) and "Rappaccini's Daughter" (1844) in *Mosses from an Old Manse* (1846). As a group the three stories develop refinements of theme beyond the scope of any one of them alone. "The Birthmark" and "Rappaccini's Daughter" are more explicit in attributing man's suspicion of woman to her physical characteristics, but other themes not considered here, such as intellectualism and pride, complicate the later stories.

11 *Works*, II, 55.

12 *Ibid.*, II, 145.

13 *Ibid.*, II, 69.

nothing is left for Beatrice but to "bathe her hurts in some fount in Paradise . . . and *there* be well" and that Giovanni would have been wiser to attach his faith to her future purity and thus to accept the bittersweet of mortality.[14] Lacking such a faith, Brown can neither fully accept nor fully deny his wife. Despite his compromise, however, his choice, in a way, is wiser than Aylmer's or Giovanni's. If his life is devitalized by doubt of human nature, his skepticism is restrained by a compulsion to live. He can continue in his generation only as previous generations have done, caught between the theological and marital ironies of his title "Goodman" Brown.

---

[14] *Ibid.*, II, 139, 145.

James W. Mathews

Antinomianism in "Young Goodman Brown"*

Almost everyone commenting on Nathaniel Hawthorne's "Young Goodman Brown" has noted that its general theme is the loss of personal faith. On the specific application of certain symbols, however, there has been a good deal of disagreement. Some time ago Thomas E. Connolly re-asserted the paramount allegorical significance of the character Faith and justifiably concluded that "this story is Hawthorne's criticism of the teachings of Puritanic-Calvanism,"[1] though he limited the object of Hawthorne's criticism to predestination. Giving further scrutiny to Faith can establish a more specific probability of meaning, which converts to theological terms Hawthorne's ubiquitous thesis that the most serious personal evil is retreat from reality and responsibility.

A doctrine of one group of Calvinists during the time depicted in the story was Antinomianism,[2] which insisted that salvation was of faith, not of works. If good works existed, they came only as a secondary by-product of the mysterious divine grace; personal volition was de-emphasized, if not completely eliminated. Grace itself was contingent on the degree of the individual's faith; and a strong faith, which usually resulted in an emotional experience, was evidence enough of one's predestined salvation. According to Perry Miller, one question inherent in Antinomianism was "since the recipient of grace is assured of salvation without ever doing anything to deserve it, should he not

* James W. Mathews, "Antinomianism in 'Young Goodman Brown'," *Studies in Short Fiction*, III (Fall, 1965), 73–75. Reprinted by permission of the journal and of the author.

1 "Hawthorne's 'Young Goodman Brown': An Attack on Puritanic Calvinism," *American Literature*, XXVIII (November 1956), 375.

2 That Hawthorne was aware of the furor caused by Antinomians in Massachusetts is evident in his highly ironic sketch of Mrs. Hutchinson. See *The Works of Nathaniel Hawthorne*, George Parsons Lathrop, ed. (Boston, 1883), XII, 217–226.

113

surrender to the intoxication of certainty and give no further thought to his behavior?"[3] Extreme Antinomians among the High Calvinists believed that "if a man was elected and predestined to salvation, no power in heaven or on earth could prevent it; and hence, no matter what the moral conduct of a man might be, his salvation was sure if he was one of the elect; the wicked actions of such a man were not sinful, and he had no occasion to confess his sins or break them off by repentance."[4]

"Young Goodman Brown" depicts a man who is so confident in his recent union with faith that he walks superciliously into the devil's own revival /74/ without any fear whatsoever. Hawthorne tells us nothing of Goodman Brown's earlier life and acts. Though Brown seems to enjoy a good reputation, there is no reference to his good works. Unlike Everyman, he does not produce them as a last-minute testimony to his worthiness. Only his faith exists, deluding him into passivity. Faith's admonition to "put off your journey until sunrise and sleep in your own bed tonight"[5] suggests that the influence of Faith over Brown is essentially negative. The insubstantiality of Brown's religious faith manifests itself in the pink ribbons of his wife's cap; their texture is aery and their color the pastel of infancy.

Brown is aware that his secret nocturnal journey is for an "evil purpose." He does not enter the forest ignorantly or under duress. He is prepared to witness evil and perhaps partake. But as an Antinomian, he would believe that no evil is charged against those with faith: "I'll cling to her skirts and follow her to heaven," he cries. He is quick to exonerate himself and brand the others faithless despite his own deliberate act of keeping the evil rendezvous. He has his Faith, and the devil leads him into false confidence early when he says: "I would not for twenty old women like the one hobbling before us that Faith should come to any harm." Faith is secure at home and is Brown's supposed mystical shield against whatever may menace him. In explaining to the devil why he is late, he says that "Faith kept me back a while." Faith, thus, is temporary protection, functioning only in isolation. Her own apprehension over Brown's leaving points to her lack of remote spiritual control over her husband.

Since Brown is confident that the faith of his ancestors has protected them from the devil, he feels that he too will turn back in time or at

---

[3] *The New England Mind: The Seventeenth Century* (Cambridge, Mass., 1954), p. 369.

[4] J. Macbride Sterrett in *Encyclopaedia of Religion and Ethics*, James Hastings, ed. (New York, 1928), I, 582.

[5] All quotations from "Young Goodman Brown" are from *Works*, II, 89–106.

least avoid permanent harm. As evidence of the righteousness of his people and of his righteousness, he stresses the theoretical side of religion with the practical as secondary: "We are a people of prayer, and good works to boot, and abide no such wickedness." Then amid suggestions that his own ancestors have been prone to evil notwithstanding their faith, Brown indignantly asks whether such is "any reason why I should quit my dear Faith" and join their company. Further, he asserts, "with heaven above and Faith below, I will yet stand firm against the devil." The poignant irony in Brown's show of certainty is that he lost the protection of Faith the very moment he left the confines of their cottage. Soon he hears the "voice of a young woman, uttering lamentations, yet with an uncertain sorrow, and entreating for some favor, which, perhaps, it would grieve her to obtain; and all the unseen multitude, both saints and sinners, seemed to encourage her onward." Faith is now not only a symbol of Brown's tottering assurance; she also reflects the lost hope of all who have suffered the Antinomian delusion of the abstract.

When Brown identifies this voice as that of his wife, he declares that "Faith is gone" and he becomes "maddened with despair." Now, he thinks, "there is no good on earth"; and in the sudden divestment of his old theology, his negative conclusion is understandable. Faith, who has appeared invulnerable at home removed from any encounter with sin, has become one of the devil's disciples. And as Faith is, Brown is. They stand together: ". . . the wretched man beheld his Faith, and the wife her husband, trembling /75/ before that unhallowed altar." Brown concurs with the devil's declaration that "evil is the nature of mankind." To a relativist and not a dogmatist, this recognition would be taken in stride. But the inverted Brown retreats. With one final, desperate attempt to preserve his heretofore comfortable doctrine of assurance, he urges Faith to "look up to heaven, and resist the wicked one." Here he voices the passive Antinomian means of salvation: the union of faith below and grace from above.

Though he does not see whether Faith follows his advice or not, Brown has evidence enough that passive faith is ineffectual. Hence his silent disdain of his "pious" forebears and contemporaries; in his condemnation of them he circumstantially accuses himself. He thereafter becomes "a stern, a sad, a darkly meditative, a distrustful, if not a desperate man," and he dies in "gloom." After his experience he becomes as passively cynical as he has been passively trusting. He knows that Faith has been false; but what he never fathoms is that her weakness (and the repulsive grossness of all mankind) is the result of his own theological error and is exaggerated by his continuous passivity.

Paul J. Hurley

Young Goodman Brown's
"Heart of Darkness"*

The critical controversy which has centered on Hawthorne's "Young Goodman Brown" seems to have reached an impasse. Critics have usually seen the story as an allegory embodying Hawthorne's suspicions about man's depravity.[1] This interpretation implies that the Devil's words to Goodman Brown—"Evil is the nature of mankind. Evil must be your only happiness."—echo Hawthorne's own attitude. R. H. Fogle, for instance, writes, "Goodman Brown, a simple and pious nature, is wrecked as a result of the disappearance of the fixed poles of his belief. His orderly cosmos dissolves into chaos as church and state, the twin pillars of his society, are hinted to be rotten, with their foundations undermined."[2] Hawthorne, Fogle says, "does not wish to propose flatly that man is primarily evil; rather he has a gnawing fear that this might be true."[3] And Harry Levin has unequivocally stated, "The pharisaical elders . . . meeting in the benighted wilderness, are doing the devil's work while professing righteousness."[4]

On the other hand, F. O. Matthiessen and W. B. Stein have resisted the majority consensus and suggested that it is Goodman Brown who purposely seeks for evil.[5] Recently David Levin has attempted to void

* Paul J. Hurley, "Young Goodman Brown's 'Heart of Darkness'," *American Literature*, XXXVII (January, 1966), 410–419. Reprinted by permission of the journal and of the author.

[1] Among them: Q. D. Leavis, in "Hawthorne as Poet," *Sewanee Review*, LIX, 179–205 (April–June, 1951); Harry Levin, in *The Power of Blackness* (New York, 1958); and Roy Male, in *Hawthorne's Tragic Vision* (Austin, Tex., 1957).

[2] *Hawthorne's Fiction: The Light and the Dark* (Norman, Okla., 1952), p. 79.

[3] *Ibid.*, p. 16.

[4] *The Power of Blackness*, p. 54.

[5] Matthiessen, *American Renaissance: Art and Expression in the Age of Emerson and Whitman* (New York, 1941), p. 283; and Stein, *Hawthorne's Faust: A Study of the Devil Archetype* (Gainesville, Fla., 1953), pp. 6–7. Unfortunately, neither of these critics offered a sustained analysis of his reading.

both points of view by insisting that Goodman Brown is misled by the Devil who conjures up apparitions to befuddle his innocent victim.[6] The idea is comforting but not convincing. To take guilt away from human beings in order to place it on infernal powers is not a satisfactory explanation of the /411/ story. To the modern mind (and I suspect that includes Hawthorne's) either Abigail Williams and her Salem playmates were irresponsible, hysterical little liars, or Martha Carrier and Goody Proctor really were witches.

If I am correct, David Levin's contention is misleading, and we must return to the original argument. He writes, "Asking whether these people were 'really' evil is impertinent, for it leads us beyond the limits of fiction."[7] Confessing diabolical inspiration, I shall take a chance on being impertinent because I am not convinced that questions dealing with man's nature and the human heart are "beyond the limits of fiction." I believe the reader has every right to wonder if the townspeople are actually cohorts of the Devil. After all, if Young Goodman Brown did not have a nightmare or experience hallucinations, Hawthorne has created a fearful indictment of humanity. But if Goodman Brown did "dream," then the evil he saw, like the witchcraft reported in Salem in 1692, was the product of his own fancy with no reality save that supplied by his depraved imagination.

My point here is that "Young Goodman Brown" is a subtle work of fiction concerned with revealing a distorted mind. I believe the pervasive sense of evil in the story is not separate from or outside its protagonist; it is in and of him. His "visions" are the product of his suspicion and distrust, not the Devil's wiles. Goodman Brown's dying hour is gloomy because the evil in his own heart overflows; he sees a world darkened by the dreariness of sin. Hawthorne has given us every reason to read the story as a revelation of individual perversion (the story, after all, *is* entitled "Young Goodman Brown"), and speculations about man's nature or the talents of the Devil are out of place.

The tale begins with an account of Goodman Brown's departure from his home in Salem village in order to keep a strange tryst in the forest. He prepares to leave "at sunset," an hour when the world is about to be plunged into darkness. Faith, "as the wife was aptly named," begs him to "put off [his] journey till sunrise"; but he replies, "My journey, as thou callest it, forth and back again, must needs be done 'twixt now and sunrise." Like Richard Digby, the intolerant religious

---

6 "Shadows of Doubt: Specter Evidence in Hawthorne's 'Young Goodman Brown,'" *American Literature*, XXXIV, 344–352 (Nov., 1962).

7 *Ibid.*, p. 351.

fanatic of "The Man of Adamant" who /412/ "plunged into the dreariest depths of the forest" and was disappointed that "the sunshine continued to fall peacefully on the cottages and fields. . . ," Goodman Brown's alliance with evil is suggested by contrasting images of light and dark which intimate a symbolic opposition between good and evil. These images of shadow, dark, and gloom become more frequent and persuasive as the story continues.

Hawthorne makes clear at once that Goodman Brown's purpose on this night is an evil one. The fact that he is aware of the sinfulness of his trip destroys any belief we may have in Goodman Brown's "simple and pious nature."

> "Poor little Faith!" thought he, for his heart smote him. "What a wretch am I to leave her on such an errand! She talks of dreams, too. Methought as she spoke there was trouble in her face, as if a dream had warned her what work is to be done to-night. But no, no; 'twould kill her to think it. Well, she's a blessed angel on earth; and after this one night I'll cling to her skirts and follow her to heaven."

Aside from the interesting emphasis on dreams, the passage is noteworthy for several reasons. Goodman Brown's conscience is troubled by his departure from Faith. He realizes that it would "kill her" if she were to know the purpose of his trip, but he assumes that his absence (his departure from faith) will be only temporary. Goodman Brown's first mistake is to imagine that faith (which, most readers are agreed, must be interpreted as faith in one's fellow men as well as religious faith) can be adopted and discarded at will. The irony of the passage resides primarily in the implication that Goodman Brown intends to get to heaven by clinging to the "skirts" of faith rather than by virtue of his own character or actions. The ironic implications become almost playful in the following sentence: "With this excellent resolve for the future, Goodman Brown felt himself justified in making more haste on his present evil purpose." Despite Fogle's concentration on the ambiguities of the story, it seems clear that Hawthorne means us to be in no doubt that Goodman Brown has already had some contact with the forces of evil and does not hesitate to renew that contact, because he feels that he will prove superior to the temptations which may assail him.

The suggestions that we are primarily concerned with the char- /413/ acter of Goodman Brown, with some secret concerning his mind and heart, become stronger as he journeys into the forest, which functions as a symbol of withdrawal into oneself. Goodman Brown's isolation, his retreat from normal human intercourse into the strange dream world of the subconscious, is intimated by the imagery which describes his journey. He takes "a dreary road, darkened by all the gloomiest trees of the forest." Goodman Brown there encounters the man whom he has journeyed into the forest to find. The man appears to be the Devil himself, and he expects Goodman Brown.

The forest, symbol of Brown's retreat into himself, is associated with images suggestive of evil. "It was deep dark in the forest, and deepest in that part of it where these two were journeying." Hawthorne also insists on the similarity between Brown and the Devil—"the second traveller was about fifty years old, apparently in the same rank of life as Goodman Brown, and bearing a considerable resemblance to him. . . ." And we are informed that "they might have been taken for father and son." Despite David Levin's reminders of the Devil's wiles and powers, this personage is so curiously described that he is indisputably Goodman Brown's own personal devil.

Goodman Brown's faith may be "little," but it is not nonexistent. His "devil" knows, just as Goodman Brown or any contemporary criminal subconsciously knows, that belief in the morality of society must be destroyed, rationalized away, before total commitment to evil is possible. When the young man is chided by his companion for his tardiness in keeping their appointment, he replies, "Faith kept me back awhile"; but faith was not, of course, strong enough to prevent his journey. Goodman Brown's "lonely night of the soul," his pathetic struggle between good and evil, is dramatized in his dialogue with the Devil. At first he protests that he intends to return at once to the village. " 'Sayest thou so?' replied he of the serpent, smiling apart." The Devil, it seems, knows his victim well. He urges the young man to walk on, insisting that they are "but a little way in the forest yet"; and Goodman Brown goes with him, not realizing how far into the forest of his own evil he has already traveled.

The Devil then begins a sly temptation of Goodman Brown, but /414/ it is a puzzling temptation because the only rewards Goodman Brown is offered are the aspersions cast on his family, his neighbors, and his church. Strangely enough, he accepts without question the words of the Father of Lies. The temptation is actually a kind of interior monologue, a debate which Goodman Brown holds with himself. He asks the Devil several questions whose purpose seems to be to keep him from evil. The questions, it is interesting to note, suggest the three institutions to which man is morally obligated: the family, society, the church. Goodman Brown asks, in effect, "What would my family think? What would the neighbors say? How would the church react?" But the Devil (or psychic rationalization) assures him that his family, his neighbors, and the leaders of his church are far more stained by the blackness of sin than he.

These questions are projected into vivid, concrete form in the visions which follow. As they walk on into the forest, Goodman Brown and the Devil come upon a woman whom Brown recognizes as the venerable and pious Goody Cloyse. Fearing (or pretending to fear) that she will question his being out so late in such strange company, Goodman hides himself. The Devil, however, advances on her; she recognizes him and they hold a short conversation in which the old woman reveals that she has long been on familiar terms with Satan. The young man never pauses to consider the reality of Goody's appearance, even though such consideration might be expected of any well-trained Puritan cognizant of the Devil's powers. Hawthorne's use of Goody Cloyse and her reference to Martha Carrier remind us that they were actual historical personages unjustly accused by twisted "youngsters." That Goody Cloyse's appearance is part of Goodman Brown's psychological self-justification seems clear from Hawthorne's statement in the following paragraph: "They continued to walk onward, while the elder traveller exhorted his companion to make good speed and persevere in the path, discoursing so aptly that *his arguments seemed rather to spring up in the bosom of his auditor than to be suggested by himself.*"[8] The biblical echo of the Devil's exhortation to Brown "to make good speed and persevere in the path" appears to be Hawthorne's ironic parodying of the situation since it is the path of *self*-righteousness to which Goodman Brown adheres. /415/

When Brown finally refuses to go any further, the Devil seems entirely undisturbed by the news: " 'You will think better of this by and by,' said his acquaintance, composedly." Sitting by himself, Goodman Brown experiences his second "vision." He imagines that he hears the voices of the minister and Deacon Gookin, as they ride by, talking about the devilish communion which they plan to attend. Goodman's reason for believing what little evidence his senses afford him is even less good in this instance than it had been in the previous one:

> owing doubtless to the depth of the gloom at that particular spot, neither the travellers nor their steeds were visible. Though their figures brushed the small boughs by the wayside, *it could not be seen that they intercepted, even for a moment, the faint gleam from the strip of bright sky athwart which they must have passed.* Goodman Brown alternately crouched and stood on tiptoe, pulling aside the branches and thrusting forth his head as far as he durst *without discerning so much as a shadow.*

---

[8] Italics here as elsewhere are mine.

Fogle has alluded to this passage too as evidence of Hawthorne's ambiguity, but there is no ambiguity in the fact that Goodman Brown actually *saw* nothing at all. Nevertheless, he stands "doubting whether there really was a heaven above him." Goodman Brown makes one last desperate avowal of his resistance to evil: " 'With heaven above and Faith below, I will yet stand firm....' " But he has already departed from Faith. Goodman Brown then thinks that he hears the sound of voices: "The next moment, *so indistinct were the sounds*, he doubted whether he had heard aught but the murmur of the old forest, whispering without a wind." Hearing "one voice of a young woman," he immediately assumes it is his wife, and he cries her name. Suddenly he catches sight of an object fluttering down through the air; he clutches it and discovers it is a pink ribbon. Associating it at once with the ribbons his wife had worn that evening, he shouts: " 'My *Faith* is gone!' ... 'There is no good on earth; and sin is but a name. Come, devil; for to thee is this world given.' " Goodman Brown accepts his wife's guilt without ever having seen her.

Faith's ribbons have proved bothersome to several critics. F. O. Matthiessen objected to them because they seemed too literal and concrete; they appeared to him out of keeping with other sugges- /416/ tions that Brown is having an hallucination.[9] Fogle has noted that they are mentioned three times in the opening paragraphs of the story, and he feels that "if Goodman Brown is dreaming the ribbon may be taken as part and parcel of his dream."[10] At any rate, "Its impact is merely temporary"[11] (a peculiar statement in view of the fact that these ribbons appear, at last, to convince Goodman Brown of man's depravity and so "color" the rest of his life). Hawthorne concentrates so insistently on Faith's ribbons, and their effect on Goodman Brown is so devastating, that one may assume they were intended as an important symbol. If we remember that Faith is primarily an allegorical figure, an answer suggests itself. Goodman Brown, we recall, intends to get to heaven by clinging to Faith's skirts; in other words, he feels that the mere observation of ritual will insure salvation—good works have no place in his (as they had no place in Calvinistic) theology. Faith's skirts and her ribbons fulfil somewhat the same function. The ribbons, with their suggestions of the frivolous and ornamental, represent the ritualistic trappings of religious observance. Goodman Brown, it seems, has placed his faith and his hopes of salvation in the formal observances of religious worship rather than in

---

9 *American Renaissance*, p. 284.

10 *Hawthorne's Fiction*, p. 18.

11 *Ibid.*, p. 19.

the purity of his own heart and soul. This interpretation is supported by the fact that what he has seen and heard of Goody Cloyse, the minister, and Deacon Gookin, even though it may condemn them as individuals, can hardly be used as a condemnation of religious faith. Goodman Brown accepts the metonymic ribbon, Faith's adornment, as reality—just as he has accepted the "skirts" of religion as a means of salvation.

Has Goodman Brown really been subjected to visions which imply the universal prevalence of evil? Has the faith of a good man been destroyed by a revelation of the world's sinfulness? It would seem not. If one accepts the fact that Hawthorne gives us no valid grounds to believe in the reality of Goodman Brown's visions and voices, he must either believe, as Fogle does, that Hawthorne feared his own knowledge of the world's evil; or he must treat those events as emanations from Brown's subconscious which intimate the corruption of Brown's own mind. Why do the young man's visions of evil concern only Goody Cloyse, the minister, /417/ Deacon Gookin, and his wife? One answer, of course, is that they represent an exceptional piety which makes their participation in evil dramatically more effective. But if Hawthorne's theme concerns the universality of human sinfulness, should we not see a wider manifestation of that evil? The only scene in which such a manifestation occurs is the Devil's communion, but that takes place *after* Goodman Brown has declared his loss of faith; and the scene of that vision, Hawthorne tells us, was "in the heart of the dark wilderness," a setting whose significance is so inescapable that Joseph Conrad would later echo Hawthorne's words (unknowingly?) in the title of one of his novels.

A more significant reason for Hawthorne's choice of those four characters occurs to us if we return to a consideration of their relationship to Goodman Brown. They are the four people in Salem village to whom he is morally responsible. Goody Cloyse "had taught him his catechism in youth, and was still his moral and spiritual advisor, jointly with the minister and Deacon Gookin." His wife is an even more important representative of the forces of morality and virtue. It seems obvious that they are the four people whose respectability must be destroyed before Goodman Brown can fully commit himself to a belief in the wickedness of the world.

The remainder of the story continues to emphasize Goodman Brown's surrender to evil. Rushing through the forest "with the instinct that guides mortal man to evil," Goodman Brown, the man who has lost faith in his fellow men, "*was himself the chief horror of the scene.*" "The fiend in his own shape," Hawthorne tells us, reminding us of the similarities between Goodman Brown and the Devil, "is less hideous than when he rages in the breast of man." The communion scene in the forest, which Roy Male finds "essentially sexual," seems to me to be entirely the product of a dream fantasy, a blasphemous parody of a religious service. In this "grave and dark-clad company" Goodman Brown, his faith totally destroyed, fancies that he sees every person he has ever known. When a call is made to bring forth the converts, "Goodman Brown stepped forth from the shadow of the trees and approached the congregation, *with whom he felt a loathful brother-hood by the sympathy of all that was wicked in his heart.*" When the converts look upon each other, Goodman Brown at last sees his wife. They are told /418/ that "Evil is the nature of mankind. Evil must be your only happiness. Welcome again, my children, to the communion of your race." But as if in denial of the Devil's assertion, just as they are about to be baptized into "the mystery of sin," Goodman Brown cries out: " 'Faith! Faith!' . . . 'look up to heaven, and resist the wicked one.' Whether Faith obeyed he knew not." Goodman's cry breaks the spell of his hallucination: "He staggered against the rock, and felt it chill and damp; while a hanging twig, that had been all on fire, besprinkled his cheek with the coldest dew." That Goodman Brown has been experiencing hallucinations or dreaming seems unquestionable. The details concerning the rock and the twig are surely intended to signal Goodman Brown's return to a "rational" state of mind.

The most striking quality of the paragraph which describes Goodman Brown's return to the village of Salem is its tone. No longer are there any suggestions of the weird and incredible. The dreamlike quality of Brown's adventure in the forest is replaced by purposefully direct and forthright narration. Life proceeds in the village as it always has. Only Goodman Brown has changed. If the events of the night before had been real, or even symbolic of reality, would not Hawthorne have indicated in some way a shared knowledge between Goodman Brown and the townsfolk whom he sees? Hawthorne has told us that Brown did not know whether his wife obeyed his cry to look up to heaven. Nonetheless, he passes her without a greeting when she runs to meet him. His own distrust and suspicion have assured him that she is sinful, even though, as Hawthorne is careful to note, she is wearing the pink ribbons which Goodman Brown thought he had grasped from the air. Nor is there any change in anyone else. The minister seeks to bless Goodman Brown, but the young man shrinks from him; Deacon Gookin is praying and even though Goodman Brown can hear "the holy words of his prayer," he still thinks him a wizard. Goody Cloyse is catechizing a young girl, and Goodman Brown snatches the child from the old woman's arms. The corruption of his mind and heart is complete; Goodman Brown sees evil wherever he looks. He sees it because he wants to see it.

If Hawthorne had wished to intimate that the events of the night were real, it would hardly do to confuse us with suggestions /419/ about dreams (unless, as Fogle thinks, this was Hawthorne's method of escaping the implications of his own insight into man's depravity). A more acceptable interpretation of the ambiguity of the story is to see in it Hawthorne's suggestion that the incredible incidents in the forest were the product of an ego-induced fantasy, the self-justification of a diseased mind. It seems clear that these incidents were not experienced; they were willed. The important point, however, is that Goodman Brown has accepted them as truth; and the acceptance of evil as the final truth about man has turned him into "a stern, a sad, a darkly meditative, a distrustful" human being. Goodman Brown does not become aware of his own kinship with evil; he does not see sinfulness in himself but only in others. That, perhaps, is his most awful sin. He has lost not only faith in his fellow men but his compassion for them. And so it is that "On the Sabbath day, when the congregation were singing a holy psalm, he could not listen because an anthem of sin rushed loudly upon his ear and drowned all the blessed strain." Hawthorne never tells us that the anthem, loud and fearful as it must have been, ever reached the ears of any but young Goodman Brown.

Frederick C. Crews

Escapism*

> "The moment a man questions the meaning and value of life,
> he is sick . . ." —FREUD, letter to Marie Bonaparte

Hawthorne's plots, we begin to see, are very much alike in their psychological patterns—perhaps monotonously so. The monotony, however, ought to be blamed as much on our critical method as on Hawthorne's literary effects, which are notoriously ambiguous. Yet I am not quite willing to grant that our stress on sameness has kept the reader from appreciating Hawthorne's ambiguity. What, we may ask, is the source of this quality? Is it simply a matter of Hawthorne's teasing the reader with double explanations and significant omissions? Or does it rather spring from uncertainties of attitude on Hawthorne's part—uncertainties that his conscious tricks of plotting only begin to suggest? The most crucial of his ambiguities, that of moral intention, has escaped most of the critics who assure us that he is ambiguous. They say that he was ambiguous *and* Christian, ambiguous *and* didactic—in other words, that he wasn't very ambiguous at all. Let us take seriously the fact that intelligent readers have arrived at opposite notions of Hawthorne's "message," and ask if this fact cannot be explained in the terms we have previously established.

In this chapter we begin to treat a character-type who embodies the whole problem of Hawthorne's genuine moral ambiguity. This is the idealist who has determined to learn or do something that will set him apart from the /97/ mass of ignorant men. Moral interpretations of Hawthorne's purpose invariably turn upon analysis of this figure, for he

* Frederick C. Crews, *The Sins of the Fathers: Hawthorne's Psychological Themes* (New York: Oxford University Press, 1966), pp. 96–116. © 1966 Frederick C. Crews. Reprinted by permission.

125

always seems to teach a lesson. Since he usually comes to a sorry end,
and is sometimes explicitly criticized for his pride and isolation, he is
most often interpreted as a cautionary example; in his death or mad-
ness or chagrin we are meant to see that the bonds of common humanity
are not to be severed. Yet Hawthorne sometimes lends encouragement
to an exactly contrary reading. In his "strong and eager aspiration
towards the infinite" (II, 61; the subject is Aylmer of "The Birthmark") the idealist does succeed in differentiating himself from an
ignorant and timid humanity; and what he learns is sometimes hinted
to be a truth deeper than any that is available to more "normal" characters. The latter are never granted profound insights in Hawthorne's
fiction, and occasionally they are shown—*by* the tormented idealist—
to be wilfully self-deluded about their buried selves. Thus one critic
can plausibly find an ennobling tragic quality in a hero whose failure
is taken by another critic as a negative reminder that we must love
(and resemble) our neighbors.

This contradiction plainly has its source in Hawthorne's mixed
feelings. As an artist whose province was, as his publisher, James T.
Fields, observed, "the sharp, penetrating, pitiless scrutiny of morbid
hearts,"[1] he was committed to a cynical brooding about the inner
quality of human nature. As a man who aspired to normal happiness,
however, he was committed to the opposite, a mindless contentment—
an abstention from thought. The chasm between deep knowledge and
normality is unbridgeable in his fiction; the few "knowers" who become satisfied, such as Holgrave in *The House of the Seven Gables*,
do so by forswearing their mental powers and surrendering themselves
to timid, conventional brides. This reflects a sense of reality on Hawthorne's part that can only be termed neurotic: the /98/ truth is so
frightening and the process of seeking it so crippling that one had better stay well deceived. The idealist frightens Hawthorne by falling prey
to obsessive ideas that are indistinguishable from Hawthorne's own,
and for the same reason he has a claim on Hawthorne's sympathy. "Perhaps every man of genius in whatever sphere," Hawthorne admits,
"might recognize the image of his own experience in Aylmer's journal"
(II, 62)—the record of a monomaniac who is about to give a fatal
potion to his wife.

Our position, then, is not that Hawthorne approves *or* disapproves
of his driven heroes, but that he is ambiguously involved with them—
and that he thereby has an intuitive grasp of their motives. The idealist
is invariably an escapist; his quest for truth or power or immortality

---

[1] Quoted by R. H. Pearce, ed., *The Blithedale Romance and Fanshawe, C*, III,
xixn. [In Crews' footnotes *C* refers to the Centenary Edition, Ohio State University
Press.]

amounts to regressive flight from the challenges of normal adult life, and the knowledge he acquires or embodies is nothing other than an awareness of his own guilty fantasies. The nature of his inhibition, furthermore, can often be shown to coincide with the pattern we have been examining: figures of detested paternal suppression occupy a mental landscape which fairly pulsates with an unnameable, forbidden longing. As Richard P. Adams says of the early Hawthornian hero, "incest, parricide, and fear of castration" stalk him wherever he chooses to flee.[2] And yet all Hawthorne's irony of characterization cannot prevent him from secretly agreeing with what his escapists discover about the "foul cavern" (II, 455) of the human heart. His plots enact a return of the repressed, and the repressed is the truth. Neurotic terror, for Hawthorne, underlies every placid mental surface, but it reaches consciousness and corrodes sanity only when summoned forth by intolerable conflicts.

These conflicts are perhaps most fully observable in "Young Goodman Brown," a patently symbolic story /99/ whose atmosphere and import resemble those of "My Kinsman, Major Molineux." Like Robin's, Brown's ordeal is useful for us because it is uncomplicated by assertions of high conscious purpose; the hero simply and "inexplicably" undergoes a dreamlike or dreamed experience that permanently alters him. Yet he becomes what other and seemingly nobler Hawthornian escapists become: "a stern, a sad, a darkly meditative, a distrustful, if not a desperate man" (II, 106). This fact suggests, but of course does not prove, that Brown's case offers a psychological paradigm for the others; and this is just what we shall argue.

It is worth stressing that "Young Goodman Brown," which has teased its numerous critics with ambiguous hints of religious allegory, has a reasonably literal starting-point for its dream experience. If Brown loses his "faith" in mankind or salvation, he does so by fleeing from a normal, loving wife named Faith. These newlyweds are not yet fully acquainted with each other's minds—and, we can infer, not yet sure of each other's commitment to marriage. This is established with some subtlety:

"Dearest heart," whispered [Faith], softly and rather sadly, when her lips were close to his ear, "prithee put off your journey until sunrise and sleep in your own bed to-night. A lone woman is troubled with such dreams and such thoughts that she's afeard of herself sometimes. Pray tarry with me this night, dear husband, of all nights in the year."

---

2 "Hawthorne's *Provincial Tales*," *New England Quarterly*, XXX (March 1957), 39–57; the quotation is from p. 52.

"My love and my Faith," replied young Goodman Brown, "of all nights in the year, this one night must I tarry away from thee. My journey, as thou callest it, forth and back again, must needs be done 'twixt now and sunrise. What, my sweet, pretty wife, dost thou doubt me already, and we but three months married?" (II, 89)

Here, as so often in Hawthorne, the two-dimensionality of the scene, with its stylized reply and its want of overt motivation, has the effect of guiding and heightening /100/ our psychological expectations. Faith's whispered plea to Brown, "sleep in your own bed," has a distinctly sensual overtone that Brown himself picks up in his mocking question about "doubt"; a causal connection appears to subsist between Brown's mysterious rendezvous with the Devil and his flight from his wife's embraces. The very absoluteness and seeming arbitrariness of his decision to leave makes us look for such a hidden connection. Again, Faith's confessing that "a lone woman is troubled with such dreams and such thoughts that she's afeard of herself sometimes" places the ensuing plot in a suggestive light. Brown, too, will be troubled with a "dream" that will make him afraid of himself and indeed afraid of Faith. Hawthorne is evidently implying that when a newly married pair are separated, each may become subject to unpleasant ideas that under ordinary circumstances are kept in check only by the reassuring presence of the other.

Hawthorne reminds us in various ways that Brown is facing embodiments of his own thoughts in the characters he meets in the forest. The Devil's inducements are spoken "so aptly that his arguments seemed rather to spring up in the bosom of his auditor than to be suggested by himself" (II, 95). The haunted forest is horrible to Brown, "but he was himself the chief horror of the scene . . ." (II, 99), and he races toward the witches' sabbath screaming blasphemies and giving vent to demonic laughter. Hawthorne comments: "The fiend in his own shape is less hideous than when he rages in the breast of man" (II, 100). This makes it clear that the presumptive appearance of devils in the story is meant to refer to Brown's subjective thoughts. No wonder that when he arrives at the sabbath and sees the damned congregation, "he felt a loathful brotherhood [with them] by the sympathy of all that was wicked in his heart" (II, 102). Under these conditions the appearance of Faith in this company can have no bearing on her actual virtue or lack of it; she is there because /101/ Brown's inner *Walpurgisnacht* has reserved a special role for her.[3]

---

[3] Some critics have argued otherwise on the basis of Faith's pink ribbons, whose tangible reality in the forest is taken as evidence that she is "really" there. As David

What does the Devil offer Goodman Brown? There is no ambiguity here. Having assembled likenesses of all the figures of authority and holiness in Salem village and treated them as proselytes of hell, the Devil points them out to Brown and his fellow initiates:

"There," resumed the sable form, "are all whom ye have reverenced from youth. Ye deemed them holier than yourselves, and shrank from your own sin, contrasting it with their lives of righteousness and prayerful aspirations heavenward. Yet here are they all in my worshipping assembly. This night it shall be granted you to know their secret deeds: how hoary-bearded elders of the church have whispered wanton words to the young maids of their households; how many a woman, eager for widows' weeds, has given her husband a drink at bedtime and let him sleep his last sleep in her bosom; how beardless youths have made haste to inherit their fathers' wealth; and how fair damsels—blush not, sweet ones—have dug little graves in the garden, and bidden me, the sole guest, to an infant's funeral. By the sympathy of your human hearts for sin ye shall scent out all the places— whether in church, bedchamber, street, field, or forest—where crime has been committed, and shall exult to behold the whole earth one stain of guilt, one mighty blood spot. Far more than this. It shall be yours to penetrate, in every bosom, the deep /102/ mystery of sin, the fountain of all wicked arts, and which inexhaustibly supplies more evil impulses than human power— than my power at its utmost—can make manifest in deeds." (II, 103f.)

Knowledge of sin, then, and most often of sexual sin, is the prize for which Goodman Brown seems tempted to barter his soul. In this version of the Faustian pact, the offered power is unrelated to any practical influence in the world; what Brown aspires to, if we can take this bargain as emanating from his own wishes, is an acme of voyeurism, a prurience so effective in its ferreting for scandal that it can uncover wicked thoughts before they have been enacted.

Thus Goodman Brown, a curiously preoccupied bridegroom, escapes from his wife's embraces to a vision of general nastiness. The accusation that Brown's Devil makes against all mankind, and then more pointedly against Faith, clearly issues from Brown's own horror of adulthood, his inability to accept the place of sexuality in married love. Brown remains the little boy who has heard rumors about the polluted pleasures of adults, and who wants to learn more about

---

Levin correctly maintains, however, if the Devil is anything more than a fantasy of Brown's he can conjure pink ribbons as easily as the more visionary part of his spectacle. See "Shadows of Doubt: Specter Evidence in Hawthorne's "Young Goodman Brown,'" *American Literature*, XXXIV (November 1962), 344–52. Brown shares Othello's fatuous concern for "ocular proof," and the proof that is seized upon is no more substantial in one case than in the other.

them despite or because of the fact that he finds them disgusting. His forest journey, in fact, amounts to a vicarious and lurid sexual adventure. Without insisting on the extraordinary redundancy of phallic objects in the tale, I shall merely cite the judgment of critics who do not share the bias of this study. Roy R. Male finds that "almost everything in the forest scene suggests that the communion of sinners is essentially sexual . . . ," and Daniel G. Hoffman, after reminding us that a witches' coven is, *prima facie*, an orgy with the Devil, finds that "phallic and psychosexual associations are made intrinsic to the thematic development of [Hawthorne's] story. . . . Brown's whole experience is described as a penetration of a dark and lonely way through a /103/ branched forest . . . At journey's end is the orgiastic communion amid leaping flames."[4]

If Brown's sexual attitude is that of a young boy rather than a normal bridegroom, we may be permitted to wonder if parental, not wifely, sexuality is not the true object of his prurience. This supposition is strengthened by the virtual identity between the Devil's convocation of damned Salem dignitaries here and the comparable scene in "Alice Doane's Appeal." In both cases the exposé is of "all whom ye have reverenced from youth," and in the earlier story an Oedipal theme is made all but explicit. "Young Goodman Brown" is subtler but not essentially different. The Devil, the carnal initiator, happens to look exactly like Brown's grandfather, and he and Brown "might have been taken for father and son" (II, 91). This Devil, furthermore, persuades Brown to join the coven by feeding his cynicism about all his male ancestors—who turn out to have a connection with Hawthorne's own ancestors. After declaring himself to be as well acquainted with the Browns as any other Puritan family, the Devil adds, "I helped your grandfather, the constable, when he lashed the Quaker woman so smartly through the streets of Salem" (II, 92). If forefathers are fathers at a slight remove, both Brown and Hawthorne are leveling circuitously filial charges of sexual irregularity here. And the charges become more pointed when the witch Goody Cloyse recognizes that the Devil is "in the very image of my old gossip, Goodman Brown . . ." (II, 94). It is not difficult to see the sense in which Brown's grandfather is alleged to have been the "gossip" or confidant of a witch who is met on the way to an orgy. If Brown must now believe this of his grandfather, he must also have some doubts about his father; for his earlier statement, "My father never went into the woods on such an errand, nor his father before him" (II, 92), has already been half-refuted. /104/

---

[4] *Hawthorne's Tragic Vision*, p. 78; *Form and Fable in American Fiction*, pp. 165f.

It would seem, then, that "Young Goodman Brown" offers yet another instance of Hawthorne's practice of denigrating fathers *in absentia*. As usual, too, the missing literal father is replaced by numerous authority-figures who can be regarded as his surrogates. Few pages in the tale lack some accusatory reference to a king, a governor, a minister, a deacon, or an elder of the church. When Brown, in a frenzy of self-induced despair, cries "Come witch, come wizard, come Indian powwow, come devil himself, and here comes Goodman Brown" (II, 99), he has not simply given himself over to hell, but has done so by aligning himself with unscrupulous male authorities—the evil counterparts of "all whom ye have reverenced from youth." Having recognized in his elders the very impulses that filial respect has inhibited in himself, he declares himself free to indulge those impulses without punishment. "You may as well fear him [i.e., himself]," he tells the anti-authorities, "as he fear you" (II, 99).

Brown's fantasy-experience, like that of Robin Molineux, follows the classic Oedipal pattern: resentment of paternal authority is conjoined with ambiguous sexual temptation. In both instances, furthermore, the hero's attitude toward womankind is violently ambivalent. A general slur on women is implied when Brown sees that the forest sinners include virtually all the respectable women he has known, from the Governor's wife and her friends through "wives of honored husbands, and widows, a great multitude, and ancient maidens, all of excellent repute, and fair young girls, who trembled lest their mothers should espy them" (II, 101). The near-universality of this company reminds us of the two critical figures who are missing: Brown's mother and his wife. Yet Faith does arrive, only to disappear at the hideous moment of initiation—as if Brown were not able to stand a final confrontation of his suspicions about her. And he has been led to this moment by reflecting that the woman who taught him his catechism as a boy, Goody Cloyse, is a witch; this is to /105/ say that maternal authority is as questionable as paternal authority.[5] Like Ilbrahim, how-

---

[5] Brown resembles Robin in allowing his general faith in women to be shaken by his acquaintance with one degenerate woman. In reply to his objection that Faith's heart would be broken by his joining the sabbath, the Devil says, "I would not for twenty old women like the one hobbling before us that Faith should come to any harm" (II, 93). This insinuation that the loved woman is somehow linked to the despised one is picked up by Brown. "What if a wretched old woman do choose to go to the devil when I thought she was going to heaven," he tells himself; "is that any reason why I should quit my dear Faith and go after her?" (II, 96). Like Reuben Bourne's anguished question as to whether he should desert Roger Malvin *because* Roger has been a father to him, this sentence hints at unconscious motivation. Brown is beginning to see Faith under the aspect of the evil-maternal Goody Cloyse; and he puts "a world of meaning" (II, 95) into his astonished reflection that it was she who taught him his catechism.

ever, Brown finally absolves his mother, but not his father. Just as he is
about to join the congregation of sinners, "He could have well-nigh
sworn that the shape of his own dead father beckoned him to advance,
looking downward from a smoke wreath, while a woman, with dim
features of despair, threw out her hand to warn him back. Was it his
mother?" (II, 102)

The general pattern of "Young Goodman Brown" is that fathers
are degraded to devils and mothers to witches (both attributions, of
course, are confirmed in psychoanalysis). Yet the outcome of that
pattern, as is always true of Hawthorne's plots, is not simple degrada-
tion but a perpetuated ambivalence. Brown lives out a long life with
Faith and has children by her, but entertains continual suspicions
about her virtue. In retrospect we can say that the source of his uncertainty has been discernible from the beginning—namely, his insistence upon seeing Faith more as an idealized mother than as a wife.
She has been his "blessed angel on earth," and he has nurtured a trans-
parently filial desires to "cling to her skirts and follow her /106/ to
heaven" (II, 90). A bridegroom with such notions is well prepared for
an appointment with the Devil.

Nothing can be gained from disputing whether Brown's forest experience was real or dreamed, for in either case it serves his private
need to make lurid sexual complaints against mankind. Yet the richness of Hawthorne's irony is such that, when Brown turns to a Gulliver-
like misanthropy and spends the rest of his days shrinking from wife
and neighbors, we cannot quite dismiss his attitude as unfounded.
Like Gulliver's, his distinctly pathological abhorrence has come from
a deeper initiation into human depravity than his normal townsmen
will ever know. Who is to say that they are exempt from the fantasies
that have warped him? The only sure point is that by indulging those
fantasies Brown *has* become different; at least one case of human foul-
heartedness has been amply documented, and for all we know, Salem
may be teeming with latent Goodman Browns. In examining his own
mind, I imagine, Hawthorne found good reasons for thinking that this
might be so.

Exactly parallel to Young Goodman Brown's case is that of the
Reverend Hooper in "The Minister's Black Veil"—a story that has
provided much doctrinal ammunition for critics who are predisposed
to see Hawthorne's ideal as a mild-mannered bachelor in clerical garb.
If Hooper is not, as some maintain, "a preacher who preaches on
behalf of the author," neither is he a perfect Antichrist in his pride

and despair.[6] Both interpretations ignore Hawthorne's evasiveness about ultimate truth and his meticulous concern with ironies of motivation. As in Brown's case, what we learn about secret sin from Hooper is only what Hooper becomes, not what he believes. He is a pathetically self-deluded idealist who, goaded into monomania by a cer- /107/ tain incompleteness in his nature, ends by becoming the one obvious exemplar of the vice he rightly or wrongly attributes to everyone else.[7]

Perhaps the best way to see the parallelism between Hooper's case and Goodman Brown's is to remind ourselves of the religious consequences of the two revulsions against mankind. We are not likely to call Brown a religious sage, yet his attitudes are no less "holy" than Hooper's. Why should we lend a transcendent aura to Hooper's gloom while regarding Brown's, quite rightly, as pathological? The fact is that Brown's mania takes the form of a super-piety scarcely distinguishable from Hooper's:

> On the Sabbath day, when the congregation were singing a holy psalm, he could not listen because an anthem of sin rushed loudly upon his ear and drowned all the blessed strain. When the minister spoke from the pulpit with power and fervid eloquence, and, with his hand on the open Bible, of the sacred truths of our religion, and of saint-like lives and triumphant deaths, and of future bliss or misery unutterable, then did Goodman Brown turn pale, dreading lest the roof should thunder down upon the gray blasphemer and his hearers. (II, 106)

It is fairly clear that the "anthem of sin" assaulting Brown's ears is a projection of his own half-repressed fantasies. Yet in taking a radical view of man's sinfulness Brown is being an orthodox Calvinist; as several critics have noted, one of the beauties of "Young Goodman Brown" is that the Devil's role is to persuade the hero to take his religion seriously. We might therefore say that the tale is psychologically if not theologically anti-Puritan. But if this is so, it follows that we are under no obligation /108/ to admire the same radical pessimism in Hooper simply because Hooper is a Puritan minister.

In one sense Hooper's "eccentricity" (I, 52n.) appears to be without direct motive. Like other Hawthornian monomaniacs, he points to

---

[6] See Levin, *The Power of Blackness*, p. 42, and William Bysshe Stein, "The Parable of the Antichrist in 'The Minister's Black Veil,'" *American Literature*, XXVII (November 1955), 386–92.

[7] Of all readings of the tale, that of E. Earle Stibitz does best justice to this quintessentially Hawthornian situation. See "Ironic Unity in Hawthorne's 'The Minister's Black Veil,'" *American Literature*, XXXIV (May 1962), 182–90.

a mysterious external necessity when asked to explain his behavior, and we are permitted no glimpse of his mind before he dons the veil. Yet Hawthorne's visual presentation of him is a distinct sketch of a familiar character-type. The minister is "a gentlemanly person, of about thirty, though still a bachelor . . . dressed with due clerical neatness, as if a careful wife had starched his band, and brushed the weekly dust from his Sunday garb" (I, 53). From these few words we would expect Hooper to display a fastidiousness in his personal relations as well as in his dress. And indeed, the note of tidy womanliness here runs through the tale in a faint, suggestive undercurrent, particularly in the continual mention of the veil. As one parishioner remarks with unconscious acuteness, "How strange . . . that a simple black veil, *such as any woman might wear on her bonnet,* should become such a terrible thing on Mr. Hooper's face!" (I, 56f.; my italics).

Such innuendoes become significant when we learn that Hooper is engaged to be married. His consummately normal fiancée, Elizabeth, cannot persuade him to remove the veil, with the predictable result that the marriage is called off. Hooper's reaction to Elizabeth's farewell is to smile, despite his grief, at the thought that "only a material emblem had separated him from happiness, though the horrors, which it shadowed forth, must be drawn darkly between the fondest of lovers" (I, 63f.). This smile, which recurs so often that it acquires a quality of daffy abstractedness, is Hooper's substitute for considering Elizabeth's reasonable plea. It could be plausibly argued, I think, that Hooper has donned the veil in order to prevent his marriage. On the one hand we see that he is already quite prim enough without a woman in the house, and on the /109/ other we find that he broods over dark, unspecified horrors that must separate the fondest of lovers. Where have these horrors come from, if not from his own imagination? It is possible that Hooper, who like Goodman Brown is obliged to confront the sexual aspects of womanhood, shares Brown's fears and has hit upon a means of forestalling their realization in marriage. His literal wearing of a veil, like Brown's figurative removal of it to leer at the horrid sexuality underneath, acts as a defense against normal adult love. No wonder that the topic of his first "veiled" sermon is "secret sin, and those sad mysteries which we hide from our nearest and dearest, *and would fain conceal from our own consciousness* . . ." (I, 55; my italics).

Now, I do not care to lay very much stress on the indications of sexual squeamishness in Hooper. They are there, but they command much less attention than the comparable elements in "Young Goodman Brown." But the very ambiguity in Hooper's motivation enables Hawthorne to offer us glimpses into the minds of the people who must form their own theories about their minister. This is true, for example, at the funeral of the young lady with whom Hooper seems to have had some connection, if only in his thoughts. Poe and others have made much of Hooper's uneasiness in the presence of the corpse, and have intimated that Hooper, like his later counterpart Dimmesdale, must have been tempted into sexual indulgence at least once in his career. Yet the hints of an explicit liaison are supplied by the highly suggestible bystanders to the scene. It is "a superstitious old woman" (I, 58) who thinks that the corpse has shuddered at Hooper's aspect, and it is "a fancy" (I, 58) of two parishioners that Hooper and the girl's spirit are marching hand in hand in the procession. That the fancy is shared is no sign of its truth. Simply, Hawthorne is exposing a preoccupation in the collective mind of the town.

This preoccupation might be said to be the chief object of Hawthorne's scrutiny in "The Minister's Black Veil." /110/ From the beginning he is concerned with the telltale responses that Hooper's "ambiguity of sin or sorrow" (I. 65) elicits from his fellow men. In the sermon on buried sin "each member of the congregation, the most innocent girl, and the man of hardened breast, felt as if the preacher had crept upon them, behind his awful veil, and discovered their hoarded iniquity of deed or thought" (I, 55). By joining young virgins with old sinners Hawthorne is placing his customary emphasis on the universality of human nature; no one is completely free from the urges that are gratified by only a few. Hooper's parishioners would prefer not to acknowledge these urges of which he has become a visible reminder. They begin slighting him,[8] making fun of him, fleeing his presence, calling him insane, and inventing sexual rumors about him that will cancel the relevance of the veil to their own latent thoughts. Of all the busybodies in the town, including a special delegation whose task is to uncover the mystery, no one is able to face Hooper directly—and even Elizabeth shows herself susceptible to the "whispers" (I, 62) of an obviously sexual scandal. When she too is suddenly terrified by a hidden meaning in the veil, Hawthorne has capped his demonstration of general *malaise*, for Elizabeth possesses a steady, cleansing love that seems unique in the town. Hooper is doubtless the supreme example of isolation "in that saddest of

---

[8] A particularly interesting early example is Old Squire Saunders's forgetting to invite Hooper to dinner after the Sunday service—a slip that is said to occur "doubtless by an accidental lapse of memory" (I, 56). It is clear that Hawthorne's interest in such "accidents" was parallel to Freud's in *The Psychopathology of Everyday Life*.

all prisons, his own heart" (I, 67), but his difference from the others
is only a matter of degree.

Thus the world of "The Minister's Black Veil" is one in which a
man can reasonably be "afraid to be alone with himself" (I, 57).
The real struggle in the tale is not between Hooper and the others
but between conscious and unconscious thoughts within each individual. Total repression is /111/ restored in everyone but Hooper, and
in his case, as in Goodman Brown's, the truth is permitted utterance
only in the form of symbolism and accusation. Hooper has a sympathy
with "all dark affections" (I, 65), but he lacks the courage to confess
their hold upon his own imagination. He too is one of those who are
frightened by the veil, and understandably so, for he has had clear
intimations of what the force of civilization must contend with in its
effort to remain the master. Hawthorne leaves us with the Swiftian
idea that a little self-knowledge is worse than none, and that the
best approximation to happiness rests in an ignorant, busy involvement
with a society of unconscious hypocrites.

In proceeding from sexual fear to obsession and misanthropy, Brown
and Hooper may stand for Hawthorne's escapists generally. Sometimes,
as with Ethan Brand, the hint of twisted sexuality is offered almost as an
irrelevant afterthought; we learn in passing that in his search for the
Unpardonable Sin, which is of course finally located in his own breast,
Brand has taken an innocent girl and made her "the subject of a
psychological experiment, and wasted, absorbed, and perhaps an-
nihilated her soul, in the process" (III, 489). More often, as in "Ego-
tism; or, "The Bosom Serpent," "The Birthmark," "The Artist of the
Beautiful," and "The Man of Adamant," the hero is facing a matrimonial challenge like Brown's or Hooper's. Either he is evading
marriage, or he has been discarded for a better lover, or he is a
strangely uneasy newlywed, or his wife is simply temporarily absent.
However sketchy the connection between the hero's lovelessness and
his zealous project or phobia, that connection is always indicated.[9]
/112/
In all these tales it is possible, indeed traditional, to ignore the
sometimes obscure hints of regressive motivation and emphasize the
hero's moral achievement or failure. Cumulatively, however, the

---

[9] As Harry Levin remarks, Hawthorne's tales are "rife with matrimonial fears"
(*The Power of Blackness*, p. 58). Levin alludes to "Mrs. Bullfrog," "The Wedding
Knell," "The Shaker Bridal," "Edward Fane's Rosebud," "The Wives of the Dead,"
and "The White Old Maid"—a modest beginning for an inventory of the relevant
works.

examples of sexually odd escapists amount to a virtual demonstration that Hawthorne regarded fear of normal adulthood as the *primum mobile* of all alienation, whether that alienation results in scientific study, art, or simply derangement. It is also noteworthy that the authorial moralizing in these tales is never translated into action. Hawthorne can say, for example, that Aylmer in "The Birthmark" would have done better to "find the perfect future in the present" (II, 69) than to kill his wife; but everything that precedes this final sentiment reduces it to impertinence. On the first page of the story we are warned that Aylmer's marital love could prevail only by "intertwining itself with his love of science" (II, 47), and such intertwining always points to unconscious compulsion. Hawthorne has written a tale of psychological necessity, not of moral error.[10] Similarly, Ethan Brand can interrupt his progress toward self-destruction long enough to draw a moral from his "sin of an intellect that triumphed over the sense of brotherhood with man and reverence for God" (III, 485); yet this awareness does not alter his behavior in the slightest degree. He is a passive, even a sardonically amused, spectator of his own damnation. If we ask why this must be so, the only available answer is that moral understanding does not reach low enough into the region where the hero receives his incontrovertible commands.

Our argument, however, is not that Hawthorne ingeniously constructed traps for the unwary, moralistic reader; in all likelihood he was as anxious as anyone to view his heroes superficially. Our argument is that he *represented* their motives, whether or not he meant to. And in this spirit we may remark that his tales of sexual embarrass- /113/ ment are full of sexual symbolism. It is hard to decide whether he would have been appalled or amused at recognizing this feature of his art, but its prominence in the tales of escapism corroborates our view that sexual obsession is a governing force in those tales. The example of Young Goodman Brown is typical; flight from the marriage-bed is rendered in terms of symbolic decor whose phallic quality is apparent to most modern readers. Brown's talisman, the writhing serpent-staff he borrows from the Devil, calls to mind the bosom serpent of Roderick Elliston. The latter is invited by Elliston's "diseased self-contemplation" (II, 319) in his wife's absence, and it disappears magically at her return—a pattern that might well be characterized as masturbatory. Again, Ethan Brand, having scientifically abused an innocent girl, ends by leaping into a lime-kiln whose door "resembled nothing so much as the private entrance to the infernal regions" (III,

---

10 For evidence, see p. 126 of this work in its original source.

478). Hawthorne is paraphrasing Bunyan, but the lurid atmosphere of the tale encourages us to see a genital reference in the image.[11] And something similar may be said of the Reverend Hooper's mouth: by feeling a need to veil it he imparts a vaguely repulsive horror to it— one that is altogether in keeping with his effeminate nature.[12] Hawthorne's fastidious idealists always flee from the modest sexual demands of actuality into a world of symbolism in which sex has usurped or "intertwined" itself with every other concern.

I grant that in some cases the context is insufficiently erotic for us to insist on these readings. If we interpret "Ethan Brand" in sexual terms, it can only be by frankly applying the fallacy of analogy with similar tales. And yet /114/ the analogy is a powerful one: the stamp of a single obsessed imagination lies upon all Hawthorne's stories of escapism. Roughly the same imagery and atmosphere, the same absence or absurdity of conscious motive, the same ambiguity as to whether the hero's idea of human depravity applies to others as well as to himself, the same immunity of his compulsion to moral influence, occur in every tale. Given this sameness, it seems permissible to use the obviously regressive cases as explanatory of the less obvious ones.

Hence the usefulness of the most grotesque and openly pathological of all Hawthorne's escapists, Richard Digby in "The Man of Adamant." Like his counterparts elsewhere, Digby is upset by the general wickedness of mankind, and more especially by a normal woman who offers him a prospect of married love. To escape her he sails across the ocean and searches out a special refuge—a dark cave with "so dense a veil of tangled foliage about it, that none but a sworn lover of gloomy recesses would have discovered the low arch of its entrance, or have dared to step within its vaulted chamber, where the burning eyes of a panther might encounter him" (III, 566). From this dubious bastion of purity, whose details suggest something less abstract and less exalted than communion with God, the hero delivers insults to his persistent admirer. " 'Off!' cried he, 'I am sanctified, and thou art sinful' " (III, 569). When he eventually dies, calcified by the atmosphere of his refuge, he and the cave together become more urgently symbolic than before. The mouth of the cave-sepulchre is gradually concealed by darksome pines and a further "thick veil of creeping plants" (III, 572). Over a century after Digby's death, some playful children pull aside this veil, find the petrified corpse, and race homeward "without

---

[11] For a recurrence of the identical phrase in a less ambiguous context of sexual ambivalence, see "Rappaccini's Daughter."

[12] A more distinctly genital veiled mouth is very much at issue in *The Blithedale Romance*.

a second glance into the gloomy recess" (III, 572). Their father is braver, yet his reaction is strangely irrational: "the moment that he recovered from the fascination of his /115/ first gaze [he] began to heap stones into the mouth of the cavern" (III, 573). And though hardly anyone will admit to believing that the cave exists at all, "grown people avoid the spot, nor do children play there" (III, 573). "Friendship, and Love, and Piety," Hawthorne adds with emphasis, "all human and celestial sympathies, should keep aloof from that hidden cave" (III, 573).

Here sexual symbolism has wrenched itself away from moral or allegorical meaning. Though Digby is a Puritan fanatic and his rejected lady a type of true religion, their theological contest is outlasted by the genital obsession that underlies it; Digby's fear is so compelling and contagious that it appalls a new generation of anxious mortals. No reading in realistic or religious terms can account for Hawthorne's admonition that Friendship and Love and Piety should keep aloof from the cave. This tale offers an extreme version of the pattern we have found in others: the hero *becomes an image of what he loathes*, and his fellow men try to erase this image from their minds.

Let us understand the full implication of Hawthorne's advice to shun Digby's cave. "True religion" is not involved; it is simply a question of maintaining a happy ignorance of real psychic terrors. Hawthorne's counsel is not to refute or reject the monomaniac ideas that rule his plots, but to avoid them—not to light a candle in the dark, but to heap stones into the cave's mouth. This attitude, which we may call both heterodox and neurotic, will prove to be his greatest liability as an artist. Secretly entertaining the worst fantasies that drive his heroes to escapism, Hawthorne will begin to lose the courage necessary for creating such heroes. His entire plots, rather than merely his protagonists, will flee from themes that become more inescapable in symbolism as they become more intolerable to conscious thought. The result will be, not an ambiguous and energized study of obsession, but ingenious hypocrisy and aesthetic confusion. Before this phase of shadow-box- /116/ ing is reached, however, Hawthorne remains capable of great psychological fiction. It is no coincidence that, as the next two chapters [of *The Sins of the Fathers*] will show, the ironic figure of the sexual escapist stands at the center of one of his richest tales and his indisputably best romance.

Suggestions for Papers

For another series of topics, some of which might overlap with those here suggested, see Agnes McNeill Donohue (ed.), *A Casebook on the Hawthorne Question* (New York: 1963), pp. 345–346.

Short Papers

Consider the various religious interpretations of "Young Goodman Brown" and analyze and discuss them.

Compare and contrast the views of David Levin with those of D. M. McKeithan, T. E. Walsh, Jr., and J. W. Mathews.

Compare and contrast the interpretations of this story advanced by Hoffman and Crews.

What does Goodman Brown mean when he says, "My Faith is gone!"?

Is Hawthorne more concerned with "sin" than with "morals" in "Young Goodman Brown"?

If Goodman Brown did lose his faith, what filled the vacuum? Can a vacuum be filled by a negative quantity?

If Goodman Brown dreamed, indicate the exact point in the story at which the dream began and defend your choice.

Critically evaluate the interpretations of "Young Goodman Brown" contained in this volume. Make value judgments and defend those judgments.

Does Goodman Brown ever use his head or lose his heart? (An answer of more than one word is expected.)

Which critical position in this volume do you prefer to all others? Why?

Long Papers

Compare and contrast "Young Goodman Brown" with *Hamlet.*

"Young Goodman Brown" and "Wakefield" were published in the same year and in the same magazine. Write a critical evaluation of both stories.

Is "Young Goodman Brown" more particular or more universal in its treatment of sin than *The Scarlet Letter?* (Give some thought to #5 above.)

Discuss all the ramifications of the symbolism of colors in "Young Goodman Brown" and *The Scarlet Letter.*

Is "Young Goodman Brown" a tragedy? If so, in what sense of the term is it? If not, why is it not a tragedy?

What elements would have to be altered in the story to make it comic?

We have some indication of the way in which Goodman Brown spent the years between his forest experience and his death. Project an estimate (essay or short story) of the way in which Faith Brown (and perhaps others) passed those same years.

Did Goodman Brown commit the "unpardonable sin"?

What was Goodman Brown's mother like? (Essay, short story, or one-act play)

Chronologically, Goodman Brown could have been a descendant of Hester Prynne. Explain, on other than biological reasons, why he could or could not have been her descendant.

Compare and contrast Goodman Brown with Quentin Compson.

Compare and contrast Goodman Brown with Meursault.

In what boat would Melville have placed Goodman Brown—Starbuck's or Ahab's?

Additional Readings

Books

Arvin, Newton. *Hawthorne.* New York: Russell & Russell, Inc., 1961.

James, Henry. *Hawthorne.* New York: Harper & Brothers, 1879; Ithaca, New York: Cornell University Press, 1966.

Levin, David. *What Happened in Salem?* New York: Harcourt, Brace & World, Inc., 1960.

Levin, Harry. *The Power of Blackness: Hawthorne, Poe, Melville.* New York: Alfred A. Knopf, Inc., 1958.

Male, Roy. *Hawthorne's Tragic Vision.* Austin, Texas: University of Texas Press, 1957.

Matthiessen, F. O. *American Renaissance: Art and Expression in the Age of Emerson and Whitman.* London and New York: Oxford University Press, 1941.

Stein, William B. *Hawthorne's Faust: A Study of the Devil Archetype.* Gainesville, Florida: University of Florida Press, 1953.

Stewart, Randall (ed.). *American Notebooks.* New Haven: Yale University Press, 1932.

————. *English Notebooks.* New York: Russell & Russell, Inc., 1941.

————. *Nathaniel Hawthorne: A Biography.* New Haven: Yale University Press, 1948.

Taylor, J. Golden. *Hawthorne's Ambivalence Toward Puritanism.* Logan, Utah: Utah State University Press, 1965.

Turner, Arlin. *Nathaniel Hawthorne: An Introduction and Interpretation.* New York: Barnes & Noble, Inc., 1961.

Van Doren, Mark. *Nathaniel Hawthorne.* New York: W. Sloane Associates, 1949.

Waggoner, Hyatt H. *Hawthorne: A Critical Study.* Cambridge, Massachusetts: Belknap Press of Harvard University Press, 1963.

Warren, Austin. *Nathaniel Hawthorne.* New York: American Book Company, 1934.

Articles

Chandler, E. L., "A Study of the Sources of the Tales and Romances Written by Nathaniel Hawthorne before 1853," *Smith College Studies in Modern Languages*, VII (1926).

Cherry, Fanny N., "The Sources of Hawthorne's 'Young Goodman Brown'," *American Literature*, V (1934), 342–348.

Cochran, Robert W., "Hawthorne's Choice: The Veil or the Jaundiced Eye," *College English*, XXIII (1962), 342–346.

Cohen, Bernard B. "*Paradise Lost* and 'Young Goodman Brown'," *Essex Institute Historical Collection*, XCIV (1958), 282–296.

Connolly, Thomas E., "How Young Goodman Brown Became Old Badman Brown," *College English*, XXIV (1962), 153.

Davidson, Frank, " 'Young Goodman Brown'—Hawthorne's Intent," *Emerson Society Quarterly*, No. 31, pp. 68–71.

Doubleday, Neal F., "Hawthorne's Use of Three Gothic Patterns," *College English*, VII (1946), 250–262.

McDowell, Tremaine, "Nathaniel Hawthorne and the Witches of Colonial Salem," *Notes and Queries*, CLXVI (1934), 152.

[Whipple, Edwin P.], "Nathaniel Hawthorne," *Atlantic*, May 1860.

Winkleman, Donald A., "Goodman Brown, Tom Sawyer, and Oral Tradition," *Keystone Folklore Quarterly*, X (1965), 43–48.

Other Books by Thomas E. Connolly

The Personal Library of James Joyce: A Descriptive Bibliography (Buffalo, 1955, 1957; Ann Arbor, 1967).

From Ararat to Suburbia: The History of the Buffalo Jewish Community (Philadelphia, 1960), with Selig Adler.

Scribbledehobble: The Ur-Workbook for Finnegans Wake (Evanston and London, 1961), editor.

Joyce's Portrait: Criticisms and Critiques (New York, 1962; London, 1964), editor.

Swinburne's Theory of Poetry (New York, 1964).

77 1517 33